THE FANATICAL
PURSUIT OF PURITY

Jonathan Bowden

TSTC

First Edition
Published March 2008

Printed in Great Britain

Cover design and layout by Daniel Smalley
Cover painting 'Medusa Now Ventrix I' by Jonathan Bowden

ISBN 978-0-9557402-3-7

The Spinning Top Club
BM Refine
London
WC1N 3XX

www.jonathanbowden.co.uk

"The Beautiful Rafaela in Green" (1927)
by Tamara de Lempicka

She lies astride a mantle
naked as the day she was born
Covered in nought but swards
emerald to its vagina's cusp
rust, lust, bust, thrust, speedy onrush!

Dedicated to Dorothy Bowden (1931-1978)

Jonathan Bowden
Photo by Andrea Lioy

THE FANATICAL PURSUIT OF PURITY
a novel

DRAMATIS PERSONAE

Heathcote Dervish
Phosphorous Cool
Bounteous Elsa Hapgood
Butler James
Mastodon Helix or Spyros/Skyros
Warlock Splendour Thomas
Tumble-weed or Hermaphrodite X
Moustachio Brave Herring
+
Ms. Igor
Baron von Frankenstein (MD)

An epigraph:

"And he laid hold on the dragon, that old serpent, which is the Devil, and old Satan, and bound him a thousand years."

Revelation 20:2
The King James Bible, (1611)

ONE PART DICKENSIAN: (1)

It began in the mind of someone who has not been born yet, and it reared up like a miasma or the merest dream. A phantasm of non-identity it was; in that one puppet dangled from a string of fives. These ropes cascaded from the back of a stage's hands and they were always beholden to the touch of a puppet-master, such as Eric Bramall and his theatre of yesteryear. It had existed in Colwyn Bay up on the north Welsh coast – or otherwise adjacent to a plunging sea. All of a sudden, a silvery puppet loomed up against a dark green background. It roofed off the immensity of its enclosure; and this was probably by satisfying the deepest, most verdant allure. Moreover, against the tincture of such a moon, the cords on our silvery titan were hardly discernible: they blew hither and thither as so much spume. Be quiet now… For – simultaneously with a streaked disc – various tendrils of night-time smoke crossed our vista. These built up so as to afford a climax in the sky; they also affrighted any nebulous intelligence whatsoever. Behind them – and at the centre of this congruence – a witches' stove was seen to boil. A cauldron it proved to be; the like of which flickered in the moonlight garishly.

Arrest any sense of fortitude now: since flames licked at the edges of this particular bowl. An extremely bright or lemon yellow (they were), in a manner which pitched sulphur against magnesium's maximum. Around this bay of plenty, betimes, a coven of witches have gathered; they happened to be both male and female. Each one of them screamed, whelped or let go a gnarled hand; it clawed the air with the sanctimony of an unused cry. Do you detect its vision? Their faces waxed a deep shade of rum; at once Khitian in aspect as well as being aggressively perspectival. Every one of them appeared to be strongly etched before a mildewed crowd. A gathering swoon or secret English coven could be articulated here: it let rip around Stonehenge and came aslant of many an arrested evening.

At the heart of their deliberations, however, a monstrous apparition had begun to unfold. It flavoured the aftermath of a puppet; or it looked out over the conspectus of a noon-time devil. Regardless of which, this puppeteering blob manufactured an orange hue. Its musculature was highly developed and rippled beneath a manikin's hide. Against this gesture, though, the jaw stood open or slack before the Fates – it relieved a process of unBeing as it travelled towards wilfulness. No – if we happen to be more accurate about it – then it measured the finality of Time before Hades' gates. Also, lower than the mouth slanted the teeth of a rippling surd; these characterised a debenture's losses. Abundantly therefore, such steroid protuberances cast forth a daemonic lustre which re-entered themselves. It gave a notice of ecstasy – only to furrow a brow or cast off before an opening maw. In short, its titanic molars stood agape; together with a crenellated forehead, masculine thews and agate preponderance. These (effectively) had nothing to do with the barrel-like bulk which cascades away towards its legs. Their number proved to be Hyperborean. Could they be mysteriously active?

LET US PERSEVERE WITH OUR TAROT: (2)
Yet even a puppet's consciousness can have a reverse side – at least in terms of who's prepared to gainsay a wooden figurine. In this case, the silvery one saw its *alter ego* enter into a magisterial building… It waxed Georgian or gave out the immensity of those dwellings around London Fields, Hackney. Are we to spy smoke or dry-ice crystals that festoon its base (?) – these tendrils rise up around lower-case windows. While – analogous to the above – our shape-shifter enters a portal dressed in black. Does he endanger a shadow: the highest plenitude of which stands before our Gods? *Avaunt thee*, an enabling act passes above us. It unloads a new mesmerism: since our puppet has shed those skins that tie it to dreams… especially now that a witches' coven exists down-town, spectrally. For – on this plane – one's Klavern becomes disembodied or no longer needs strings… and each one basically floats free from the heavens. What can the collective

anima – or *anima* rising – of a penumbra be like? Never mind its hinterland… Well, it embodies new fractures – but glides abreast. And this is primarily because (contextually) our coven exists as a blanched face that twirls. It was ethereal. Our visage exalts a lunar conspectus – one with red orbs, distended eyelets, gigantic teeth, lavender skin, and the rippling glow of a von Hagens' plastinate. (Note: these showed themselves to be inanimate corpses, *a la* Vesalius, which slither under ultraviolet light. Did they occasion a blue temperature?)

THIS FIRST ACT DAMNS A HARLEQUIN[!]: (3)
Yet enough of these introductory forays… no matter how hypnotically registered they might prove to be. Let's commence: at the centre of an English coven a male witch stands aloof; all the rest subsists on Wiltshire's moors. His name is Heathcote Dervish and he's just cast a spell in ancient Enochian. Around him a rabble have gathered in their sepulchral hue. "Listen to me!", he cries agape. "Our Jaggta-Noga lilts after no such involvement. Let the wraith appear from subdued depths of chasm. Do you detect that he cuts up his enclosure's miles? Desist from your dreams or pornographic abandon! HE'S HERE! Awakest thou a rage in sulphur --- particularly as it pertains to one who crosses dimensions in order to be? Listen…"

During this intervention, though, our warlock holds up his hand – the outermost fingers of which are extended. These virtually scrape the surface of the Heavens… conceptually speaking. He also wears a lengthy robe; the farthest or outer lineaments of it sweep down to his feet. Beyond this two sandals or slippers peep out. A cowl is then seen to douse his head; in a situation where his features are limned against a pumiced cloth. Oh yes --- here he prances before a cauldron; a vessel of the stoutest iron that possesses a round handle on its side. It looks heavy and proficient. While the entire tube glows at red heat – so much so that a nimbus radiates around these flames… Each and every one of them then pours successfully from every side. Such a vortex entrances its wonderment... does it likewise seal its fate before the facts? All of a sudden, a ghostly face emerges from this bubble or steam: it moans and quivers. Its features are blurred by congestion; and yet a doleful mouth, orb, twilight and sceptre looms up. They count to ten, basically in terms of the nearest indifference. Could this incarnate a Gothic sliver by Fuseli? Anyway, as the death's-head materialises these witches gather around in thraldom. Each one successfully envisages an astral belch or flame. They are eight in number – at least when viewed from a distance. Every one enjoys a covering before a bridge (betimes); and they represent a Dominican order in reverse... often down to minor details. These votaries prance, leer, caterwaul, gibber and let loose a hullabaloo! Oh my; since --- for today's Comus Rout --- such events were a dream's culmination. Hermetically speaking and all...

Whilst – beyond our expectant throng of magicians or musicians – an immense zero gathers. It proves to be an infestation. It is all signalled by a shuttered wall, mortar, brick-dust and scraggy trees: these limn the sky or delineate a presence. All of it measures a dotage unto ash: it's against such vapour at any rate.

TWO HEADS ARE BETTER THAN ONE STILTON: (4)
To complete our picture now... the warlock, Dervish, stands screaming before a scarlet haze. At the edges it tapers into turquoise, indigo, magenta and a brilliant or refulgent orange! His cowl moves back slightly on his scalp, but it still just about gives one balm, phrenologically speaking. Whereat his shoulders lift up in ecstasy – in this they recall a diver without complete control over their anatomy... as seen in Leni Riefenstahl's *Olympia*. Nonetheless, his mouth rests open, his robes billow expansively, his radiant orbs streak back fire and the mage's chanting reaches a crescendo. It remains both hermetic and hieratic. While either of his arms, windmill-like, find themselves thrust out as stick-insects before the dawn. At last the wraith – curdling amidst Greek Fire – becomes temporal enough to

materialise. Does it atomise unbelief's frequency? A rainbow then cheats the heavens of its vista – and this appears as either a snout or a pedigree nostrum. Above such a saurian two slit-eyes poke forth --- they are Mongoloid in aspect. Furthermore – at the base of this indent – a savage mouth cuts against the ether. All in all, our Flame-face floats free of every support. It interprets a disembodied mask or filter – let's call it Hermaphrodite X or Tumble-weed. Our Warlock continues his bleat: "Behold brethren, I have achieved my fondest desire – a wraith evinces its temperature; it tumbles forth aflame. Listen, heed its bark or cry! (Note: like the demon-king in many a good pantomime, our shade or presence from the other side speaks in rhyme. His couplets trip off the tongue as so much goodness to dross. He bathes in the sardonic quips of a debased ironist. Can't you see the puppeteer's strings going up behind 'it' --- at least in terms of our toy-theatre of yesteryear?)

Tumble-weed or Hermaphrodite X:~

'A spell is cast
by any repast
it delineated a task
--- only to ask.

Do not forsake
the prospects of a bake
which ends in a lake
perchance of all slake.

Cauterise the blow
let alone the flow
it can never really glow
leastways not slow
but by all means GO!'

10

A SIAMESE TWIN HAS AN IN-GROWING TOE-NAIL: (5)

As precipitously as his arrival, our demon king or wraith vanished. Abruptly a golden vapour, mist or silent trail fills the space which he once occupied. The drunken shell of a building is all that remains; it lists vacantly from side to side. But – in all truth – its static projection fulfills an unknown promise. A spiral of smoke ascends from this tambourine man's gesture – it has to be a tendril which limits its dissolution. An inner wreckage or decay cauterises it, especially given the lop-sidedness of those turrets. They speak of a broken husk. It looks out on the blasted nature of a heath further on; a kindred of this sprouts whey grass or split bracken. Would it be too onomatopoeic to speak of its taste, lustre or Imperial purple? The mage continues to stand as a dark shape – or a nineteenth century silhouette – within a dwelling open to the elements. His arms straddle a lofty competition, given over, as they are, to the reality of an incomplete fastness. All the other occultists lurk furtively around a well – and a tower/its circular brick-work hoves into view, in terms of so much darkling air. A brief and magnificent spasm passes across the moon: itself a cellular orb or shift that reflects orange against turquoise. Look at this now, Heathcote Dervish's returned to the verbal fray:~

"*Avaunt* a lost witness to expectancy, brethren… No-one can effectively take away from a memory which is ours. Oh my yes – the wraith has gone back to its solitary sphere of absence. Who but us may tear away the veil of these secrets? Tumble-weed or Hermaphrodite X lists where it wilt, as regards a cosmic finality or its precision. Yet our monstrous or thwarted mask's boomeranged home – in whichever dimension that may be said to reside. It reverses its ascent by way of a cast dye; it traverses once again a Masonic coffin which litters a vatic space. No matter what relief… and given the nature of its unquiteness, as it comes to be played today. Could we be speaking of a Mediaeval passion or mystery play? Don't its nails percolate now amidst wood, balsa or tenderness? They spread a deluded word – only to

11

kilter before its speed. It limits its projection or penetration into the oak, thereby. Will you correctly configure it? For a tunnel, a prick or a pin casts an indent before Golgotha: it merely mounts to the glory of puissance. Now let's loosen a charred fabric, it helps to give a costive or bluish glow to caskets, the nature of whose bark curls under each knife! Yes indeed, those screws that turn on the tap of plenty are bound to unlock a woodchip's offering. The grain or texture leans sideways; primarily in a way which lifts up one strut in order to massage a spendthrift plenty. It is all held too deeply within those trees."

DO NOT BORE US WITH SLEIPNIR'S EIGHT LEGS: (6)

Heathcote Dervish pulled down the cowl from his darkly illumined robe. Didn't it resemble a reddish hue in a cauldron's last or fluctuating breath? Behind him a bright yellow panel indicates its transport: it struck up before a ceiling's livery. Various planks or heavy buttresses, irrespective of purchase, existed beyond his left shoulder. A woman is also observed from afar. She has de-cowled, at least when taken together with a slightly owlish face – it proves capable of looking spectral, even beady-eyed. A pair of expensive and reinforced ear-rings are also seen: and these ramify with a devil-may-care set of eye-brows, themselves merely captured before one's view. (Just for a moment, one of Richard Linder's exercises in Pop Art veers into the frame. Many of his canvases were used to illustrate Vladimir Nabokov's prose, after all). Against this, the female had a shock of white hair which passed through her scalp's central axis: it ricocheted from one's brow like a silk handkerchief's tail (…) Her name, you ask? It patterned to Elsa Bounteous Hapgood. "My husband", she beamed, "you have forever vanquished the toils of Reason. One must care for an abruptness which travels aslant a balustrade. Never mind… since a Y has been carved deep into this sand-stone's interior. It widened out towards the cement of an outermost wall. Such a walkway carried away its dispensation --- most sheer. Again, a disillusioned or carved rubber – squared off with mathematical precision – hindered the foreground. It related to a black pastel square beyond its linkage; one which arrested the signature of a forgotten diary. Likewise, a brick, lozenge or sponge disfigured the whole: it had to pick up the skeleton lurking inside this stone. No matter how articulately its roughage can be yielded! Moreover, the icon of a wizard --- or possibly a salamander without fire --- cast itself adrift from this unribbed mortar. It all seemed to hint at a saurian indifference *avaunt* one's grave. Nor can we forget, necessarily, the skeletal outer limbs… when taken together with its bulbous orbs (at once insect-like) and the bird's rib-cage. It up-ended a vice, triangular in its certainty or rigour, and Palaeolithic in frequency. Surely H.P. Lovecraft's *Rats in the Walls* digs deep enough for us?"

DO NOT GO GENTLY INTO THAT ACID BATH: (7)
For his part, Heathcote Dervish manifested a powerful visage; it looked on the world in a misanthropic way, definitely so. The brows were beetling, the eye-sockets sunken; especially when taken together with lugubrious skin around other apertures. His hair also delineated a slant; being coiled, silken, black and closely etched upon the scalp. Whereas outer extremities – like ears – proved to be made of heavy porcelain, metaphorically so. (This recalled Dennis Wheatley's novel *The Haunting of Toby Jugg*, rather helplessly). Meanwhile, his lips sundered flesh or they happened to be full, ripe, discursive and non-pursed. They definitely resounded to a strong chin's character; whilst his snout indicated narrative drive. It drove home its point in a way which appears beaky, truculent, vulture-like and aristocratic. (In terms of a fictional correlation, Alan Sillitoe's novels *The General* and *The Loneliness of the long-distance Runner* come to mind). His teeth, less remarkably, gave an impression of Vorticist angles: that is, they gyrated towards a steel grimace. Here we find that Caro's lightness of touch misfires with genetics…

AN ANGEL BURIES ITS NOSE-CONE IN THE EARTH: (8)
Another individual stares on in a grimacing way – his features are desperate, cloven-hoofed and unperturbed. They seem to

kindle memories of a concrete slab which was possibly off to one side. Furthermore, these detours into identity, phrenologically, appear thick-set, graven, slip-streamed or trog-like. His name intoned the following accent: Warlock Splendour Thomas – it happens to be. "Bravo", he thundered in a deep, bass voice. "None could have served such effective witness as Heathcote Dervish. He (alone of all doubters) reaches beyond oblivion's curtain in order to summon this wraith. It came at his call and in accord with his prime o' life – only then to susurrate the wind. Can the late symphonies of a post-modern like Richard Simpson cast a beat? Whatever the cause: a hollow reaches out before one's background; it strives to be deep or mole-like under the ground. Likewise, the darkest mud and earth limbered over it; thence occasioning a relation to wires of red. These came to illustrate a clock's outermost features; itself closely bound up to or broken in terms of a face... at least on one side. This sun-dial's white frontispiece was chipped, peeled or salutary in scope. Whereupon its innards spiralled out of control. They addressed the certainty of a witness too far... even though each coil, helix, comfort of many and compression-spring toiled to reconnect with its aftermath. These internal devices (you see) affect to be modulated; at once bearing a carnival's imprint... even the sea-side resort or comedy circuit of yesteryear."

WE SHALL BURY NUDE CARDS IN A VACUUM: (9)
Our narrative travels on, however, with Heathcote Dervish striding away from his cauldron... it continues to splutter and smoke on a brick altar. Its votaic patterning adopts a form that's silhouetted, darksome, rigid and squared in its quilt. A vapour trail rose up successively from its hearth. Assuredly, the sky broke to the remit of its orange – if only by virtue of incense swirling below. Heathcote moved forward with a bowed head now – almost as if the man's visage became frozen, congealed, progressive and determined. A dark nimbus plays about his brow, casting it in a silhouette's form. In any event, some wooden debris --- when mixed with stone --- lit up our view's

14

left-hand corner. Certainly, one woman (a nameless votary) looked on dispassionately --- all of this religious circle's experienced a shock, after all. Whereupon another monk drifted in and out of consciousness; he came to abreast of the right-side. In reflective mood, Elsa Bounteous Hapgood opined: "Some day the world shall understand, husband of mine. It will broadcast such results as these on children's television. Isn't it obvious? Since two pillars stand alone before a moon's opalescence (now). They disagree with what may or may not exist within one. The twin columns rise like sentinels in England's darkness; while a shadowy or liquid orb slips upon furtive ground. Don't chase it again... because fictive shapes cross the screen of a dawn's mantle. They live out their subsistence on an electric terrain; the like of which refracts onto a falling wall. This telescopes a graph of many bricks – all of them releasing deep grooves into Byzantine concrete. It seems to be a million miles away from Sir Frank Brangwyn's oil sketch, *The Lemon Pickers*, in 1908. Although a rough-cut suffused this stone; it drove a bargain and etched its stillness. Definitely now, such a mural levered its absence towards the wood: thereby reflecting on such deep incisions."

NO WARRANTY SURPRISES PARADISE: (10)
Over and again, our mage chooses to intervene: "Listen to me, woman, we need to break out of our enclosure – it offers us nothing but purple. The rottenness of one hand may not limit entreaty, particularly if our feeble will halts before Fate. In any event, mankind mocks at us by way of surcease. They imagine us to be fools or worse, in terms of our adherence to these mystic arts. You speak --- Bounteous Elsa --- of a time when knowledge or illumination comes; but favourably cast aside such Masks. None surrounds us with a hundred pigs here: since any swine-herds on stakes recall William Golding's *The Lord of the Flies*. Insufficient recognition awaits us; it passes off into ready grievances – only to fail at a feast of Yorkshire's art. Whereby – like a painting by Atkinson Grimshaw – Aphrodite gestures

ethereally across a tidal scope of red. It lumbers up above the horizon – thus escaping from any final curtain-call by Arthur Sutro. Truly wife, what we require is a sigil's power --- not a Pope's indulgence. We need a sign that comes to us from out of the aeons; or quite possibly it's the nimbus of a new decay… one which scrapes the maggots from expiring meat. We have to prove to our fellow doubters or sceptics, locked into modernity as they are, that this knowledge registers in our breasts. It pertains to us alone."

In his mind's eye, though, Heathcote approaches a double-breasted door… Next to it – and availing itself of all mythology – a pattern of mist swirls around its angles. Leaning against one of these posts stands a Clown; he seems to indicate infinite cruelty or a Pueblo's response to lust. Do such peons learn morality through a carnival of play? Anyway, our character is seen to incarnate Glock's absence or estrangement – even the tell-tale covering at the end of Trevor Griffith's drama, *The Comedians*. Certainly, a circus' sinister aspect travels beyond our avatar. But no matter… for our version of Magnasco's *Punchinello* remains arbitrary in his dismissive air.

A MAQUETTE OF DELUDED LOOPS OR EYES: (11)
A car's indifference attracts one's attention to it – such a futurist racer lies to one side of a funeral block made from stone. It casts the net wide before a phantasy (herein). To notice our hullabaloo: all of these denizens, led by Heathcote Dervish and Elsa Bounteous Hapgood, make their way towards a bevy of vehicles. Expensive limousines find themselves arranged next to several collapsed walls. Didn't Dennis Wheatley declare that those engaged in the mystic arts are often wealthy? Abundant materialism always breeds such immaterialism, you see. Nonetheless, Wiltshire's mists gather around a burnished Rolls-Royce; while, to one side, a silver cloud or lotus effectively locks in its own seating. Various subdued panels fall away; their sides are crenellated to a lost magnificence… and each one looms up

16

before its witness. Occasionally, a brick becomes discernible amidst porous granite; it comes laced with the odd neighbouring hole. A cavernous window (this) which peeps out of such hollows; it straddles a parchment via many stones. Do they scream in silence, in accordance with so much feminist dictum?

Anyway, our two main protagonists, whether male or female, walk between these barrows. They pick themselves up over such hewn rocks and head for the cars' running-boards. As usual, Heathcote Dervish is talking: "We must accomplish a great feat, wife... one that cuts against the very root of Life's tree. Oh yes – if one of our number brings down to earth, even momentarily, some sort of sun-spot... then all corners of the globe shall bear witness to it. Not until such Power has been manifested will we encompass our due. What we require involves an object for both passion and thaumaturgy." As he said this, Heathcote strode forward purposefully. Furthermore – in a glowering template – his face stood out starkly; it seemed to be limned or even haloed. A ruddy effulgence covered all of its aspect; whilst a scorbutic rim hastened to chastise those roundabout. Seen in this way, he effectively betokened a shaman's features: at once masked, effigy-like, fixed and full of blood. To wax Mediaeval about it, his humours were unbalanced and thus led onto a situation of excess choleric.

All this time though, our worshipful master has a dream or fantasy on the go. It relates to a past Clown or one who chooses to brush aslant us... albeit when beholden to a shadow's bliss. This big-top monger --- or companion from out of left-field --- gestures wildly. Yet still, all things considered, we continuously return to his face. It depicts an unalterable act – whether spliced, immobile as to grease-paint, and transformed by degrees. Let's sort it out, if you will. For our Grimaldi's tone seeks oblivion's rescue. It can be seen in profile, hectoring from a booth or otherwise akimbo. Needless to say, all of these Glocks look macabre over a potential for masking up – that is, for foot-wear worn over the face. Yes: our patience has worn thin... because the bulbous nose, red-letter day, rouge, thick lips (abreast of silence) and paint-wheels all speak of chaos. Or – to put it another way – they indicate nought but an anarchic potential in tom-foolery. It happened to be a feast of fools which ventilates the aperture of a new beginning. What goes on here? Nothing really; our scenario just understands that a mountebank engages in assault and sexual ragging: it all proceeds darkly under glass... nay, even smoothly betimes. Like all relics that die in a child's arms – it contrives to induce an innocent fording, possibly a rind stone amid a darkling glass.

UNDER A SMILE, A MECHANISM BETRAYS ITS GREASE-PAINT: (12)

Our warlock, Heathcote Dervish, walks to a brocaded car through some indifferent mist. It all speaks of unhallowed offerings before various bull gods and others. Somewhat reluctantly, his wife steps out with him, although already his mind happens to be elsewhere. One experience before all others risks its temperature across from his brows. It seems to encompass the following: in this programme a lonely waif, Heathcote in another life, wanders Whitechapel's streets bereft of care. Isn't this where those 'sexist' mutilations and slayings took place – all between the 31st of August 1888 and November the 8th of that year? Watch Heathcote Dervish, though – for he's attired in a triangular dome independently of any trespass. An old great coat – of the sort worn by a Boer war veteran – surrounds his lower appurtenances. But any mask (hitherto mentioned) comes surrounded by a further infraction. This enables one to breathe under a muslin extremity; it seeks to whisper against its own claret. Needless to say, a great swathe of bandages hides the cusp within... or could it be a Pinocchio who's been shorn of all his lies? In any event, the mummified rictus swirls apace – if only to bury a scarab's entombment. It rightly decides to go on before the draft; at once disabled, frigid, falsely congealed, sarcophagus-like and ameliorated. In this advent, you see, one's verso or 'the sinister'

18

has been raised to a nethermost power; it chalks off any semblance to lint. Let's see now --- a gas-light glimmers in the distance, nearly always adjacent to a pea-souper. The briefest of blue scarves then uncurls from Heathcote's neck in a serpentine fashion.

LAUGH, LAUGH YOU HOLLOW SCARECROWS[!]: (13)

"Numquam potest non esse virtuti locus."

'It can never be that for courage there is no place.'
- *Medea*, Euripides

Bounteous Elsa Hapgood, his wife, has been meaning to accost him for some time. Perplexed, she stands her ground like a four-fold tree. "Husband of mine", she averrs, "all semblance of torture must cease to be articulated by these lips. Your importance in our community stands recognised... and vast wealth surrounds you --- what more do you crave? Surely, you can wax satisfied with these inner furnishings of Pandora's box?"

For his part, Heathcote remains still or mute. His mind cannot readily free itself (you see) from those fancies which come laced in an alien *Victoriana*. By virtue of them, a close-up is observed around his bandaged eyes. These stare manically ahead of themselves – whilst coming wrapped in a magenta's haze. Each eye-ball looks avid, unremembered, and all requesting in terms of a sacrifice. But where can a wickerman be found in this unlikely fog? Altogether now, his mummified appendages speed on lightly to their task. Like a satanic easter egg, these outer wraps encode one betraying silence or other.

A MINUTE TO SAVE THE UNIVERSE FROM CAVEMEN: (14)
Still Bounteous Elsa Hapgood, who has refused to quit her post, makes fine her entreaty. To which her spouse responds brusquely

and with brutality. "It dissatisfies me over provender, woman. Do you hear? I cannot bear to be scoffed at by my peers o'er performance of the ancient rites. More than any Dion Fortune novel, we are the true custodians of animal magic!"

Despite this though, the wizard's mind seems to be penetrated by Whitechapel's fog. His *alter ego* has turned his back towards a dark pregnancy, only to then give a rejoinder to a back-line of gloom. Basically, he continues to wander forth, the triangular tapes and bandages trailing behind him. All around his 'dead man walking' there subsists an uneven glow; it lops off one final disaster before another... even though a decayed wall or fantastical mural slips along beside them. It drips with entreaty or hidden expectation. Hark (!), might those prove to be figurines up front or in the darkness? He can hardly make them out, but somewhere he knows that he's seen them already.

AN ADVENT WITNESSES GOITRE PRIOR TO MARTYRDOM: (15)
Like always, Heathcote Dervish is bluff and unapologetic with his social inferiors. While almost unbeknown to him his chauffeur, Butler James, holds open a carriage's exit so that his master might enter. "I trust all went smoothly at the ceremony, your worship", cooed the Butler. "Verily, underling, show all speed so as to position us before the mansion", snapped his bad-tempered owner. Butler James – irrespective of what he actually thought – held open the door for his lord and lady. A league beyond this certain other couples were likewise disembarking. Furthermore, the vehicle in question proved to be an old silver ghost; what with spoked wheels, tiny palisades and shimmering glass surrounds. All the time a heavy and impenetrable mist came down around them; it appeared to register the trick known as Pepper's Ghost in the theatre.

MULCT THE PREY WHICH MUST BE YOURS: (16)

Heathcote Dervish knew – with all sincerity – that to feed on your own kind was an obvious moral necessity. Yes indeed; but who or what were those dimly discerned shapes ahead? In one sense, identification luxuriates in straightforwardness… since two bourgeois figurines stood out amidst a pea-souper. Its resultant colouring – when bereft of all toads – had to speak of cerulean's mock-majesty. Now then, in the distant confusion, Heathcote makes out various sparring partners. They prove to be differentiated versions of Butler James and Elsa Bounteous Hapgood. They stand, in pre-Edwardian fancy dress, in front of a rather stark building with a golden door. What might it signify, possibly? Again, desultory gas lamps shimmer from above, and each globular yellow speck looks to be cast away in ones and twos… This is it: yet one enabling factor foxes our consciousness. It has to involve the figure of a small ragamuffin or street urchin who runs from our respectable duo. Do they come to represent or illustrate the middle-class couple on Munch's bridge, irrespective of his screamer? Never mind: since our street-child involves a bit of stray ectoplasm or sensory protoplasm. This may well have been cast adrift by Bounteous Elsa in the course of her researches. "Come back, return to us, ol' Jenny. Let there be no hard feelings or recriminations. Can ya credit it?", opines a dead butler. "Cor mister, not likely", hums our Jenny. "Haven't you heard that there's a monster abroad – around aways and about these backstreets, themselves encased in fog? He be a ghoul, a watchman, a Ripper or Walter Sickert without the acrylic grief, my lovelies. Lor' above, me ducks…" – it's then that she spies Heathcote D. Abreast of mummifying bandages (he is), although not necessarily liable to stop aside of a triangular convex.

DEVIL DOLL, DO YOUR UTMOST TO UPSET THIS APPLE-CART: (17)

In our dimension (or its twenty-first century compass) this couple's limousine races ahead. Deep inside its upholstery a husband and wife converse. "I'm afraid that you worry me on occasion, my lord", insisted Elsa. "Let's give it a go abreast of Hans Jurgen Syberberg's cinema… for, in truth, your pursuit of magical salves started almost accidentally. It went under the christening of a hobby --- nothing more. Now it seems to have completely taken over your existence, dear." In saying this… one just has to remark upon the emboldened mask which is her face. It happens to be blanched, replete, effulgent, clipped as to tone, aristocratic and spartan in its training. Was it anything other than an Aristo's visage, to be sure (?): if we might make use of a phrase drawn from John Fowles' non-fiction. Nonetheless, nacreous ear-rings float in her lobes (depending); they carry forwards Leni Riefenstahl's Olympic torch, thereby.

BETRAY THE DEATHS OF A MILLION GNATS, WHY DON'T YOU[?]: (18)
Irrespective of any of the above, my friends, Jenny ran smack into Heathcote Dervish's mask. He stood out starkly when limned against an ebon ground; in a scenario where his orbs glowed like coals. They transfigured such darkness within a shining esplanade – especially now that a gas-jet lit up the rear portal. It gave off a stroboscopic pulsation none too easily. Likewise, his features showed through the triangular hood underneath the bandages… Could H.G. Wells' description of *The Invisible Man* have been a psychic transcription of this? In any event, his Lon Chaney grimace passed muster with the sepulchral; and it denoted an off-shoot of Bram Stoker's discourse over those seven stars, or such-like sigils. "Lor'", betokened our Jenny in innocent blasphemy. Had a vampiric nemesis struck from out of the pages of James Hinton's philosophy – leastwise, when it came to deal with female redemption?

DO NOT DISILLUSION THESE POST-MODERN STAVES: (19)

The lord of the manor, Heathcote Dervish, remained oblivious to his surroundings – while concentrating on an innermost project. "Most assuredly", he responded to his wife, Elsa Bounteous. "Covenship (or the practice of the mystic arts) has become my life, veritably so. Nor will any dare to mock me for it – irrespective of aught else. Do the heavens mark my cry?" In this instant, Dervish's voice rises to a crescendo; it both rasps and shouts. Whilst his upper-class patina (to look at) recalled Lord Lucan's after a Saturday night out at one of John Aspinall's gaming emporiums. Abruptly then, it reached out as expansive, costing plenty, robust, truculent, awkward, plummy and magisterially alone. It sort of intoned a David Cameron look without the wetness, effeminacy and liberal bias. No temporising stood out here from afar: in that Heathcote Dervish came across as a preacher man Riley, a fanatic or a customary mystagogue. (You don't need to have read Flannery O'Connor's *Wise Blood* to have arrived at this conclusion). All and everything stares clearly up at you from these waters, yes?

SPARE A SECOND THOUGHT FOR A RUINED TENNIS-BALL: (20)

In a parallel universe to our present one (circa. the London of the eighteen eighties) a street-child backed away from us. Might she interpret the role of one of Pasolini's rag-and-bones, particularly when illuminating the forsaken identity of 'Kathy Come Home'? No doubt about it: her liquorice treatment seemed to suffice for some instant or other on the board. It waxed beastly before its own inanity, therefore. As to hair, the girl sought out a rubicund offering – with her mane frazzled under a temperate dose. "Lor'", she insisted, when addressing the bandaged carapace before her. "Are you a make-belief or a shape-shifter; that is, one who plys the by-ways of the soul looking for victims?" For a moment, Heathcote's *doppelganger* remained silent, but he then repeated in a dulcet whisper. "Lor', Jenny, old love... it's time for socio-biology to take effect – just think of me as your reaver, claustrophobic entry and Maudsley hospice. Truly, I shall release you from your mortal coil." In uttering this, he incarnated a wraith's imprint – what with his glaucous spirit, husk, rotting cadaver exterior and Anne Rice look. Certainly, he bore his mummification lightly – if only to retrieve its essence at day-break.

LISTEN TO A CANNON'S JOYFUL WISDOM: (21)
We move now to embrace another character's development... For a silvery puppet, by the name of Phosphorous Cool, hangs from the back-frame of one of Eric Bramall's marionette shows. Like a toy-theatre it was; in that our silver manikin danced above a globe – the latter jigging away before a transparent screen. Could it be little more than a prop vest; or a painted door at the back of a performance house? Let's loosen such a witness – when we remember that a swirl of the Heavenly firmament exists outside: within which one glacier after another shifts its transparent non-ice. It fuels the fire of teleology or a prior purpose, you see. Yes again; each planet twinkles before the stardust of its available canopy. While – to one side of these developments – Phosphorous gazes at an enclosing white hole. A centre-point of non-darkness (this happens to be) which eludes its own sun, choosing instead to fire off around a planet. Such an imprint sought to give a fiery halo to a visiting orb; it composed an aureole that transfigures its stillness.

EAT A GOLF-BALL WITH A PORCUPINE'S MOUTH: (22)
Entreat me now and forever, why don't you? For our bandage man continues to subsist in a rival dimension. It paints up the posture of its latitude, indeed... especially since Heathcote's auxiliary consciousness strikes muster in its mirror. May this object be one of those fair-ground glasses which disfigures the body – by means of optical trickery? Never mind: this has to be due to the fact that Mister Bandage is adjusting a cantankerousness in his hand; one which casts a Doctor

Kevorkian shadow. Do you detect its lustre? Let's examine this forethought again… particularly when his adjustment filibusters an eye: the kindred of such a loss betokens a poison within each valve. Whilst concentrating on this debenture Heathcote Dervish registers a manic gleam – it's merely non-spectral, undistanced and puissant (to say the least). "Lordy", whispers Jenny. Her slightly hoarse Cockney accent is reduced to a croak now. "My Lor', no, no, Jesu; you must be the harbinger, phantom or monger of solids. Hazard your worst, Mr. X!" "I shall, dearie", responded Heathcote D., "have no doubt about that."

VISIT OUR ENGLISH *COMMEDIA DELLE'ARTE* FOR THE FIRST TIME[!]: (23)
What does Phosphorous Cool look like? Well, he continues to ply a trough into innocence – if only to remember a maintenance of prisms. Instead of which, however, we notice that his eye-sockets are absent to an expectant retina: they achieve the grave of one unknown too soon. Most definitely, since the dome of the puppet's head glistens like a billiard ball in those stage lights – each one of them twinkling from this comedy theatre's wings. Never again though, *quod* our marionette's visage recalls the architectural purity of Botticelli; wherein idealism comes transfused in one face (*a la* Riefenstahl's yearning). To be true: the cosmos radiates unreality behind our figurine's head-piece; possibly due to its articulation out of papier-mâché.

ONE PICK SEEKS A SAND-CASTLE TO KNOCK OVER: (24)
Against our witness statement here, Bandage Man prepares his pipette for the final count-down. Irrefragably, his finger-tips, covered in lintel, reposition the plunger within this particular dial. Moreover – culturally speaking – his demeanour has much to do with Professor Moriarty's obsessionality in a film like *The Woman in Green* from the nineteen thirties. To be faithful to its memory, you understand? Meanwhile – and viewed as a close-up – Jenny stands before this dark doctor with a funereal 'plaint.

Surely, she represents a Pre-Raphaelite virgin who's badly out of focus? Yet again, we find that her mittens were clasped together, the tresses badly dishevelled, the eye-pits sunken and her skin sallow. Furthermore, the mouth depicted an oval or rectangle – almost pleading, empty, redundant or forlorn (it was). A passionate dimness then gripped all around this fog; it limbered up to a neighbouring building's absent prospect, effectively speaking. "Let me inform you of who I am", registered our Band-aid top.

MARIONETTES SQUEAK BEFORE THE LIGHTS, MIND EACH FIRE: (25)
Underneath our jigging figurine, Phosphorous Cool, a silk backcloth superintends; it provides a fitting terrain for this character. Almost immediately Phosphorous hunkers down; he seems to be regretting something whilst remaining speechless. Above his pointy head a meteorite shoal glimmers; it carries forth a transpondency... even a reluctance. Let's forgive its overall vista once in a while... Likewise, our puppet – although a manikin and not a glove – realises that he can't break free. Most assuredly, he must be stuck in an assembly of stick-men or corn-dollies (forevermore)... and don't forget the restiveness of Mister Punch, irrespective of his violence, once the old Italian called Porsini brought him over from the continent.

FLOW RIVER, FLOW THROUGH MERCURY'S VEINS: (26)
Back in a prismic recapturing, then, Heathcote's bandaged saliva manages to fill this wreckage with fear. It rears up as a tubular encastellation of rags; each one delimiting the tower in such a Babel. It decides, most considerably, to leaven dysgenics with the promise of an after-life. Again now, a variant on Breugel's tower of many tongues leads to some sort of closure: it essentially finishes off the space around our plunger. Also – and akin to this – the atmosphere swirls pulsatingly like a piece of Op art. Mightn't it encode one optical illusion amongst many? Although the hollowed out cheeks of our Jenny back away; and

26

this is oblivious to the fact that her Joker's turned up… albeit in a game of solitaire. "No, please, master of diffidence, 'ave mercy on a poor waif and stray. Do ya find it so?" "Forget the bleating, oik of a crimson plenty", enjoins our Strangelove's tissue. "Your reaping of the whirlwind is a gain attributable to my particular life. Mark it so: the provision of slaughter – for these new Gadarene swine – has to be either a misadventure: or a desire to place a porcine head upon a wooden staff. For – only by virtue of sucking the marrow out of you – can I liberate myself from the doldrums. No mere psychic vampirism, *a la* Dion Fortune, may satisfy me and mine. Not half…"

ONE STRATAGEM EXISTS FOR A BOUNCING SILVER BAUBLE: (27)

One has to listen to what's going on in order to really understand, you know? While – during this rival tournament – Phosphorous clenches his fist in an expectation of nothingness. A burst or susurration of speed surrounds him – all in accord with reverse trigonometry; it actually favours one capture ahead of another one. During this enclosure, the puppet's jaw hardens with new resolve, albeit pugnaciously. It similarly argues for a split humidity around the eyes, within which one star-cluster can coalesce. It burns – akin to magnesium oxide – at some time in the future. Maybe Ray Bradbury would not approve – but, in all honesty, Phosphorous Cool had decided to break free from Eric Bramall's chains. He wishes to blurt out from one theatrical backing or story-board… at large. Again, such a toy-theatre – as chronicled by George Speaight – was made by Elsa in West Germany (sic). It betokened some wood, came flat-packed, stood erect up to six feet when mounted, and consisted of heavy velvet. A colour scheme of red-and-blue intruded --- complete polar opposites, you see!

AGAIN, TO BREACH A PANTALOON BETRAYS A CACTUS: (28)

Assuredly now, way back in the nineteenth century Jenny staggers away – together with a golden pulsation surrounding her lights. Before her form, Heathcote Dervish, bandage swathed, prepares to administer the *coup de gras*. "Your worthless life (Jenny) must furnish fuel for my becoming… it illustrates the ability to replenish existence with naught but a sausage. A naked tableau of meat spits in the pan – always broiling over the embers of unnatural fires. In its way, therefore, it proves to be adjacent to that scene in a Howard Brenton play; wherein the mass murderer Christie rises from a den of rubbish. He forsakes the articulation of so many crazes – it also reaches out in order to refute Brenton's doctrine of 'practical communism'. Nonetheless, a mask on Christie's psychopathic features betrays its innocence. It listened to the adventure of so many gates; even if nemesis rises up from crumpled issues of *The Daily Star* – rather than *The Morning Star*. A bobble-hat and scarf around his upper body – possibly with the colours of Reading FC in blue-and-white – passed underneath Christie's second skin. Conceptually speaking, Christie's facial covering looked rasped, Mediaeval, boy-hooded and somewhat naïve. It doubtlessly travelled via this travail *in lieu* of pain; it also speaks to nothing save a salve in an empty mirror."

With this repast, *ergo*, Heathcote Dervish slid through Jenny at a run; and his syringe proved to be the weapon of despatch. Listen to me: a sacred scream is heard… one which happens to deliver its provender from the ground. Everything else really tips away from its offering now; despite the fact that Jenny's demise takes place before a bar of newsprint. A rectilinear blast at the Hackney Empire followed its suit… whereupon a thousand-and-one vaudeville shows, *artistes*, and such-like entertainments, littered its boards. Didn't these betray the inner dimensions of the Actor's Club off the Strand, as well as being pursuant to those early Max Wall farces of yesteryear? Jenny – at a milk-top's

28

finality – cried out: "Help, murder, police... cor, not half."
Finally, the two shadows merged into one. A rooted hood and a
minor earthling combine in their shapes – and the cry of a lynx
comes to be heard at a falling night-time. It yelps, roams and then
turns mute. Likewise, a policeman's whistle may be listened to in
the distance, but who will truly obey its sound?

CRUMPLE BEFORE A HURDY-GURDY MAN'S
LISTENING: (29)
Phosphorous Cool has jilted himself free now... He accosts or
limbers his body up, thereby, and this is in order to let off steam
from a deluded turbine. It travelled up one's left-side in terms of
one geyser too many. Whereas just behind Phosphorous – and to
the right side – there stood something of a pitted planet. In a
Herculean firmament... it seemed to speak up for ultramarine,
sapphire, cerulean and French Blue. Despite the fact (we must
say) that this globule undulates like an asteroid – what with
craters, dips, declensions and other inclines. (In truth, such an orb
took us back to those moon globes care/of Sir Patrick Moore's
Sky at Night). Needless to say, a pitch black or ebon back-screen
limits our theatre. Phosphorous Cool sets himself against it. May
he be a rebel with or without a cause?

COCKNEY EELS WILL MAKE YOU PAY, MAKE YOU
PAY: (30)
Our narrative continues in another dimension, but now it takes a
different tack. It's not Heathcote Dervish's consciousness this
time; no, the development which enters here has to do with
another character altogether. For Phosphorous' transliterated
dreams come to the fore – especially when a turbo-charged
hansom cab repositions itself above the stars. All of this leads to
a situation where the Thames levels out below: and it sheers off
to the side, if only to escape from the glittering lights. Contrary
to Bulwer Lytton, these reflect back from a spangled or
bedizened river. *Tout court*, the People's Palace is lit up adjacent
to Pugin's Big Ben; the latter cascading into the sky by dint of its

hours. Sundry air-ships or balloons are also seen; they move effortlessly across between the north and south banks. Irrespective of this, Phosphorous belabours his point by motioning to the cabbie. He stands, whip in hand, at the back of the vehicle. All in all, he sets himself over a Phileas Fogg extravaganza – even a rival child's intervals of play. Yes indeed, he stood upright like one of those figurines in a toy-theatre which Montague Summers made so much play with at the twentieth century's advent. Could a connexion also be established, perchance, between this drama and Terry Gilliam's Pythonesque bravura…? In any event, a picturesque *Victoriana* continues to intrude. It's best illustrated by those gas-lamps whose illuminations flicker on the Thames; the water then glistens, ethereally, in a haze. Mark it!

TO ESCAPE AN IRON-MAIDEN TASTES OF HONEY: (31)
Do you wish to remember such a velocity? Phosphorous has speeded up now and he is just a blur of motion. A literal quick-silver weapon he might well be – one which chooses to render indistinct its momentum towards a goal. Certainly, various planets and cellular orbs twinkle on, plus a negative reverberation in relation to the silences of these interstellar gulfs. Didn't such planetary correspondences become frightened at day-time? Furthermore, our marionette wants to break out from Eric Bramall's world --- freedom is sought, thereby. It wishes to strike out along a ventriloquist's lonely path. Don't you know that a puppet-master's voice ultimately originates from the stomach? Regardless of which, Pascal still seemed to be affrighted by the ache in these gulfs and their ignorance over mankind!

Some time later, Heathcote Dervish enters a pub down in the vicinity of Bishopsgate – it's called "Jack the Ripper". (Although – unknown to many of its participants – an inn with a similar name would be forced to change its title. It did so during the nineteen seventies and under feminist pressure.) Heathcote nimbly entered the tap-room – with his bandages prominently displayed around his pyramidal cone; within which his eyes burnt on like coals taken from a living fire. Various gas-lamps illumined the scene; and they had VR picked out on their glazed surfaces. It stood for Victoria Regina. Inevitably though, this pub appeared to be heavily lit – what with solid wooden panels all around its walls. A few mid-century pictures – such as one or two Constables – lay about the room's far-flung vicinity. Yes truly, they came encased in gilt or ormolu frames of some grandeur. A large collection of creatures filled the bar; they wore frock coats, top hats, cravats, bow-ties and even cloaks. A few of them dissolved before one's gaze – becoming shape-shifters or semblances *a la* David Icke. What might this hint at? The possibilities are obviously multiple – it's true. Yet a captured disfigurement hints at a lack-lustre glass. Around Heathcote Dervish (and to the side) stood his two accomplices: these were Bounteous Elsa Hapgood and Butler James. Although formally dead – he'd changed little down the years, but she looked altogether like a little madam. A virago authoress of yesteryear – she was definitely U, to make use of Nancy Mitford's term. Various buns adorned her scalp (thereby); itself replete with an off-the-shoulder fur coat. Less Pre-Raphaelite than mildly Audrey Beardsley in manner – that's how she proved to be!

ENOUGH OF THESE STRATAGEMS WHICH ENCASE OUR THOUGHTS: (32)
On Eric Bramall's imaginary stage-set, then, Phosphorous Cool comes unstuck; in that his body caroms back from an after-screen. A terrific conundrum ensues… Alack (!), a reverberation impacts upon this puppet cradle with almost physical force. Again, a brain-dwelling SPLAM (!) notates this mark… it also raises the moniker of a spendthrift Golgotha (here). Surely, the barrier at our set's rear preserves a forceful imprint – one which lends a corporeal lustre to what might otherwise be a doll's tabernacle? For a moment our figurine looks stunned or sleepy – yet one cannot help but notice that the strings which tie a marionette are broken. Unlike Gerry Anderson's *Thunderbirds*,

or a barge-theatre in Henley-on-Thames, this glove seems to have slipped 'his' armature. No-one really knows any more at this juncture...

Meanwhile – back in the ecstasy of Heathcote's forgotten dreams – he espies a tap-room's mortal saw-dust. Yes indeed, various trans-mortals sup up their cups in the bar's recesses; in a situation where each one measures a cloud's aberrant silver. In one corner, a spheroid-headed mugwump downs an ale; while his companion grows a pineal eye from its compress. Do we really mean 'its' forehead? Again now, the public house's back-sweep waxes poignant in its intrigue: and it shadow-boxes over an array of figures who could have come out of a Beresford Egan drawing. Regardless of all this, a number of pre-Edwardian yokels bite the dust – they also sit around circular tables in a low light. Listen to our mementos: since a man in a cylindrical top-hat slumps in a recessed booth, and the head-gear in question is bright green. Whereas – on the House's other side – certain couples relax before pint glasses... or a jar of viands fills the space next to them. Although it appears to be obvious that one of them has a misshapen head; it flutes away to a turnip or trumpet *a la* Cesare Lombroso. Further, his companion in this endeavour downs a milky stout – a monk's habit and hair-cut are numbered among his possessions.

DON'T FORSAKE US IN OUR LETTUCE HOUR: (33)
Forever and a day, Phosphorous Cool's silvery form floats in space. He's at once up-ended and unresourced, but with a trail of vapour crossing his prow amidships. It definitely maps out the silhouette of so black a night; the curtains of which have been pulled down as a tribute to Pepper's Ghost. Look at this: a stillness supervenes in a puppet's world or show, and it grew angry at such a sallow hindrance... Despite the fact that Phosphorous drifts gloomily in space, or through a disacknowledged template under its sound.

32

WE WILL CONQUER ONCE MORE, ABREAST OF SULPHUR: (34)

Let it ride now: when we discover that a bandaged Heathcote sits next to Elsa and his butler, albeit a transformed one. A hint of frustration enters his voice here – yet he does well to conceal it. To speak of his head, though, Heathcote Dervish's cranium is adjusted to the triangular; it also came swathed in bandages. He illustrated an Egyptian mummy... possibly one which had been characterised by Budge, the Egyptologist. Still – underneath Anne Rice's accoutrements and gear – Heathcote's orbs festered away: and they summoned up fiery marbles to one's memory. In the farther environs of our public house, some desultory spectres sat at their drink. Although – and close to hand – Elsa Bounteous Hapgood and Butler James whispered in his ear. As a penitent, perforce, he had no choice but to consider their objections. One by one they laid them out before him... can we consider it as some fallen architecture aslant its deliverance? Her form looked most apt, wrapped up, mesmerised, intense and concentrated on one final effort. Similarly, she wore a studded broach or choke around her neck; it reflected a pale white lustre this even-tide. Are the eyes a window into one soul's leaving? In her case, then, such cerulean offerings paid the price of their own intrigue. It definitely outshone any Aphrodite of Melos out back – or contained on a salutary grass-land. Do some refuse to call it the Venus de Milo? Against this, however, E. Bounteous' moral jigsaw showed off; it sloped to one side and carried away Stan Barstow's carrion. Likewise, such a carnival knew no surcease and it exhibited its contempt --- even playfully. But such slits gathered some witnesses: and each one atomised an agency of change. They similarly refused to come down from the moon... especially when each one threw over a domino's heart. Surely, we can declare that her eyes foiled a slain witness (?); they were hard, twin-pointed, dark, enveloping and vulpine. Do they witness the star-lit status of a silent-screen goddess from the nineteen twenties? Oh my yes...

LET'S INDULGE TRUMAN CAPOTE'S PASSION FOR BRANDY: (35)

Within our puppet-master's purview, a meteor shower inundates the ground; it cascades to a known promontory. Nor do any ask: how can such fiery rocks fling themselves towards a toy-theatre's round-house? Never mind: since this shower of plunging granite moves on – and it tends to follow a definite pathway. Each congealed cliff carries a momentum's track (in other words); and it seems to observe a straight or propulsive energy, thereby. Furthermore, an ebon screen still sufficed to translate these puppets out into the mainstream. From the maelstrom or carnival of children's entertainment, then, it loomed up... so as to castigate a grave. Wisdom may issue from the mouth of babes, but, in this case, a circus always hints at Fear's wages! Any infantile joust doubtless contains the sinister within it...

THROW YOUR DICE, YOU MASSACRE OF INNOCENCE: (36)

Like Julian Barnes' novel about Sherlock Holmes, Heathcote Dervish and his companions sat in a Victorian pub. Each mystery solved its own defence through absence, you see. To return to the narrative, though: Butler James snapped his fingers in a clinch, but not necessarily a convulsion. Dear me no: because Butler James' look is altogether sly, inclement, listless and over-drawn. Nor can one tax a nasal feature which connects such a protuberance with his forehead... at least straight out. He chooses to wear an over-stuffed great-coat --- one that swoops down to his booted knees. In the remainder of the pub, revelry finds itself joined to an early version of a Cockney knees-up... although it doesn't necessarily feature Chas & Dave! Nonetheless, a sing-song has begun in the tap-room's farthest recesses – it helps to depict a miscellany of *fin de siecle* types. All of them happen to be hale and hearty. Do they not embody, after all, one of those Strong Men who are painted onto the wooden boards of a Limehouse show-town? Also, our collection of revellers consists of one Tommy Atkins on his own...

somewhat conspicuously. A dragoon guard possibly, his cap, uniform, braces and belt went with the sabretache underneath. He's surrounded by two charlatans in conical hats, or quite evidently they could be Pearly Kings and Queens. (A tradition which hasn't altogether disappeared from contemporary East London... an area wherein the old white population's virtually ceased to exist. It's been forced further out into Essex's marshes – primarily by dint of mass or alien immigration from the Third World). Accompanying this assembly, then, an old dame tinkles away on the sheet music's piano. She hardly looks at the score, however. A gusty tune rips from their collective throats (resultantly); and it remembers Lord Blake's biography of *Disraeli* in more ways than one.

A splendid town
a wonderful round
we'll smash our enemies into the ground...

Hurrah; hurrah –
diddly-doo...
nothing but the few can entertain you.

Rule Britannia
Britannia rules the waves
Britons never shall be slaves!

What music accompanies this ditty? Mayhap it happens to be *Standing Block* or *Stele* by Gyorg Kurtag, together with two works by Karlheinz Stockhausen: *Group* and the *Helicopter Quartet*. Dream on!

A BISCUIT CAN BE EATEN IN ONE GULP: (37)
Look at this! Our silvery puppet is caught up by these meteors and flung forth. He finds himself propelled along without either volition or will. It belabours the point of its own inauthenticity, in other words. Yet – when considered in the round – a version of

Clive Barker's *Books of Blood* crystallises here in a toy-theatre. Truly, it's an example of Angela Carter's *The Magic Toy-shop* or one of Michael Moorcock's broken tambourines. A certain haze comes over one's eyes (now) – even though Phosphorous Cool finds his velocity to be mute. Alone he is; while being cast amidships of this oblivion. It awakens before a necessary harbour. Again now, his limp body finds itself exhausted in front of such a waif. It's carried aloft or gusted forwards slightly; and the stray momentum of its entreaty measures a shaft. Does an embarkation like this require an Indo-Aryan swastika on its cover? Regardless of all else: the meteor storm turns on a cascade of rock and ice, or is it fire? During the course of it, a silver bullet seeks a were-wolf's body --- so that it might enter it. No matter: the point at issue rests with curving sun-light; it picks up our puppet and leverages him towards the earth. Moreover, our home planet looms up in the background – what with a quadrant of the night-sky blossoming from this dolls' theatre. In these moments, then, a transfiguration reckons on its aftermath: and it carries a marionette out of a mere play & into life. No longer, therefore, will the Marquis de Sade have to conduct plays involving lunatics at the Charenton asylum in the early nineteenth century. Such exercises in Artaud's Theory of Cruelty took place before Peter Weiss' version... nor did it really pre-date an expressionist vintage. In this cavalcade – together with these comets or meteors – Phosphorous Cool escaped from puppeteering AND ENTERED LIFE. (He was no longer beholden to a bald puppet-master, brandishing a mimetic trestle, and could now strike out in the dark. Surely, blindness might escape from his revolving orbs – if we consider those sculptures to be manufactured by touch alone? May his maker utilise a plasticity, stretched out on mesh or chicken-wire, and beloved of Elisabeth Frink?)

A SPARROW ALIGHTS ON A DISUSED STOVE PIPE: (38)
Further unto this endeavour, Heathcote Dervish and his fellows remain in 'Victoriana's' public house. Let it all come down

now… irrespective of a bath-towel. On his left side, Elsa Bounteous Hapgood and Butler James adopted a conspiratorial vein. They looked unapologetic, shifty, needful and full of what Titus Oates once called 'Popish Plots'. Elsa's eye-brows were arched and James' moustache-ends looked waxed, pointed and possibly insect-like. In contrast to his fellow travellers, Heathcote Dervish seemed more sinister than ever – what with those bandages shifting over the surface of a Toblerone head. Do these mummified cadavers move and slide every time he speaks? His eyes continue to glow preternaturally – by dint of a closed light. "Are you akin to our water-pistol's spout?", articulated Butler James. "Or does a poison-pellet, when delivered by a straw, leave you cold (?); especially if one shoots it like 'Just William'. What are you up to now?" "Of course I agree, my clucks", cooed Heathcote… by way of remonstrance and whisper. (He was desperately trying to reassure his erstwhile allies, you see). "Furthermore, your desire to up-end the Victorian colossus commends itself to me. I know you for what you are --- most veritably. You happen to be plenipotentiaries or representatives of the Grey Movement – an English schism, this, from the wider skinhead current. Many consider you to be an Anglo-Saxon variant on New Slovenian Art. No stuckists are you, but rather the vanguard of one collective semblance. It vaguely relates to the rock band, *Laibach*, who were part of *Neue Slovenia Kunst* – their anthem could be considered to be a version of that *ABBA* ditty: *Life is life*… never mind 'Great Man of the Nation'. In your case, however, you wish to rebel and overthrow Victoriana in order to establish modernity… albeit of a neo-classical and authoritarian vintage. Like Saddam Hussein or Gilbert & George, for example, you will use *kitsch* against itself --- in terms of reverse dialectic. One also wishes to speed the velocity of your pedal-bike more radically on its way."

NO SECRETS OF THE UNKNOWN MAY RAISE THIS BALACLAVA: (39)

Most truthfully, our comet streaks across the azure heavens above Heathcote Dervish's limousine. It is at this moment that our puppet-theatre, hitherto prior to all, crosses over into three-dimensions or real life, so to say. Look at it this way: our meteor shower blasts across the template of a thousand houses; and it stops only to bear witness before Holst's *The Planets*. A swirling impediment of mist then clears a desultory template of light. May rural England experience aught else – in terms of early morning rapture? Let's hold fast to this – for Heathcote Dervish's silver cloud passes over a mottled bridge; a structure which happens to be constructed from Portland stone. It casts a grey aspect atop a restless sheen beneath: this characterises the green scum floating on a waterway that intrudes under its arches. The limousine --- stream-lined by Tamara de Lempicka's art --- then facilitates the speed of its embrace, as well as its rectilinear outcome. Various hamlets or dry-ice shoots limber upwards here, and they surround the patterning of so many Wiltshire endeavours. Each dwelling – when one looks at it – has rain-sluiced roofs, together with laminated grills or ducts. These are occasionally illumined by one high-light too many – a torch-light to a brave insistence, this essentially is. Nonetheless, a comet offers its payload overhead and it strokes a heavenly gate with a prior anger. Looking up, Heathcote Dervish refrains from any suspension of disbelief. "Look, my husband", cries his distracted spouse. "Way out there over the moors… a hurtling thunder-bolt breaks up its essence. It champions the earth or bites at its own bit. Regretfully though, no such indulgence can affect us – since each threnody spies on our entreaties. Do you hear me, great Old Ones gathered above? Yes sir, no Babbitt may prove to be alive… given its trajectory across the moors --- but us, why are we never forlorn before those practioners of Weird?" "An incarcerated rock formation, dearest; it coagulates over unarrested flame. Nor must we know more of its advent. Let it all come down – it entreats a

38

consecutive burst of silence. Let's also survey how it plummets downwards towards the moors."

IN CHESS, A THIN WAFER THREATENS TO CASTLE: (40)
Multi-dimensionally, and listening to its quality, Heathcote Dervish turned his face slightly westwards from his guests. Still – and as before in our credited witness – the features of Bram Stoker's Mummy remain in order to entrance unborn children. It leaves nothing to be desired, you see. For the eyes stare as beadily or manically as before; and his cone's lint decides to unwrap what Jim Dewey chose to call *Deliverance*. Most assuredly, we are going to throw over politeness for the sake of war --- what Julius Evola would have called *The Metaphysics of War*, (theoretically speaking). Again, this surrender to fate involved no iron-maidens; and instead it chooses to throw a road-surface between two poles. "Are you listening to our witness before Zeus?", enquired his two correspondents – both of whom seemed to be adopting a querulous tone. (Note: peevish can never be a word that intrudes here... no sir). Why so? Because both of their faces looked calm, slightly put upon, and livid with a cold spark. Isn't its colour a natural blue? "Of course", he answers, "my attention has never remained riveted on a Chinese doll – namely, one which exists carved in wood, or spray-painted with the gold of a renewed western passage. It definitely stops before a sheen that releases demons when it cracks – these mushroom up from the artificiality of bark." To which statement Butler James averrs: "Are you barking mad?"

AN ELECTRIC-CHAIR, FROM ITS BLUE LIVERY, CASTS A POSTER'S RUSH: (41)
A large meteor lay steaming in the road; it effectively swooned in order to deliver something akin to a divine spittoon. These sulphurous breaths then raised themselves up amidships – probably to allow out such a radial gasp. Fundamentally though, its colour apportioned a spirit of rufous brown: one which chose to be hived off amid some sandy accretions. Certain other

smaller boulders – or chips off the old block – lay about its epicentre in a confused consort. Up above the sky deposited a lavender effulgence, even though the orange streaks of a breaking dawn were seen at its periphery. These cantilevered up to an ochre streak at daybreak – one which filled half the sky with rectilinear fissures. All of them waxed lyrical – via a very deep blue or cerulean at its depths. Above all else, Heathcote Dervish's limousine cut through the dimness with a yellow sword-thrust. One naked tree – rendered savage by its innocence – stood barren and without leaves on it. A mighty oak from England's past, it laid about matters from the left... bearing witness to those wooden tendrils that scraped the loam beneath. Can you see it, strange witness? Observe this as well – from one side of the roadway a lighter pall lifted --- one which casts a negative shadow that betokens warmth. What was a pulp magazine's moniker from the nineteen thirties (?) – why, it had to be *the Shadow knows*... Anyway, we mustn't interrupt Heathcote's talk. "It be a mystic sign from beyond our ken, wife. Let us look at it from the depths of one of John Dee's mirrors... therein to read the future on a piece of darkened metal or glass. An appurtenance of disorder this be, although many would mix it up by calling one a diving/divining pane. Such a blast as this has rent the curtain from beyond – it roils and writhes aslant us here. We must go to it... and those who are untroubled can lead the way. It has to involve a deliverance in relation to Dublin's pale – one which we must follow so as to reckon what it portends." His words are followed by silence in the vehicle.

SAMMAEL'S VICTORY WEARS A CONE-SHAPED HEAD: (42)
Isabelle of Bavaria had guests this afternoon... Now then, Elsa Bounteous Hapgood seemed convulsed with a near rage; in that her features were rapt, arcane, liberated and feminine in their fury. Each affidavit rose to a crucial witness – almost after one of Rodin's forgotten orgasmic studies. (These have to be works that exist prior to a sculptor's object. Certainly, no indication of relief

40

could be proffered by a maquette's advance. Can one tell? Let's overcome this pleasant even-tide together...) "I wish to make it clear, Heathcote, that our rebellion is one of pure style. Bugati racing cars and Tamara de Lempicka prints are not enough for us... Our stylistics must plumb the depths of modern articulation. It's not for us merely a matter of penny farthing bicycles – when these were themselves jet-propelled or subject to locomotion. You see, these sky-scrapers list their own tenancy --- they presumably drive their rain against pillage. Most understandably... because we can visualise aerial velocipedes, balloons, dirigibles, strange hanging baskets and autogyros. No more stilt men, hurdy-gurdy entertainers in top-hats or human bicycles shall be seen on our streets... *Au contraire*, we want a firm break with the past and regime change. For us, any transfiguration has to involve a future wilfulness – it must incarnate Liza Minelli in *Cabaret* (amongst other things). Above all else, to us she embodies a blasphemous tincture – albeit in terms of the Tofflers' futurity. For there she stands – virtually naked and with fresh thistles; together with fish-net tights, much abundant Latin flesh, a leotard or clout, choke and bowler-hat. It's what we call Weimar's diorama." "I see", purred Heathcote... while contemplating vitriol. Do you *really* see?

DON'T LIMIT THESE DRAWINGS TO B-PENCIL SKETCHES: (43)
It always exists further down and nearer the stomach's pit... Yes indeed; since Heathcote Dervish's wiry profile limits its perspective to the right. It tries to vaingloriously shift to a look which is less foregrounded, evil-like, articulate, craggy or austere. Beyond his example – and way out ahead of him in subdued mist – stood the chauffeur Butler James. No doubts can come from this parkway – by virtue of his minion's peaked cap, truss and serge overalls... themselves manufactured from rare linen. All around them, smoky English twirls lay upon their beds; it definitely chose to break up the day by a seizure in Blue. "Heathcote, sir", mumbled his minion, "nought effectively

witnesses a tell-tale sign. Do you credit its gravity? No-one lurks out there in those mists… or alternately, are you prepared to gaze beyond a perspex glass – if only to embrace nothing?" "Let me be the judge of that", snapped his charge-sheet. "Look you! The folly of inaction lies heavily on our brows. We must up and away at the assertion of these days. Remember now, it has to be far in excess of just smouldering meteorites, to be fair. Again, the listed complexity of one's allure merits caution… It also transposes dignity. Look, you fool", he cried out…"you are dead and gone in your forgotten witness before this truth. Mark it, no, no – there's far more here than entertains a fitful retina."

STAND AND DELIVER BEFORE A TRIANGULAR HARPOON: (44)

An urgent newsflash then intrudes into the recesses of this bar; it opens out so as to provide solace before a Leyden jar… no matter how prior. Indeed, the news-caster manifests a hybrid or 'twenties look – what with his slicked hair parted down the middle, plus its Brylcreem, and a white carnation conspicuous in one button hole. A pronounced banner looms up behind our Radio 4 Johnny; leastways, now that we are on the safe ground of a Task-force being readied, *a la* the Falklands, for operations in the south Atlantic. Needless to say – and during this outburst – our bandaged miscreant seemed to cut against such "Boy's Own" fervour. Can we say that we don't necessarily care for the nature of his jib? Even in another dimension – we couldn't see what these fellahs had done for Britain, you see!

A BOER WAR WITHOUT MAFEKING'S CRUMPET: (45)

These smouldering rocks continued to broil and lick their wounds – each one of them liberating a sliver of steam up above the moors. It produced a spasm of smoke over its conspectus – isn't it really like having a dentist called Mr. Angel? Never mind: because a silvery hand peeped out and was altogether discernible amid this gas. It rested almost in a disembodied way and roundabout these houses. Look at this now… Like a shed mitten from a store dummy (it lay alone); at once apposite, unconstrained, and a glove to end all other such conceits. Can you fix its astrology now? Yet Heathcote Dervish and his chauffeur stumble across this frost or opened tundra. Behind them, the sky swirls with a cerulean fixity; it demystifies its ice… Both men gingerly pick their way towards the impact crater. "Careful now", suggests Heathcote with a gentle care. "We have to ridicule any semblance of trespass – only now may we stretch over to the moon's other side, scorpionically. Yes truly, a hand or glove o' mystery protrudes from the site – it obeys Fate's linearity. Like in an Edgar Wallace fiction of yesteryear; it was ordained that I should find it."

MEN IN GIRDLES HOLD BROAD-SWORDS BEFORE THEM: (46)
During all of this commotion – multi-dimensionally – our bandaged Heathcote comes over all distrait; he properly writhes back and forth in his pub seat. Might it be a stool of lacquered or wickered extraction: one which has been given over to the balustrade of so much good? In any event, the background hubbub distills a sensibility like one of Hogarth's prints; in that a generalised din superintends. A fanciful array of British dress intrudes thereafter – it has much to do with Alexander Howard's *Cavalcade*… in which a miscellany of Anglo-celtic customs let rip. Could it be referring to the Cogers, the Festival of the Herring, cheese-rolling, the Red Quill girls or Padworth's hobby-hose… or Klansman's horse, perchance? Simultaneously, a grey palaver of sound intrudes; wherein a medley of coster-mongers, clerks, Bow Street runners, minstrels and patriotic loafers break into a song or ditty:

'Britain, Britain awaken thee…
We, we, we shall always be free
Dash the foreigner, Turk and Jew
We will forever be TRUE, True, True.'

A general chauvinism fills the air – all of which, contrary to the blandishments of a liberal like Menzies-Campbell – is a fine redoubt. But listen closer to what these yeomanry of the guard were saying. "Heathcote Dervish's the one to watch", they adumbrated. "He sneaks up on victims in the night --- he's often aware of an Enemy's plight; beware, beware a Dervish in the night! He never takes fright --- only to spite --- by one's morning light --- a semblance of the trite, just bright." Like Thyestes, in the House of Atreus by Seneca, Heathcote D. is beginning to feel sick to his stomach after this luncheon. Look you... even his companions, Bounteous Elsa Hapgood and Butler James, are starting to become concerned on his behalf. She places a dulcet right-hand on his sleeve arm; its touch was delicate, feminine and refined. "Rest easy, my spouse", she purrs. "I say, steady on, old chap. You're coming over all a'dribble. There's no need for perplexity, here – we're hardly at a Jake or Dinos Chapman exhibition, after all!", interpreted his butler.

A LAKESIDE DEPORTMENT; NATURE TRANSFIXED --- MASONIC BIAS: (47)
Heathcote's shadow leaps up abreast of a great boulder; it spray-paints its own leaving before a genuflexion of pumice. May it prove to be grey or transfigured over its likelihood? By any other circumstance, the rocks around him pitch up to a quickened brown --- could each one be rufous or genteel in its design? Several shards lie around the escarpment or floor. Nonetheless – in the centre of this tableau – one observes the recumbent form of a puppet, at once silvery in tone. Yet no strings – or puppet-master tracings – can be spotted hanging down from an invisible trellis. Such markings are going to be helpfully adorned... they are wiry over an asp's lost ether. Certainly now, our masterful wizard speaks with his destiny gathered together in both hands. "Look ye, Butler James... our pagan Gods have communicated to me across nethermost yore. It's in a situation where our puppet-head's delivered a new outpost, in terms of Eric Bramall's dwindling strings. Yes truly, never mind the

Edwardian artist Charles Dixon's *Titanic*, painted in water-colour in 1912, this Titan rises from its own depths. The more so, my dear James, when we consider that this mysterious menace from another world has fallen into our lap. Veritably, my friends and witnesses, we have worked no magic to secure this bounty --- it is the Will of the Gods! Most magisterially... since our string-fellow remains subject to scant restrictions; given that few have come across him outside a booth or fair-ground. A likelihood which means that this *deux ex machina* gazes solely in our direction: it understands that no-one must pass these Masonic portals other than us... In a perspective where classical pillars are raised up before a shimmering cloud of Blue; an anchor and cup were then seen to move, guardedly, atop David Blain's trespass."

GO AHEAD; GO AHEAD; AN ARMADA OF SONG IN ITS COFFIN: (48)

Let's rise above this restitution of 'Beowulf'... because the singing in our East End boozer has become over-powering. This Chas & Dave knees-up now re-opens many an old wound; it possibly reeks with noisy self-satisfaction. In one corner, various denizens with Brylcreem or parted hair... why, they sprout into song. A definite filibuster eventuates – irrespective of where-ever it starts in the tap-room. Do you notice its discharge... minus any cymbals? Against such wishes, though, one character wearing both a cravat and a carnation raises a glass. While – simultaneously with the above – another jar of real ale is hailed by a bewhiskered fellow in a tall, conical hat. A following-on subaltern, who possesses a waxed moustache, likewise breaks into song. Other subjects of the Crown who join this merry chorus are as follows: an aged or retired colonel, a bow-tie wearing nerd with a pointy head, a monocle sporting rugger player, a smoker of Bradley's rolled cigarettes; together with a cup-wearing trooper. He's alone out in front and his sword's drawn. It happens to be short, thick and blunt: a sabretache then follows on behind him on the floor, needlessly. All those foregathered here pick up the following ditty:~

45

"Britannia, Britannia, Britannia
We are the way
Forever to stay
Nowhere to play
Always and every day
Nothing to pay:
Irrespective of the Krays
Release all our stays:
No-one can match our rays!

Hip, hip, hooray!"

ONCE UNTO THE BREACH, DOLLY HARPER: (49)
"Come, carry him forth amid these tendrils of mist, Butler
James", uttered Heathcote in a steely voice. "We must lever our
puppet-man from the impact crater. Nature has set him amongst
us here --- but we shall travel on to the end of this particular
night. Like Louis Ferdinand-Celine, our misanthropy must find
its ripeness unconstrained. Gather up this manikin – let us deliver
his slumbering body to the car! Its capacious door swings open
behind us; and now we must escape from one venture into
another's trap. A great prize has been lifted from one chariot to
its twin; it crosses over such pillion... nor can any doubt my
future destiny. Every such register on our unconscious had to
summon up the Ancient Ones... they are the custodians of sleep
and wake. Oh my yes..." With this affected disregard, both
practioners raise the stringless puppet from his pallet. Lying
prone on the rocky ground (he once was), now he sways between
two human passengers surrounded by fog. The blue-garbed
chauffeur follows on at the rear – with a silver-smith cast before
him, his hands are effectively 'neath the other's shoulders.
Whereas a cloaked mage contrives to carry his charge aslant both
knees.
+

A veritable commingling of rain, mist and morning vapour
surrounds our ambulance crew. They proceed in silence.

46

WEAR A MASK, TASK, RASP, CLASP, STEAMING ASK: (50)

At the sound of such a chorus… our bandaged carouser becomes increasingly agitated. A glass of wine or pellucid cider sits uneasily in his hand; it happens to be mummified against the implementation of any surgical instruments. Nor can such a living sarcophagus commandeer our attention: it merely looks down from above, face about apex. Don't we understand that these heads – sarcophagi and all – merely look over from a cascading height… with each carved identity lining up from floor to ceiling? By any reckoning, the tension around this fluted stem becomes more and more pronounced; it causes the glass to whistle and even crack. This pressure looks progressive in its offending curve; it approximates to the unforgiveness of a new resolve. "Steady on, Dervish ol' Heath", murmurs a butler… by way of a mild imprecation. But it's all too late. Yes indeed, the fructified sand – like under a sonic scream – shattered into a thousand shards in Heathcote's mitten. The anger remained within, however; it had yet to find a ready outlet.

DEVIANT SPIDERS DEVOUR MUSHROOMS: (51)

It is now dawn on the planet earth. A roadster then speeds across a slope towards some brooks; a trajectory which seems to be chiselled out of the landscape. It has to be an English rural scene early in the morn. A sweeping panorama of arable land lies to one side – wherein, shooting across it like a brazen deer, comes a white strip of road. On it one discerns a hurtling silver-cloud… together with a smoky trail of exhaust which curls out of its back. Various old-fashioned English dwellings – many of them worn out of grey slate – add to this abode. Likewise, these cottages and bungalows pop up amid rich foliage; to the lee of which arises a constellation of cliffs. These reconnoitre a structure or assemblage of granite; at once inundated to its wrath or Vorticist, spiritually speaking. As such, each lineament cascades to a vertice: it also feeds geometric abstraction at one remove. Like one of Nevinson's indents – it adds to its glory through refracted

47

lustre. No doubt… a discerning on-looker then checks a river flowing aft. A few boats find themselves marooned on it – and they signal one remit too many. (A case-study by the *naif* painter Wallis looms up here, somewhat expectantly). Let it fall or all come down now… no hindrance may be given to our resultant sky. It silvers a distaff: and is ready to cross or circle cerulean's lines. "Quickly, my servant, we must rush on to my ready manse… already a fantastic plan breeds in my brain. Away, we shall endeavour to coax a feverish future."

TWO GAMES OF SKITTLES MURDER NINE-PINS: (52)
Our soldier or Victorian dragoon brandishes his sabre – he holds it before an ornamental vest or surcoat in the tap-room. Against this, a pint pot of heavy liquor soaks a moustache; its under-side finds itself whetted by Brakespeare's… a real ale brewed in Henley-on-Thames, Oxfordshire. Furthermore, our cavalryman sings in a gusty humour, sword-in-hand and tassels aplenty: what with ornamental stuff and flummery all over his surplice. It's a bedizened jacket, to be fair. A deep purple sash – of woven silk and vaguely recalling the Orange Order – crosses his mid-riff. Slightly drunk on the mead… he launches into a vaudeville air; a deep bass voice then fills the mint…

Heathcote Dervish, Heathcote Dervish
carapace and spite
by no means let's fight
it's alright
to creep up on a foe in the dead of Night.

Heathcote Dervish, Heathcote Dervish
we're coming for you ---
with no mean crew…

But he gets no farther than this. A shot rings out and this trooper crumbles forward dead. Could it embody a different version of Heathcote Williams' *The Speakers*? Anyway, our attention is

48

diverted by the figure of Heathcote Dervish. He stands triumphantly before us, a cocked machine-pistol in his bandaged fist. His lint appears to be luminous in the vague or darkling light. Immediately afterwards, various women start screaming in the saloon bar. Can we interpret its flexed illumination? Although Heathcote Dervish continues to look saturnine: what with a Toblerone head (bandaged) and a grilled grin, a great coat and one billowing automatic. Vengeance has spoken: IMPERIOUS REX!

A MIRROR CASCADES VIOLENCE FROM SPENT RAIN: (53)
In the back of a careering cabin, then, Heathcote and Elsa look aprey; each one gazes at a silvery puppet-head... it chooses to wait on a stray bullet, though. Despite the fact that a morning praise (or its glory) seeps in from an aperture – the environment is subdued and off to one side. Rather like the circular mirror in a ship, it flickers like a candle... whether deluded of all mist or not. During this intervention – our husband and wife gibber like two ghouls; their avidity truly plagues them like a sport. To adapt a line from *King Lear*: 'As flies to wanton boys... are we to the Gods; they play us for their sport.' Wasn't this aught like Edgar's original rasp? "Look ye, wife", commanded Dervish with aplomb. "We shall use this good fortune as luck, kindred or insult... He has been placed amongst us by the Gods' lap – but not in accord with Matthew Arnold's verse. No. Let us examine this: we shall use Phosphorous as a make-shift, even a cavalcade. For – whether through him or no – we establish a nostrum. It alone can prove a moral taxidermy which is less than Kevorkian... but more than Galen. Since this doll without strings surprises us: and he wanders out --- somewhat forlornly --- from a heavenly keep. Essences and expectorations (thus apprised) we shall use him to prove our magic circle. No mistake can prevent us from offering this hand in Ombre or Brag."

TOGETHER AGAIN WE STORM SAX RHOMER'S BOUDOIR: (54)

Outside these step-overs (and in a late Victorian alley) two figures approach a pub called "Jack the Ripper" in the fog. It curls or curves around their feet in wisps; & each tendril then seeps out like a snake's armature. Maybe a copperhead's nectarine is otherwise hinted at? Certainly – my friends – we need to recognise that one figure was Phosphorous Cool; the other a mechanical variant on a former wraith known as Hermaphrodite X. Our nacreous puppet glistens in the mist with his head on one side; while X recalls Dr. Caligari's box plus a cylindrical skull. Against this travelling circus or carnival, an old-fashioned cab or four-wheeler disappears. It finds itself to be engulfed in mist. Likewise, an insolvent picture feels the point of this and it reeks of one sacrifice too many. Even though bits of newsprint blow about in the dust – our caleche has already beaten an unashamed retreat. Our travelling post emboldens one back portico or curtain, and this exists in its rear when betokening a Punch & Judy booth. A gas-lamp flickers in its tracery next to such an incline.

REBUILD CHAOS WITH ARISTOPHANES' LOGIC: (55)

By this time, our coven-leader and puppet-thwart have carried Phosphorous over a threshold; the latter evinces a subtle radiance or glow. A whiff of brackish incense covers the portal – it helps by adding a mesmerism to our abstract. Momentarily though, various out-buildings and possibly a cathedral close rear up in an undefined mist. This curtain or rain-dust floods the aisles; while all of it belabours some stillness. One tall lamp-post starkly neighbours the limousine; and it proves to be a vehicle which has been left near to the curb. A side-door then comes to well up in an eminent pile; it's a heavy brass aperture to the Masonic temple that betrays a classic façade or solidity. Gathered together as a group, now, the three figures of Heathcote Dervish, Elsa Bounteous Hapgood and Butler James rush into a side-entrance. It opens out onto some Saxon flares, one of which bears an impress on it of Cool's features. Yet again, our threefold protagonists found themselves bent over or put upon. "Many have --- in the depths of pantomime --- tried to stop or arrest our guest. All have failed... at least until now. Our manikin has avoided all attempts or capturing nets up to this moment. Let's examine this, comrades: a token of the divine or intelligent design caused him to alight here... circumambient to our prey."

SLIP THE NOOSE FROM A PRACTIONER'S ARM-PIT: (56)
In a plateau of silence, Heathcote Dervish fired at pace and each bullet ricocheted around the pub's precincts. He also appeared to be using a machine-pistol or a device where the carbine existed beneath the knee. Look at this: any *art nouveau* drawing of the period – whether by Mucha, Beardsley, Redon, Klimt et cetera – didn't do justice to it. For Heathcote Dervish's bandages swarm aplenty – they definitely contrived to spiral or create a rumour around Heathcote's triangular head. A certain circular nimbus – or affidavit – buzzed around now. Again, a mummified Dervish was heard to roar at all and sundry: "I will cleanse everyone who stands in my way. None may mock the power which levels behind one particular throne. Do you hear me? The ukase that springs forth – in this nobility – is divine. It wastes away upon a plate of indifferent fayre. No sir... you should rather choose to survey the insistence, the puissance, which lurks behind one's blackened fingers. It all aids the pillion of a new awakening." With this outburst (then) quietness continues to reign.

A DETOUR AROUND THE HEAVENS SEEKS AN ALABASTER IN PINK: (57)
A tableau now unfolds... it places an exorbitant price on Heathcote's living room. He sat there, stern-faced, with one fist cupped at the shoulder of his chin. Meanwhile, his features looked saturnine, grave, brooding, magically inclined and even lugubrious. Oh yes, it suffices us to know whether he remains one of Saturn's children under those beetling brows. A bow-tie can be seen around his neck, but on closer inspection it comes to

be spotted with pink and blue dots. Next to him a lamp peels off; when taken together with a grated fire-place, coal scuttle and pincers. Several classic pictures by various artists – Reynolds, Ramsay, Gainsborough, Constable – provide appurtenances. These line the walls. A new threshold can be crossed and this was primarily by pointing at one's butler across a room lined by bric-a-brac. Twenty-twenty vision indicates (moreover) that some of these artefacts happen to be stuffed birds in cages. Isn't taxidermy a privilege of the aristocratic nature? Anyway, a sibyl sits across from our thaumaturge and her name proves to be Elsa Bounteous Hapgood. Next to her – and within this unfolding panorama – one notices James, the butler. He stands like a manikin and he betrays the stiff manner of servants the world over... no matter how tendentiously. Yes again, the latter's starched collar, black tie, jacket and striped leggings are all of a piece. Open your eyes now and then – do you recall the figure of Parker in Gerry Anderson's *Thunderbirds*? You'll continually find that estuary English invades everything these days, you see...

+

"Our way into the future becomes clearer with each passing millisecond", ventilated Heathcote. "We must learn to strike using Nature's hottest brands. Furthermore, Phosphorous Cool's power – even to morph between dimensions – cannot be used against us. He remains out of Time... not exactly powerless, no, but profoundly indifferent to causality. It's an unknown secret – my friends, servants and allies. Or, if we were better armed by a reluctant Fate, then a marionette's strings might be cut on a theatrical barge. They trailed on the ground like so many wires or snakes. We are still Seven now --- do not forget it." (This latter is in answer to Elsa's questioning; or by way of a Socratic preamble. She had basically wanted to reflect on a puppet's strength and indestructibility – or its ability to shape-shift into an insect at will. Truly, Kafka's *Metamorphosis* has nothing on this...)

ONE WOOD-PECKER BLINDS A BLAST-GUN'S RAPTURE: (58)

Back in our public house – "Jack the Ripper" – all hell finds itself breaking out. It definitely issues forth as an example or illustration of Armageddon's village. Then again, there is a mysterious cachet here – if we were to be honest about it. For example, why does Heathcoat's *alter ego* attack these revellers? Well, it must have to do with a mixture of alienation, mystification and respect. Surely, you can understand now the inner meaning of Hermann Rauschning's *The Revolution in Nihilism*? To be sure: they reject Heathcote Dervish because of his zombie-like status; while he, on the other hand, finds himself enraged by Kronos' dreams. All of which necessitates a casual disregard, even a delinquency. Because one element alone suffices and it revolves around a modernist bias – possibly a refusal to dream. Maybe – in this context – Heathcote Dervish's phantasm might make a puppet-theatre too real, too three-dimensional (so to say)? In real life, therefore, Herge's *Tintin* wouldn't care for being humanised by c.s.i or computer software imaging.

+

In spite of all else, a ground-breaking out take to Lucius Annaeus Seneca's *Thysetes* comes about at this time. For Heathcote Dervish fires repeatedly at the pub crew gathered roundabout... and we also see a dum-dum/perforated bullet pass through a miscreant. This exploding slug took off the man's back in a scarlet welter. Likewise, a character in a fluted hat endured a multiple smash-up. His head rocked back – when splintered to smithereens and illuminating Peckinpah's slow motion (thereby). Against this, a trained hussar reared up in the twilight. He manifested the livery, braid and sabretache of Sir Nigel or Brigadier Gerard – as contained in Conan Doyle's now forgotten historical novels. Meanwhile, a subdued frenzy curdles the air; it sets the seal on upturned tables, desks and splattered gore. Could this abattoir interpret one of Felix Labisse's paintings back onto itself? Although perhaps this charnel house indicates Rouault –

what with circular flutes, columns, shattering VR glasses and exploding wood-chip. Several denizens cower behind some chairs and return fire. They sport antique revolvers in doing so. All of these weapons seem to be fit for purpose; and this vaudeville atmosphere becomes quickly crossed with Stephen King's *'Salem's Lot* as a result. It subsists in a puppet-show… wherein manikins die, besport themselves and are genuinely undone by Antonin Artaud's Theatre of Cruelty!

ONE MIMESIS LISTENS TO A SINISTER TALE: (59)
Heathcote Dervish continued his rambling screed, irrespective of all else. "We must use his presence amongst us as a Parthian shot", he said. "Do you understand? Such ukase as he possesses will not be turned on us – instead all his strength shall be required to greet the coming ordeal. Yes again, we repeatedly dwell upon a beautiful misstatement – especially when this globe realises that wicca defeated him. A masterful puppet of yore or the olden days sacrificed its essence in transit, even while being retrieved from the wood." "But, my dear husband", expostulated Elsa Bounteous Hapgood, "any accusation of a like kindred testifies falsely. Kenneth Grant's or MacGregor Mather's sack-cloth and ashes fails to subdue him. No mage would willingly meet him on a path after darkness. We found him out there by ourselves…" To this rejoinder, Heathcote Dervish replied: "Refuse the foolishness of Windsor's merry wives, my girl, and wait till you have heard of my plan. Its boldness tempts the sprongs of Heaven's trident… Butler James (he turned now to the servant) you shall prepare a potion: one that contains henbane, Fulbright's lotion, static electricity, bluestone, and the marrow of a baby gorilla's bones. I beg you to wait upon its hardship!"

DOWN THE LYON'S TEA-BAR, GLADIATOR'S PRANCE: (60)
In "Jack the Ripper" – a pub which only served real ale – all pandemonium continued to break out. Instantaneously, a range of

bullets hurtled through Heathcote Dervish – they passed outwards via his bandaged and great-coated form. Let's have a look at this incident: since any necessary wraps rose above his teeth – and the latter became grilled in terms of a triangle's head-stone. No matter: any passageway that exists between one dimension and another falls sheer. It also affects those mad eyes; and both of them stare out engagingly from amid mummification. Furthermore, this phantasm's carbine or tommy-gun repeatedly splutters in his hand – somewhat like a sten gun on a previous naming of parts. "Cor blimey, mate", ejaculated a rival shooter. "His companion-in-arms looks close to a reaver, wolverine or lycanthrope. Truly, the slayer of those young *demi-mondes* in the East End happens to be a species of Pakenham's reckoning. Maybe they had to make do with a kick from a false pair of scissors? For it's obvious that he stalks sewers as yet unplastered over. Whereupon – in a forgotten vista – one alternative Kratos looms upon him with a sepulchral eye. It bears across it a red of the deepest hue. Oh my, this wraith allows a slug or bullet to pass through his anatomy. Could it recall Lon Chaney's performance in *Phantom of the Opera*, or alternately, has Hermaphrodite X stolen up on us awhile? With this abatement in intent, then, Heathcote D. rushes for the exit followed by tracer fire. May it all come down now – without let or hindrance…?

DO NOT DELAY A RECKONING WITH PURPLE: (61)
Certainly now, our puppet has wakened to consciousness for the first time. He finds himself awake in an ornate room – one which possesses gables, a four-poster embrasure and an ornamental door. An aperture through whose gap Heathcote Dervish and Butler James make a grand entrance… Both of them are then found to be dressed in a baroque or early twentieth century vogue. Perhaps it's got to do with Tamara de Lempicka's agenda; or possibly an effortlessness of sheer style that typifies the Ritz? In any event, he wears a studded collar of an old-fashioned cut – plus a thick black-tie, almost a cravat. A silk morning coat or smoking jacket – much after the impact of

Nayland Smith or a bachelor in an H.P. Lovecraft story... why, these are what he besports! A keen observer would also reckon on the dressing-gown he carries... which happens to be slung casually over one arm. A pair of shiny ebon trousers made up the last of this particular couple... a companionship that has to do with one of Ian Fleming's dress-suits, possibly worn out of tune. Behind him comes the butler, James, who holds a tray on which a tureen or mug waxes clean. A fine vessel (this) it's probably made from Spode china; and it comes dressed in a brilliantly white adornment, thereby. Next to this Toby jug (sic) on the salver, and by way of a silvery trace, there registers an upturned dish: its companion appears to be a saucer beneath it. All of this may presumably be accounted for by an Anglo-Saxon delicacy; as well as a scenario where the soup or consommé's heat needs to be kept in. To one side of these walkers – and in contrast to a prone puppet – a heavy gilt frame exists around a Gainsborough portrait: it doubtless depicts a Lady walking in woodland with or without a parasol. A pot-pourri cover-all lies adjacently; and it testifies to an absent odour that wins one over resultantly. A companion-piece in chaos also attracts our attention, however, and this relates to a candle in an up-turned or louvered jar. Again – my friends – all of these appurtenances stretch to the left of our speakers. Phosphorous Cool, on the other hand, rests prone in the middle of the bed, and finds himself to be barely covered by a blanket of Scotch plaid. Or could it involve one of those rags or thick coverlets used in séances? Our main character's skin then shines like some worn or glimmering pumice; it exists primarily in order to reflect away all doubt. Both of his legs suddenly stir under the covering; and this is no matter how briefly Phosphorous waxes lyrical (to speak of). Surely Grendel didn't really tarnish a mother's spite?

BRING ON THOSE MOUNTEBANKS WHO DANCE AND WOOF[!]: (62)
Heathcote Dervish finally vacates "Jack the Ripper" at high speed... and he trails many a rifle's discharge behind him.

Outside all of this, a spectral block progressively glimmers in the darkness – while our bandage fetishist refuses to look askance. Especially when we consider a backwards glance from our anti-hero in terms of a pyramid's pace (withal); and aren't his eyes twinkling like rivets? Does one enjoin Wyndham Lewis' painting of a Canadian munitions factory as an afterthought? Likewise, Heathcote glowers back at his pursuers gun-in-hand – a few shards of glass circle around him as he does so. "Stop him, interdict or desist from such out-pourings, my brothers", intones a voice which heralds from the pub's interior. Above a retreating Heathcote D(.), though, a cylindrical setting adjusts its bearings... and it just happens to render a mezzanine redundant. All around him, then, one swirl betokens some early Edwardian designs --- it contrives to lose itself in a morbid thriller *a la* Patrick Magee, the Irish actor. Didn't Samuel Beckett hear his gravel-like tones as a diction in his own ears? Anyway, a bandaged waif soon passes out of a portico'd entrance.

A LYNX LIES IN THE LONG GRASS; IT BARKS IN THE NIGHT: (63)

"Who are you; and why have you contrived to bring me here?", demanded our shiny puppet with some asperity. Yes indeed, his diction customarily intoned a thousand bells or more – rather like a Khitian temple in the dark. Might it endorse such a hollow tinkling? We can see it all now... But Heathcote Dervish's quick to cover his tracks by barking thus: "In answer to your ready affidavit, we found you out upon the roadway and purloined of all purposes. You were steadfast and yet mildly injured, so like any man of esteem and goodwill I brought you here. Amidst much relative chaos – I heard you ask after my name... 'tis Heathcote Dervish, Baronet of the realm." "Sanctimony or moral conscience? Bah!", scoffed Phosphorous Cool in a light humour. "My, my... how mortals change their ethics like a weather-vane or possibly with their socks, perchance. Given this eventuality, how on earth can you simper on about boon favours? For everything that Man does – from whatever perspective – involves self-interest and war-like ardour. All else comes close to poppy-cock and lavender; it rejoices at a dog's wheedling."

RUN, RUN HAVOC BEFORE THESE PRINCES: (64)

By the by, Heathcote Dervish moved out through the pub's swinging doors and into a London pea-souper. It swirled all around him when concentric to a centrifuge; while gusts of wind blew newspaper about. Doubtless though, none of this meant much under a swinging pub board or arch... could it be an awning which spoke of "Jack the Ripper" with a question mark appended? Likewise, a flaring gas-mask lay above our heads in a crown or a fluted overhead jar. Heathcote Dervish then burst forth from the pub with a bandaged surplice in tow; whereupon a great-coat and scraggy scarf made up his accoutrements. Our anti-hero stopped quite short in the available light – particularly when he spied Phosphorous Cool standing before him. Our latter presence also looked magisterial in a flowing cape; the like of such a garment closed around his mid-riff and lower extremities. Click, a broadsword or switchblade (even a cutlass) shot forth in his hand; it all helped to add a javelin or bean-pole to a silvern grasp. Whilst behind both of them our robot gazed on blankly – each one of his eyes comes to filter out beneath a breasted torment... Whereby the machine-man's orbs look rather longingly over a zig-zagging circuit board. Certainly, our Tumble-weed or Hermaphrodite X has noted down better days, whether in or out of a new cybernetics' ring. "Adopt this fiction", Phosphorous snarled in Heathcote's direction... but our other custodian proved to be too wily altogether. "Adumbrate the contrary to Abel Gance's magisterial film *Napoleon*", hissed Heathcote Dervish. "An eagle who stoops to devour his prey in sunlight – or on the stump of a tree (somewhat inevitably) knows nothing but perfection. Doesn't he collaborate with a Robinson Jeffers stanza... retrospectively speaking? No mercy subsists in Nature – nor should you feel free to consult its witness. It all goes to show – rather predictably – that only one of us can survive this incident. Our meeting – in a sunken or dripping

Whitechapel alley like Angel Alley – entails a fact which knows that just one of us shall leave it. *Touché*. "Fate decrees my overall witness statement --- not yours!" "Balderdash", indicated a vexed Phosphorous, "one of our scant forms cannot quit an imbroglio without fighting. Let it pass us by…"

PLAY IT AGAIN, RITCHIE, YOUR PIANO SNAFFLES AT MIDNIGHT: (65)

Reject not this interlude in play-time, my brothers… For – with relatively ill-good grace – Phosphorous Cool has snapped up a proffered dressing-gown. He ties its silken cord tightly around his middle and off. Against this, his silver dome of a skull looks imperial… and our puppet's overall eye-sockets are accorded no real pupils. Each one of them – in this manikin's impediment of sight – then blazes ahead like St. Paul on day-go biscuits. Twice blinded thus, he takes some time to meaningfully convert amongst Gaza's sands. Never again, he thinks… because the lush or plush interior which surrounds him antagonises a wooden sensibility. Most especially – if we take into special consideration his inner delectation as a puppet! *Avaunt thee*, Heathcote's servant, James, busily adjusts his condiments in the background – he seems to be stirring some soup. A large, pre-Edwardian barometer lies to one side of our characters: and it reaches out so as to encounter a wall in this reluctant country house. Could it be a clock instead? (Isn't it one of those stately homes, like Gray's Court in south Oxfordshire, best superintended by the National Trust?) Meanwhile, Heathcote surveys or steams on apace --- he's quite clearly the lord of this individual manor. A saturnine gleam bounces off one eye in particular – it comes to us in terms of a Son of Satan. Might Dennis Wheatley have actually been involved all along? To be sure: Heathcote's brows are seen to be beetling, straw-bestrewn, Crowley-like, and they become increasingly reminiscent of a satyr's. His orbs glowed or gleamed preternaturally; and they seem to reposition themselves within a variant of Gray's *Anatomy* – that is: one which knows nothing other than the turn of a Tarot card towards death. Doesn't the thirteenth card stand for transfiguration and joy? Phosphorous Cool, though, actively refuses to give too much credence to Heathcote Dervish – what with those avid looks which were drawn from Austin Osman Spare's *The Book of Satyrs*... his own nomenclature, (this), for a detour around a mediaeval *Book of Hours*!

+

Watch this space now: "None can trust mortals like yourself", spat our guesting puppet. "Upon your savage sphere that you call the earth nothing exists save war, peasant cruelty and rapine. Mankind does nought out of tragedy or charity --- self-interest alone recognises an outsider. It forecloses on nothing save a child's grave! Essentially though, an owl in a mildewed tree stands for wisdom, but, in this condition, nowt other than a burnt cadaver will do. In truth, you can only indicate to me Christopher Lee's crazed aristo(.) or pastor in the film known as *The Wickerman*." "Tut-tut, such an outburst", responded Heathcote Dervish after a pregnant interlude. "Remember this: bitterness ill behoves a knight-errant such as yourself. Your fame spreads before any puppet-master's crossed wires. Do you remain oblivious to the fact that in Punch and Judy, down by a sea-ground's fair, our main glove lies bathed in a Professor's right-hand? All of it excuses an oil painting devoted to Kronos' appetite; the former merely alive to these castrated off-spring. Aren't their genitals hurled into the sea in order to create teeming abundance or Life? Salute this gesture with a stiff right-arm, why don't you? James... let's have some needful broth for our brooding guest."

CAUGHT IN A CROSS-FIRE IS A PALACE OF DEAD ROADS: (66)
By main and castleguard, Heathcote Dervish finds himself afflicted with a blind fury – possibly it encodes the forgotten frenzy of a Viking berserker. He bellows and releases a strong appeal. Let it go forever and a day... since, with a guardian's pillion about the membrane, he pushes out. A triangular hood

60

slants outermost and it serves to enjoin a battle royal. Does the samurai war chant 'banzai' come to reverberate in his mind? Nonetheless, a criss-crossed boudoir contrived to rip out these guts and it came covered with bandages – albeit after a conical section. May it amount to the sadic equivalent of a garden gnome? In any event, his irises come to be convulsed like two lead pellets; while beneath both of them a machine-pistol chunters on. PUDDA-PUDDA-PUDDA(!), goes the weapon repeatedly. It happens to be directed against the Phosphorous manikin stretched out before him. "Time to die, devious one", cries Heathcote Dervish in triumph. "No warfare lifts the salience of this pastel mixture or admixture, particularly when it's run together with alkyd and turpentine. Never mind anything else, *quod* our fixity finds itself enlarged in a red eye and hemmed in around scorbutic flesh. A rejection then hastens aboard our after-taste --- now it's livid and lucky to perish."

A GUILTY SECRET PURSUES ARISTOPHANES: (67)
Back in a world of adult puppets who have come to life... a small tureen of broth is held in a silvery hand. It gingerly announces its presence – even though a svelte aroma spirals upwards towards a vaulted ceiling. Phosphorous Cool's head was thereby turned to the side... so as to put an impediment on many such dreams. Yes again, the cleavage of a polished skull closes on its point – it obviously announces its complete or spheroid quality without fear or favour. Can anyone tell the slanting lope of this glance, in that it reveals a quadrant of 'Eye' somewhere to the side? Moreover, the beaker within which such consommé is stirred looks like some pewter rendered ajar; it flatters to deceive. Nor can anyone deny whether an orange background supervenes over the whole... at a time when Heathcote Dervish's stare proves to be avid (indeed). It illustrates no self-division; primarily since this manikin has his lordship's undivided attention. He adopted the role of a nonchalant croupier therefore – what with one forefinger gesturing across his upper-lip. Did it bear astride its form the quivering antennae of an insect's

warning? As Sherlock Holmes made clear in the case known as *The Illustrious Client*, nature always builds in an alarming signal… It has to do – in the case of Baron Gruning – with those little tips of moustache which curved away from the mouth. All of this revealed the cruel gash of a murderer's forethought; and it all came to be reminiscent of those mug-shots in a crime filofax. Doesn't it betray a luminance proffered by Colin Wilson and Patricia Pitman in their *Encyclopaedia of Murder*?

+

Still and all, Heathcote Dervish gazes on in rapt awe. (A situation, my friends, where even his close-slicked black tresses add to a distaff eddy. Might they not be emblematic of some of the graphic art left by Beresford Egan?) No doubt… his resemblance to one of Montague Summers' billy-goats proved accidental. Yet a fortuitous moment needs to slacken off – and it hardly tasks itself over mastery. Most particularly, when one is given over to studying the saturnine affectations of these braves… or could they really be lost Masonic utterances? Maybe even the sensibility of Aleister Crowley's last look out – as contained in Augustus John's portrait – comes to mind? Similarly, the 'Against the Turner Prize' paintings of Steven Taylor might well figure here. Let us set up a boomeranging example!

+

"A replenishing tincture of broth slakes your strength, I'm sure", muttered Heathcote Dervish in a mild manner. Although Phosphorous Cool belatedly came to shake his head. "Any strength of mine comes borne by cosmic rays, irrespective of Eric Bramall's puppet theatre. His strings have been cut by a pair of scissors long since… Yet I will drink deeply of this draught – its aroma pleases me." (And when he speaks again our male doll does so almost as an aside… like in a Shakespearean tragedy.) "Men! Even as your entire anthropology teeters on the brink of chaos, you find a means to sustain your amenities."

LOOK AGAIN AT THIS SPARROW FALLING TO THE GROUND – IT'S COVERED IN FIRE: (68)

We now swiftly return to the adventures of the late nineteenth century, if not to those of a vouchsafed Golden Bowl. Surely the dulcet tones of Henry James composed a book of that title? It suffices to retain all of our needs prior to destruction. Any matter – in deepest and darkest Whitechapel – Heathcote Dervish and Phosphorous Cool confront one another. Albeit in a swirling fog, they both stand several paces apart… all of which responds to the shoot-out in a spaghetti western by Serge Leone. Heathcote Dervish – for his part – has a First World War great-coat around his shoulders; and this proves complementary to the lint pyramid that adorns his head. He fires bullets repeatedly from his machine-pistol, but these ricochet from a sprocket which a robot has thrust up into the air *in lieu* of a hand. This must re-confirm the existence of Tumble-weed or Hermaphrodite X, albeit cast anew in the form of a miniscule robot… possibly one that embodies nano-technology. "Mind how you transgress the Norns", hisses a grill at the front of our metal-man. Most certainly – the heroic figure of Phosphorous Cool remains alive to such dangers as these. He congratulates the android at his side: "Hail to thee, in terms of your metallic husk or rusk… let it all come down aft: in relation to a stone mason's mission or life-task. Surely it encodes that silent feature film from the late nineteen twenties with Lon Chaney, *The Phantom of the Opera*? Remember never to forgo a cybernaut's lustre, *mon ami*, since you are obviously the King of the 'droids!"

STILL-BORN, A DWARF CONTINUES TO PLY HIS SCYTHE: (69)

Take it or leave it from here on in… Our main character, Phosphorous, keels over as the quilted carpet rises suddenly to hit him in the face. During the course of this, then, the sacred cup passes from his lips – he has drained its filter to his last gasp, you see. Oh yes, only at the moment of severance does he realise whether such a fricassee has been drugged or not. No wonder the butler, James, evinced such a self-satisfied air. Do you understand? Phosphorous topples forwards onto these rugs as a result: and he does so in an ungainly fashion, surrounded by a dressing-gown. It ends up flapping around his imagined knees. Heathcote Dervish – standing directly behind him in order to adopt a lordly posture – starts to rip off his smoking-jacket. It happens to be made from rare eastern silk. He (Baron Heathcote) is extremely exultant – while his 'man of all work' shares in the glee at one remove. Again, Heathcote Dervish – an aristocrat of forgotten beginnings – proves to be the first of our figures up to or mounting the stairs. He adopts such a mainstream task – primarily because he flexes his own Masterdom at this instant. "Foolish dolt, my puppet from another stage! You certainly represent Hogarth's bountiful fairs of yore; and these help to take up many a prat fall in the circus ring. Unbeknown to you... all and every artist's figurine of your ilk tilts on destruction's brink. Heed me, silvery man of straw, I am about to call a witches' coven... a gathering which will inevitably encompass your destruction. Quick – my lackey of our feasting – draw upon the car. It stands outside and immediately favours our escape."

DERVISH PREACHES RAIN, IN THE FOG, OUT IN SHOREDITCH: (70)
With an airy gesture our protagonist, Phosphorous Cool, raises his right-hand into the air... basically so as to hurl a bolt of living flame. It serves to justify its own existence (forevermore); especially given the furious hell-storm that erupts. It shoots the dice towards a double-six in one go; particularly when one game of chance must compete with cosmic roulette. Hell's spawn and all, a shadow features its length and stage-craft; and it throws a thunder-bolt in accord with Thor's ability to do so. Yessss... this triumphal arch of Otto Rahn's fire just lets go; and it catapults molten ballast like in a mediaeval siege.
+
Moving on from these stage directions... a wall of liquid magma or Greek Fire engulfs our termagant. It sacrifices one enclosure

64

to an urgent sense of ire; only then to salve Etna's explosiveness with cotton-wool. Don't deny its compass – for this fiery furnace seems to 'do' for Heathcote Dervish, albeit unsatisfactorily. Against such a measure (now) a contrary dispensation rolls up – and it signifies nought but a mummy roiling in flame. Are Heathcote's eyes – as contained in their mask – then transfixed on cruelty's art... even though one body after another goes up in pitch? Yet this Heathcote who exists in another dimension, *inter alia*, comes to recognise his indestructibility... Not being truly alive (you see) he's incapable of smoothly fleeing from one identity into another – despite an almost plastic ability to survive. In these circumstances, then, white phosphorous or napalm doesn't burn down to the bone. It entreats silence.

COOK UP THE MYSTERY OF FISH IN A TROPICAL BOWL: (71)
Truly, junk food refuses to feast on its served excrement... *ditto*. Now look, Phosphorous Cool has tottered on this special brink or cusp... if only to reach out towards a heavily mantled carpet with a bump. Might its corners or extremities betray tassels about them? To be sure: a few moments later a limousine winds its way towards a lonely Stonehenge. On the way, it passes disused out-houses and the shells of abandoned buildings. It essentially masters its own provender – for the bracken of so many forests necessitates torment, whether or not they happen to be derived from Stoke Newington. Heathcote's vehicle chooses to drive under a wisp of smoke or carbon; the like and kindred of this circles in strange eddies over the car. It bears (loosely) a Rolls-Royce or Daimler figurine at the front. What does Dennis Wheatley have to say in his Gothic novel, *The Devil Rides Out* – namely, that only those of extreme wealth are left to practice the mystic arts? Still and all, we find an on-rushing breath and spume above the heath, as a fierce wind cuts this way and that across the heather. No gorse makes its appearance – when the silver-cloud glides by. In any event, a blasted house, turreted and with broken windows, lay half chewed over this Egdon heath – it proved to be

almost a Kellogg's box or a balsa structure ripped apart by a giant. In its loneliness it configured no wants… But – abreast of all else – Heathcote Dervish's reedy voice was heard over the air-waves. "Listen to me, mages of yore. Before this very night is done, comrades, the globe shall tremble at our power. We are the masters of coming tombs… have no doubt about it… Nor will our enemies be able to decry our curdling balm. All rapture hints at those Assyrian Bulls in the British Museum – i.e., the ones with wings and a darting magnificence, you know. Likewise, once mankind recognises our Spartan ukase – why then, nought shall hold up our route to endless dominion."

DOMINATION OVER ALL FORSAKES ITS ABSENCE: (72) Listen to me: way back in a parallel dimension a fiery Dervish races down an alley-way, and his arms and legs were a flaming cart-wheel of pitch. Could all of this indicate that J.G. Ballard's *The Crystal World* is alive and kicking, albeit in some sort of translucent posture? Nonetheless, our roulette-wheeling dervish caroms down this corridor. Might it be, in actuality, the very angel alley which runs parallel to the modern gallery in Whitechapel? Certainly, Heathcote Dervish comes mantled in flame… even though his retreating form sparks a thousand timbers. It must all align *avec* a poster that comes somewhat sign-posted on a dripping wall. A statement which asserts – in accordance with Lord Kitchener's vintage – that the female waxes deadlier than the male. Wasn't this one of Rudyard Kipling's actual see-saws? In any dilemma, now, Phosphorous Cool glowers after the reclining torch with a halberd in his gauntlet. A mini-robot, like the one drawn from George Lucas' *Star Wars*, applauds each gesture from the left's proximity. Furthermore – and next to him – the figures of Elsa Bounteous Hapgood and Butler James look on. They happen to be the first and second excesses… otherwise they are hoist by their own petard. "Begorrah", witnesses a white-skinned puppet, "his evacuating dark lordship shall not escape from me again. No untrammelled witness can outlast an altar boy's cry in court!

66

Remember this: revenge, taken cold, always turns out to be a livelier dish. Do we imbibe the following epigraph from Machiavelli's *Discourses* (?); namely, the fact that those who wish to erect a monarchy must first kill Brutus, but the citizens wanting to establish a republic shall have to slay Brutus' sons. It has been written."

TAKE CARE OF THE ICED CAKE/SLICE IT IN EIGHTS: (73)

A manifest even-tide descends on men's souls, and it alternates with the universe's regulation... at least in terms of the menstrual cycle. Let us see: our silvery puppet finds itself lain before a circumference of dust, one which travels out beyond its pedigree (betimes). A stone slab – of the darkest green hue – lies directly underneath his limbered frame. A brief wisp of mist or spume from a cauldron travelled overhead; and it also seemed to be reminiscent of a severed head in a basin of straw. This subsisted elsewhere: or in one of those caskets-cum-wooden pallets within which house removals & antiques are obtained. Deep inside it – and to one side of gilt-edged volumes from the eighteenth century – there exists a phrenological skull. Or – more accurately – it betrays the quality of a porcelain brave; that is, one which shines under lights and indicates a delicate example of Gray's *Anatomy*. Do we detect a bullet-hole smack through the centre of its scalp; a gap consequently levelling off to a red dye against magnesium's ore?

+

But never mind it: a coven of witches gathers on a foredoomed slope – and in a setting where eight mystagogues choose to travel across light years o' spirit. They do not luxuriate in the calling of those Three Weird sisters in *Macbeth*; no, even if such an eventuality came to visit in an expressionist interpretation by Steven Berkoff. Let it all ride out on this... since the faces of this clack were shocked, beaten down, estranged or put to grief. They also belittled an intemperate blaze; a factor that merrily fitted itself to a griddle yonder. A brick wall of tiled alabaster – each square peg representing a tired pavilion – lay behind Heathcote. He stood directly under a flaming trope – what with the marionette's body immediately beneath him on a dais. It enclosed the offerings of so many saviours; being both silver and white in apportioned lustre. Nor should one forget the blue… Abreast of all this magnificence – and with a fine theatrical gesture – Heathcote Dervish began. "Brethren, let us pray for rapine", he uttered.

POISONOUS MUSHROOMS LUXURIATE IN LOAM: (74)

To one side of our predicament, Elsa Bounteous Hapgood grabbed hold of James' collar – at least when given access to a world of dreams. All in all, the bell tolled for an adventurer who opened up Ouida's calm. It requisitioned or spoke up for one of Daphne du Maurier's romantic stories during a still period. "Quick", she sibilated, "everything we planned for is lost or contaminated with dirt – especially if Heathcote D.'s allowed to make passage. He must not escape, James. I'm relying on you." To the wording of this, our Butler responds in a masculine vein. Whereupon, he immediately challenges Phosphorous Cool to a duel. He acknowledges (you see) that in order to pursue one he must first vanquish the other. "*En garde*", he snorts, "none but ourselves can rescue a stargate from its past. We must be the ones who make a decision for everything which remains alive. Surely, the purpose of our efforts is to bind as well as loose on earth and in heaven?"

BACK IN PARADISE TOM-FOOLERY WEARS A MASQUE: (75)

"Potions or filters, brothers of the hearth, can be used to dampen down a prospective victim. Yet his destruction and our relative empowerment doesn't occur thereby. Can it be licit; and if so – how will his demise be brought about by witchcraft?" Heathcote Dervish speaks before an assembled throng of mages. The cowl is deep down over his eyes – only to reveal a spectral imprint; a silhouette that fuses with any sepulchral tones issuing from below. Let it trace its appendages thus... because what we are engaged upon, my fellow magicians, happens to be nothing more or less than *The Fanatical Pursuit of Purity*. Oh my yes, it all has to do with those fluted shadows which pass up a wall in flame. Never again shall we be left to subsist in the matter... but, after the kindred of the Persian author Sarban's stories, a certain exercise in Yockey's *Imperium* needs to creep in. Furthermore, does one forsake the difference between ourselves and Richter's book on Greek sculpture? In this work --- scripted by a curator of classical art --- we see an instrument of yearning. It faces off against these tomb-stones, foreshortening them and leading to arrestation... even lift-off. None may gainsay it; since the ultimate object must be a perfection beyond mankind. Its remit is to transcend – level upon level – so as to justify an eagle's affront. May we detect a refusal to bottom out into the equal or egalitarian? In such keeping, those of our kind militate against absorption... we also maximise our potentiality, thereby. Summon up the reckoning... I beg you; and forsake each spectrum along its compass. Woe to Icarus who flew too near the sun --- we shall not repeat his escapade. Do you resuscitate those visions of Parisian cranks, in wings, who fall into the Seine from bridges? In any event, our view of these kore, stele or metopes is bound to change over time. All in all, it aims at a point beyond its radius or circumference --- the truth lies in extremes, do you follow? Moderation resembles a curse; whereas a straight line traverses a circle's curve further out. Look no more, scant ones, than at the head of a giant from a metope in the F temple at Selinus: all of it originates from the National Museum in Palermo, Sicily."

+

"Viands, rare herbs and *pot-pourri* may put our manikin abed, but – by necessity – only black magic or wicca's left-side can extirpate him. Now you will witness his destruction writ large! It can only be encompassed by rejecting a Masonic grave. Nor shall it really contrast favourably with Paul Klee's painting known as *The Possessed Girl*."

WE MUST DESIST FROM EMPTYING SEVEN COFFERS: (76)

In a side-street in Victorian London (now) two figures are duelling with swords; they happen to be Butler James and Phosphorous Cool. A clash of blades takes place between them in a gathering swirl; nor can one really confront the blistering nature of such a fog. Like it or not, their scimitars clatter amid a vortex of wind – a whirligig within which various bits of newsprint get blown about. Could they possibly be Cypriot delight wrappers or examples of the yellow press? Each of their sabres continues to strike blow for blow – while, adjacent to the action, a gas-lamp flickers under a distempered moon. It waxes to an ochre tint that limns scarlet with brown hues. Again and again, these poniards of Sheffield steel break asunder; as our two characters jig about on a puppet's theatre. Maybe it emboldens a forgiven posture – given that the dolls' house so implemented could have been owned by Scriabin or Montague Summers? First Phosphorous and then James has the upper hand... albeit swerving to avoid each other's pointillism or sword-sharpening. All of a sudden these two blade-runners exchanged places – what with Butler James at magnetic north and Phosphorous Cool at magnetic south. Seeking to glean assistance from his inner mind, Phosphorous' face and eyes become luminescent – and each one holds to a hypnotic effect after Mesmer's witness! Beneath his silvery cascade of moon Butler James fights on, but Phosphorous had already begun to delve deeply into his sub-conscious. What will he imperil by finding there?

TWO AUTOGYROS COLLIDE IN MID-AIR: (77)

Heathcote Dervish stood before a boiling cauldron; and this was irrespective of the bursting steam that issues from its coals. These are fiery – purple to red – and they set off a bubbling torrent of spume. Seen in the lee of this, the figure of Heathcote Dervish rises up in a hieratic vein. He casts a scarlet mantle upon a subdued dawn; in a situation where his hands grapple with imagined goblins of the air. Like an actor from the Garrick of yore, Heathcote's eyes and eye-brows wax middling or beetling. They rear up --- after the fashion of so many cameos by Donald Pleasance, Lon Chaney, Peter Lorre and so forth, especially when playing villains. Further to this effort, the jaw is thrown back; and the hands are convulsively clasped and unclasped: while Enochian verses gush forth from his gaping orifice like a torrent. They may be said to spill the ventilation of one august rapture too far, even when it's been crossed with the diction of MacGregor Mathers or W.B. Yeats' verse.

Heathcote utters the following imprecation or chant:~

We live by a courageous splurt
it all goes blurt
but there is no time to flirt
in explanation of so much hurt.
+
Do you reckon to this drama(?)
registering in Sobibor's pyjamas
at the time of a dead lama
or with the expectation of one particular brahma.
+
Service the demands of frenzy
make way for an adventure by Henty
it notifies one special entity
by dint of running on empty.
+
We specialise in the needs of lock-jaw
in terms of a surfeit of pooh-bar
let skeletons rain down on a foot-path
and others deliberate on chutzpah
while we deliver the *coup de gras*.

Again now, let us hint at the bravery of those within a circle who find themselves surrounded by candles. They prove to be dark, lissom, chocolate-like and are made from black wax. "Harken to me", hissed Heathcote Dervish, "come at my call and within the navigation of my name! Notify your existence to us and christen our breath's shadowy utterance. Appear – materialise; even manifest a presence at my clarion; the latter being a warlock's abjuration. Come", he gibbers in rapture, "at the urging of Heathcote Dervish." Suddenly a manifestation begins.

THE FUTURE IS TODAY'S PUTTY IN HAND: (78)
Do you detect a curse beyond this horizon of even minds? Let it loose now... since Phosphorous' mesmerism bites deeply into a Butler's soul – the former a set-up in which the latter's eyes gaze on in a built-up lantern. Do you take on board its marvellous fatalism? Anyway, our glistening puppet delves deeply into the other's mind... only to allow a future inheritance to instaurate its nature. For he realises that his opponent, Butler James, wants to usher in a new world – namely: he wishes to herald an unbidden century. Might B.J. be a member of the Grey Movement without knowing it? Against all of this, a phantasm devoted to a century yet to be milks one's screen... and it encodes a digital signal from the twentieth century. (After all, this exercise in raw creation or *Art Brut* captures the post-Edwardian era... most effectively). Wherein – in his mind's-eye – Butler James delivered up an entourage of shadows. These consisted of a silk backdrop, a television screen showing *Bagpuss*, a miscellany of punks, teddy-boys, grunge types and skin-heads (*a la* Richard Allen's novels); together with Mary Quant females from the nineteen sixties. Such *demi-mondes* came garbed in short skirts, boots, felt-caps, padded belts and black mascara around the eyes – Elisabeth Taylor style. Perhaps the most arresting image of all happened to be that of Liza Minelli, when depicting the decadent artiste in *Cabaret*. She sports a feminine leotard, fish-net stockings and suspenders, choke, heavily made-up face, high heels and a bowler hat. Does James see the future in the fag-end of Weimar; rather than what follows it? Phosphorous Cool

continues to battle with his adversary, but he cannot help but think: "is there no end to this *danse macabre*?"

TIGER, TIGER RIDE SOFTLY IN LILAC: (79)
As if by magic (sic) everything gathers pace within a swirl of paint: and it husbands unto itself abstract expressionist lustre... whether white, red, green, black or indigo. Slowly a face and its gestures emerge from a bubbling pit; a license that hovers over a sacrifice which grows from a circle's circumference. Yet it no longer encompasses Tumble-weed or Hermaphrodite X, no, since a more reptilian fondue dissolves before us. Or should we say that a creature hesitates to come of age amid broth? In looks we find a saurian carapace delivering itself up to us – one that conjures up a prehistoric past well before mankind's advent. Yessir: the dragon-man floats above our hubble-bubble; and he or 'it' then has to choose his lines very carefully in this drama. It comes to quit its omens in a ready manner... For one item releases its vapours before any other: especially in relation to the brick kiln on which it all rests. A livery of such scales surrounds its mouth and these, in turn, refuse to rest unless they embody those levered up eye-lids that crush the orbs beneath. Against any redundant flavour, though, its token ears appear to be ribbed and longitudinal --- albeit after a bat's potentiality to listen into its own scream. Moreover, a swirling trail of ether surrounds this massive head; one which comes to be known as Mastodon Helix or Skyros/Spyros, (effectively so).
+
Vaguely underneath our offerant to the task, however, two cloaked arms find themselves raised up in a Heavenly direction... whilst below his cape and rapture everything else is all but turned away. Furthermore, this warlock barely flexes his back and leg muscles... before he lets out an exultant cry. It leaps out from the underside of his cowled exterior/interior. "The will of those Heavenly presences finds an object suitable to their tasking and remit. My word, a monster or Goat of Mendes rises through this mist... examine its codex, I beg you. A champion

73

has emerged; the one whom the Norns have chosen to crush our prey hovers above us. All hail…"

REMEMBER LADY MACBETH'S LEFT VENTRICLE: (80)
Meanwhile, a flaming image or Armageddon hurries down a Whitechapel alley-way; and it runs from pillar to post and filters itself in terms of a fiery crescent. In this divided medley, then, our mummy looks for a new victim amid flaming sheets. For an *auto da fe* or a climbing matador – dressed in a Klansman's body – seeks to liberate its pursuance. During the course of such a journey, then, his fiery hands clap about adrift of snow – and this is irrespective of the fact that we are dealing with extreme heat. Various posters or notices come to light on these walls now; in a tabernacle where "Pear's Soap" or some vaudeville *artiste* seeks to deliver a message… alive; alive-o. In his present fury, Heathcote Dervish understands the need to fall or alight upon a new victim – and in regular or short order. As King Lear has occasion to tell Cordelia in the play of the same name; nothing will come of nothing: speak again. Yet who should the flaming tarantella of H.D. alight on – if not the myth of a recurrent bourgeois? Might such an individual become entwined – memory for memory – with the steady couple on the bridge at the back of Munch's 'screamer'. "Good Lord", cries out the man in the frock coat and stack hat; in that he has a dim understanding of a meteoric wraith before it's upon him. Yes indeed, the territory of Hades strikes within an instant – and it also transfixes one Guy Fawkes prior to a necessary vogue. But this Scaramouch now finds ripe faggots piled up around his feet. Is he tied to the stake – by virtue of plexiglass beads or wires…? Nonetheless, a human torch falls directly upon our victim. It happens to be a refutation of Max Stirner's *The Ego and its Own*, and in a breaking moment quicklime showers upon him. A total blackness soon intrudes.

ARM YOURSELF AGAINST BYZANTIUM'S ENDURANCE: (81)

Open and aghast, Heathcote Dervish surveys the scene. A curl of hair – together with tufted eye-brows – sprouts from beneath his wizard's apparel. Now no-one should really look at things in any other way… For, rearing abreast of him in the twilight, is a mastodon or abomination – all and at the same time tendrils of smoke drift upwards. They spiral in terms of a noon-tide sign; a conundrum which doubtless has to do with a fiery cauldron further on. This unheralded figure goes by the name of Mastodon Helix or Spyros. At one time history and literature knew him by another title… one that heralded the forename: ADAM. You see, once upon a time (or abreast of such aeons) he'd known bounty… or even the rich pickings of grave-yards. (Necromancy had been numbered among his darksome urges, after all). Yet an innocent inflexion gave rise to subterfuge, primarily in terms of expectancy and loss. To rephrase the early pages of Alexander Trocchi's *Cain's Book*, every later sin or infraction came to be coruscated in his features. They bred over the lymph of so much scar tissue – only to issue from an iron mask's failure to blow with these breezes. It also resuscitated trust… or, more accurately, its absence. Because each lust, form of greed, envy, resentment, jealousy and cowardice bore a livid stamp upon 'its' features. The mask of every hate --- in other words --- may have travelled across these worlds; there to cloak a million ropes with hemp. Surely, such disfigurement indicates: what? Why, it proved to be the over-loaded bay of so much fury – none of whose circumstances can give any glory to *The Abominable Doctor Phibes*. Mark it now: one level of entropy always militates against another: it seeks to cover over such a shroud with a bloody film. Could it be construed to be rather like Marc Quinn's efforts – albeit after any taste for refrigeration finds itself forgotten?

STRAIGHTER THAN AN ARROW: (82)

Way back in the nineteenth century, a shimmering spirit chooses to enter a charred corse. It smoulders meaningfully to the side in brackish incense; and the likelihood of this proves to be a perfect foil for such a misalliance. Does one bother to recall the ancient Christian doctrine over a soul's transmigration? Let it go: since now – long after the facts of the case became known – Heathcote Dervish approaches a vaudeville's vista once again. No two matters are truly alike, you see? For a start, one is almost driven to see a circus barker's cry... despite its reversal. Will a spendthrift bill not obtain to this likelihood, in a scenario where it can only obviate the case of the Elephant Man and other freaks? (His skeleton – to this very day – speaks legions about a jar in the Royal College of Surgeons, in south Kensington, where it happened to be situated. Iain Sinclair makes use of it in his post-modern redoubt, *Whitechapel – Scarlet Tracings*). Almost as an aside to the main business, m'lud, Heathcote Dervish tip-toes towards a collection of Victorian bobbies. All of whom are busy standing around three "Eminent Victorians" – in Asa Briggs' use of the term. These were Phosphorous Cool, Elsa Bounteous Hapgood and Butler James. Our wilderness finds itself travelled across by Heathcote Dervish – a creature who definitely supports a stack hat within some unfolding mist. A few scratches or tears from the yellow press pass in the wind. Whereupon – and underneath a flaring gas-lamp – a motley crew of Peelers make their case. Bestride of any magnificence, though, a Watsonian figure gruffly approaches the prey: it manifests one frock-coat short of respect... and mantles in the Derby's direction. A heavy and woven moustache also travels around an upper casement. Does our enjoined butler stoop to hear Bow Bells reverberating in the background?

A LIZARD SEEKS ITS TISSUE IN A SLIT-EYE: (83)

A saurian raised by Heathcote's spume had already started to speak; and – rather like a monster in an H.P. Lovecraft story – his accents were guttural. Any dedication to stage fright (you see) has long since gone west, in a scene where mortal sounds welled up atonally. Resembling Arthur Schoenberg's musical diction (in short), each couplet drained a muddy silence. Every word --- therefore --- took lustre from Samuel Beckett's anti-novel *Comment C'est* or *How It Is*. Wherein shambolic denizens drag themselves across upturned earth without benefit. None knows any surcease (effectively so); yet they recognise a sibilation due to speech. It preserves the characteristics of Bim and Bom, both of whom drag their bodies aslant the loam. In a drama drawn from George Speaight's toy-theatres, however, Mastodon Helix begins to speak:

"Harken to me, drivelling poltroons! My estimation of your blood is as the thickest of lemon juice, do you hear? Now that my fury renders everything serviceable in terms of yonder matrix… since none but I can stand on the basis of its longitude. Do the mathematical formulae which lie beneath me visit a new Gorgon's sight --- to make use of a courtier's cry in *Macbeth*? But never mind Fuseli's romance; my carrion teaches the abomination of a new witness. It always supports no-one other than a curlicue or such wonderment. Indeed, the name Mastodon X ill-serves my massive frame, m'lud, and it's one that passes across the horizon like a twilight's beacon. These rough edges can often be planed down by unreason – all acting in accord with the subterranean codex of Goya's dark. Hitherto, I knew your solvent imagery and burning face masks. Yet now and all, I am well aware of George Bernard Shaw's insistence on locking himself into a shed or writer's cabin in order to compose. Whereas – in my case – a parallel with Greek legend causes us to catch our collective breath. It indicates the fact that Poseidon fell asleep on a rock in Attic Colonus – from which sprouted the first horse, named Skyphios, when his seed accidentally fell on the ground. Thus, one of those crooked limestones reached for the stars in its musculature, but it actually recalled a steroid husk under grey lights. Truly, a monstrous heap such as myself shall reach its closure under lightning – only then to see a man torched in a cage of wicker. After all, no druid has ever captured my amphibian tonsure."

BEHOLD THE MASONIC DRIFT OF A RED COFFIN; IT LIES AFT: (84)
Back in our period devoted to High Victoriana, the multiple blades of our two protagonists continue to clash. Each tungsten fillet pounds on another's indifference – if only to surmount the bravery of two rather than four musketeers. Let's go on to consider this further: the courageous edge to one's will musters up oblivion at a sword's cusp. It's in a reckoning which chooses to accede to *Beowulf's* logic, particularly in those moments where the hero takes on a fire-breathing dragon. This exists in the saga's second half; and it refuses to mix mead and water in a manner that might disoblige John Gardner's *Grendel*. A story that tells this skald's effort from the monster's perspective --- talk about moral relativism! Nonetheless – and with a sudden gesture – Phosphorous Cool's ceremonial dagger smears up and slashes across the servant's face. This errant Parker reacts in alarm, if only to examine the cut or gash on the left-side. It affixes itself to a divided thespian – especially by dint of those Hellenistic masks which weigh the temperature within. They often transfigure a golden or Grecian dawn – one that finds itself carried away towards an available purple. The whole truth of the matter relies on Loki being imprisoned one day beneath the earth – he has to be trussed up and confined concerning his bodily movements. Heavily fanged serpents then lie above him, contextually speaking, and these drip venom on our half-giant from afar. In order to avoid this molten fate, however, his second wife, Sigyne, captures such ichor in a pewter dish. But every so often she has to pour the silver dinner service away, and, in such a brief passage of time, this eldritch stew reaches Loki. Thor's half-brother screams… and the shock or reverberation of his cries issue as earthquakes. These cause geologic plates to scour, tidal confusion to rise up and the mountains to shake. Chris Bonnington's adventures of yesteryear --- in other words ---

nearly always touch the void by missing a salutary trampoline. Is it not so, Joe? But still, Butler James turns southwards with a bleeding mugshot; an encampment, most definitely, which remembers one of those criminal profiles by William Roughead. "Curse you, salt-petre", announces our underling. "The quell of your questing bell shall do nothing for these restive spirits, Khitian or otherwise. No dotard beckons danger from a false moustache; it merely serves to underscore one axiom – namely, that in a sovran tarot the thirteenth card betokens death as well as utter transformation. Belial take you and feed on your vitals, sirrah! Any such custodianship must greet the day with a severed face (sic) dancing for joy on a burning post." But Phosphorous Cool replied: "My endangering of your left-side waxes efficacious. It permits the real dimensions of one's character – outside of the brain's right-side – to find themselves revealed. Belial feeds on hungry spawn existing beneath a lake's green top. Algernon Blackwood has nought on such evidence. It raises Ragnorak – only to die."

SISYPHUS LIFTS A BOULDER UP PEPPARD'S HILL: (85)
Examine this, my brethren! It effectively freezes any temperature behind an iron face-mask. Needless to say, Mastodon Helix's physiognomy rears into view and it grimaces before a lion's advent. But – in actuality – the saurian complexion of his diatribe remains calm. It doubtless breaks from one's special patina... if only to limit spectral ears beyond the fray: these prove to be the mark of a bat's wonderment. Such offerants scream (potentially) in Gaza in order to see... even though a fragmentary license drifts up amid smoke. These gestures come to be seen later as lily-livered in their cups... doesn't each one buff the eyes with a snake's alignment? In turn, our object's orbs are convulsed, the mouth elongated and serpentine... and the teeth definite molars of decay. Do they need to be an indication of the serpent folk's cruelty? Let it all come down in breach of Heaven... I pray for such an indulgence, at once stripped and ready for this task. (These were doubtless Heathcote Dervish's ready thoughts about

79

the matter...) All of it may be resolved, however, if we understand dehiscence, crepitation, rhino skin, scorbutic lustre, reptilian husks... and Austin J. Desmond's deliberations over warm-bloodedness in lizards. Furthermore, tendrils or wafts of uneven smoke billow up around him... despite the evidence over Pacher's Lucifer being unable to turn this prayer-book's leaves. Has Mastodon Helix escaped from an Arthur Machen story, experimentally speaking? Or might it choose to rekindle Fenwick Lawson's sculptures? These either indicate or capture the power and truthfulness lurking in wood.

A FISH OUT OF WATER FRIES ITS ONIONS: (86)

Back in the pre-Edwardian fogs, a large bevy of police constables have turned up. They surround Phosphorous Cool and Butler James like a blue wave... but may these waters be lapping inwards or outwards, retrospectively speaking? Our two protagonists have likewise drawn up their sabres by this time. Meanwhile, several of the policemen are holding up old-fashioned street-lamps; many of which happen to be fuelled by a mixture of oil and resin. Every one of them glints or glistens in accordance with H.T. Flint's thesis on *Geometrical Optics*. One or other of these sapphire misfits holds a billy-club in a gloved hand; while other faces scan an indifferent future. Under their conical hats they interpret a poster painting by William Roberts. All in all, then, Butler James uses the police as his pride and joy. Pointing in the silvery one's direction, he declares: "Arrest this traveller between dimensions, men! He's the phantom of yore who's stalked the streets of Whitechapel. Many a graven image, carved from silent bark with a chainsaw, proves to be down to him. It reconnoitres such spite; nor can one spill the iodine over those wounds in Herman Melville's *White Jacket*. Take him into custody, officers; he's your chief murder suspect." "Let me be", opines the heroic puppet. "From the depths of my heart, I in no way subscribe to poisoning. I am innocent of these abominable crimes, to be sure!" In relation to which remarks... these

Victorian tokens of the 'Bill' gather round. What decision will they make?

GEORDIE FLODDIES ARE *SAUTÉED* IN LARD: (87)
A century hence – and around a cauldron of desire – Mastodon Helix continues to mouth stern imprecations. It doubtless achieves divers outcomes – all of them curdling in the lee of this particular Greek Fire. Sufficient unto this day, then … "I grew up afflicted with cosmic radiation", growled a moniker's Spyros. "Yet still, my fatalism came across the universe like a bolt from Zeus' finger. All of it gave me unparalleled strength –in terms of bringing a city to its knees. Didn't the federal authorities in Louisiana, when a hurricane struck, call it Katrina? Yes – for devilment – these escapades must wreck the future of such a frothing doll; it only twitches on the end of Hecate's string. But what of us marionettes? We barely delve into the fortune of Eric Bramall's *Puppet Plays & Playwriting* – wherein the dream phantasms of a thousand-and-one nights takes place. All told many withering happenings break free now… they line up behind a balustrade of engagement, as was foretold by a Hulton radio picture library. Here an all-father or puppet-master left our legs dangling, and these were signed up for some nomenclature *avaunt* the stage. Outside the sandy mists of Colwyn Bay it found itself to be; and in its confines mahogany stretches away as far as the eye can see. It also travels towards oblivion by way of a cascade: the chandeliers of which mellow into candle-light hours later. It figures already… for a tabernacle upon the wall called to pipes aplenty. These limited a disturbance to the gothic image of a puppet-master. His name went by the following soubriquet: Moustachio Brave Herring."

A POLICE ACTION ON ALL FOURS REMINDS ME OF THE BOER WAR: (88)
The Metropolitan police have gathered around the two parties to this dispute without knowing why. A lamp-light glows fitfully in subdued ochre; and it floats like a bubble upon a fractured

81

horizon. Listen to the following: Butler James is still expostulating – and this's irrespective of a leftwards tending scar upon the face. "Officers, I entreat your goodness and solitude… like one of those Gilbert & Sullivan policemen so beloved of Howard Brenton. For, in his marxist plays, Robert Peel's men fail to apprehend a notorious psychopath who was mentioned before as Christie, the Notting Hill murderer. Did not the latter lie covered in newsprint and old ashes – albeit before he rises aslant of a wandering finger? Likewise, his masked otherness slopes upwards in a dun-coloured mack; the likelihood of this causing a toppling, demasking and honouring of a leaping antelope beyond his fellows. "Who will you choose to believe or blather on about?", accosted a young bridge builder. On more solid ground, though, the metropolitan blues ask Phosphorous Cool and Hermaphrodite X to accompany them to the police station. Underneath this festival to cerulean lamping, however, the robot called Tumble-weed made a despairing gesture. But the understanding of a world's pockets and tactics are widely superfluous; given a man like him who flies no flag save his own." "Fillet it now, my brethren… the limbering up of such tasks helps to illumine every shadow. Surely, it proves to be an example of a resurrection's clue on even a world-wide perspective? Whereupon various plants require a husbandry that speaks nought of time; it only demands. 'Will you marry me?', undertakes our philosopher before the dam. Yet those women cascading through our drama limit its freedom."
+

Phosphorous Cool (13) has been subsequently interlarded into a skulking jack-in-apes. Do you consider iced bombs to be such a recognition of one's skald a hundred years on?
+

In expectation of the above, one of our coppers grates on a hurdy-gurdy machine: "You shall accompany us all on a visit to the threshing floor. It betokens its own basic spray – one which prevents southern politicians asking some awkward facts. Do you acknowledge our moral trampoline; at once allowing children to be destroyed before their time? A new amnesty lasted until a detergent or Sutro's raising of Count Maurice de Maeterlinck from the dead. It all has to do with William Roberts' painting of toy-policemen on a postcard... and its seemingly oblivious quality."

A WORLD IN YOUR EAR, O DWARFLINGS[!]: (89)
"Moustachio Brave Herring's face levelled up to that of a ripe cucumber; and it continued to rally around troop movements which were as yet undisclosed. His mask intoned the principles of an old man, but nonetheless retained an aspect of youth. Then again his lineaments proved to be heavy, needful, unembarrassed and grave in aspect. Less a perspective of the Christian god he was, than an illustration of Odin in terms of *Beowulf*. Even though those two don't necessarily overlap... Yes, let's see now... Perhaps Moustachio Brave Herring was a puppet-master – that is, one who existed adjacent to his cabinet of Doctor Caligari. Let's be fair, though: such a denizen indicates the wrong-headedness of Eric Bramall, in that this marionette or *artiste* never misses a trick... certainly over trestles and their ropes. Might one detect it anew? Against all this, Bramall's lustre could pick and choose from among his manikins. They basically launched themselves to such a favour of fortune. Furthermore, all of these puppeteers stand above their armatures; and adjacent to many springing back-boards. It also becomes accosted by virtue of some tacks or pins; the like of which hold up a watercolour scene by Ramsay. May it yet morph into a modernist schema by Miro instead?". You have been listening to the words of Mastodon Helix!

AGAINST A FLYING AUTOGYRO'S TROPE: (90)
In the near mist of a nether Victorian England, a reincarnated Heathcote Dervish approaches Elsa Bounteous Hapgood from a reverse direction. He or 'it' embodies --- in physics --- the convexity of so many bowls... let it lie. Again, the mist or London's pea-souper seems to have cleared; a situation that

makes the master of the house's nearness ever more discrete. Doesn't such a glory rely on his conical head-piece; i.e., a smoke-stack which stares apiece at this blustering after-life? In the background a Gothic manse raises its charm. No longer may James Purdy's imagination let rip... when pursuant to the fact that his deep fried Southern Gothic turns the tables on its English genes. Various windows or casements can be seen in the darksome interiors of such a House – it more than lights up damnation ever so clearly in order to spy on it. The policemen are off and to the side, but no-one interferes with an exchange between a husband and his wife in another dimension. "Heathcote?", she whispered semi-abstractedly, and with a slight quaver in her voice. "The very same, my darling", he insisted on *avec* a greedy billowing. Meanwhile – and to the right – Butler James stood beside them imperturbably, and with utter calm. "Cabbie", he called out abruptly to a waiting atrocity. "Let us leave this spot as quickly as possible... maybe on a rare penny farthing", insisted HD. His voice etched a muffled tambourine – even as he spoke.

TANGERINES GO PURPLE IN THE BLOOD[!]: (91)

"There's always been room for one more, my friends", intoned Mastodon Helix's guttural voice. "Yes indeedy, since a star-burst or gateway exploded before a lively portal. The semblance of a meteorite was now seen; and it risked the peak of a disabled overture... namely, one that took on a distracted element even in terms of its ransom. Such a scimitar levelled off towards the sky-line – instead of plummeting down in a rage of all witness. A brief gaze aslant this rapture saw the earth's crust peel away; it thence depicted continents and lakes beneath a misty firmament. A spume-like elemental dances under the stars; whilst a darkened backdrop of our milky way gravitated yonder. It continuously bespoke of a galaxy well beyond a satrap of nothingness... that is: a substratum which led the way to a thousand faery lights. A dispensation, this, that belabours an unsubtle point concerning Spenser's diction. One Milky Way does not a million flowers

84

make, in other words. What could this flashing comet signify? Why, it had to do with Mastodon Helix... in that the merest thought of the puppet-master, Moustachio Brave Herring, lifted him off his feet and onto another plane. Altogether now, an *artiste* who governs his charges can whisk them away uppermost; and to various points in another direction such as one knows. Further to this, he raised up Mastodon's musculature – at once carrying him to a trope and fixing on a possibility yet to be. Might it mean salvation for one who skims the galaxy like a deluded star – maybe so? For one carven idol can be moved to the Fourth Dimension just by thought; primarily so as to allow you to exist in parallel outside Time."

GUARDIANS OF SKYROS' GATE: (92)
Immediately our cab moved up from a neo-Victorian abode, and it circled London town looking for future egress. Above all though, the vehicle betokened a will-o'-the-wisp which sailed above houses and out into a dark azure. Truly, the minaret or spire of a Baptist church hoved into view: and it all bespoke one tension too many for this aftertaste. Face the facts, will you (?) – because this church's pyre extolled a secondary virtue. Analysts came to consider it as green in colour. Do you take its message forward in some way? An electronic whip cracked from above; and it was the coachman directing his flying vehicle. Especially now that an autogyro --- patented by the toy manufacturer Britons --- soared into the ether. "Giddy up, Pontefract", yelled the hansom cabbie. Didn't Wyndham Lewis posit a 'Taxi driver test' for literature in his intellectual autobiography, *Rude Assignment*? In any event, our three co-conspirators swap anecdotes. They are Heathcote Dervish, Elsa Bounteous Hapgood and Butler James. None save them may effectively register such an affidavit or molecule. "Phosphorous Cool shan't be able to use legerdemain to much purport... one feels. Extravagantly so, allow him to escape into the paradise of trying to lessen one's impact through mesmerism! Let it alone, my cousins: Phosphorous will find it impossible to sweet-talk

Inspector Lestrade over those Phantom slayings in the east",
remarked their butler.

WILL EISNER'S GRAPH LACKS SPIRIT: (93)

"Each conundrum opens up the way to a new awakening, hereby.
For – many moon-times previous to this – Mastodon Helix found
himself to be trapped in his Master's vortex. In a scenario where
Armageddon comes to deliver its offering every Thursday
afternoon. In such an advent as this, Mastodon's steroid hammer
got thrown about unnecessarily. It landed at its competitor's feet
without any surcease whatsoever. Does one know or grapple with
such a truth? Likewise, the Beast could not turn around without
knocking over a concrete pylon: and this was a structure which
transposed itself in-between Plexiglass barriers. These were
readily devoted to silence. Make no mistake about it: Mastodon
Helix found himself to be trapped in a variant of what Hubert
Selby Jumior later called *The Room*. No matter… *quod* each
strange molecular pathway triggered the actual: and these
offerings agreed to beam up a portrait *a la* Dubuffet or Hans
Prinzhorn. You see, our Puppet-monger or Master of Ceremonies
(MC) moved to quell such violence; especially when it realised
its imprisonment by the puppeteer, Moustachio Brave Herring.
'He cares nothing for my strength – measured, as it was, in
proportion to East German sprinting', cried out Mastodon in
credit and pain. The owner of this puppet show also speaks of a
'gawk' or an anonymous freak; a specimen or example of
Lombroso's kin whom you pay to look at. Above all else, any
carnival or fun-fair carries out its damage limitation exercise – at
least should one prove to be necessary. It's all part-and-parcel of
Life's sense of regret. 'He just seizes us --- out of pure thought
rather than malice. It's a sufficiency of power or puissance; and
then he leaves us to rot in prism-like dungeons. These are
narrow-sided cells whose walls are nacreous; themselves being
manufactured from pearls. Get real, *mon ami* – the way to a
wooden puppet's heart has to be to pull at its strings!' Surely,

such manipulation or chicanery had nothing to do with Donna Tart's second novel?"

A HALF-BREED'S SMASH-UP; LIMIT ITS LECTERN: (94)

Meanwhile, inside the cab our three conspirators hatch their plans – even though it was altogether less than convenient. Heathcote Dervish lay further to the left; and he was on the occult's left-side. (Again, didn't Colin Wilson in his 'sixties book of the same title look upon these malefactors and impresarios like a badly behaved sixth form?) Needless to say, Heathcote Dervish's tall hat proved to be pulled down closely over his eyes, and it certainly transformed those disfigured features that went forwards smarting. Next to him and within the relatively cramped cab sat Elsa Bounteous Hapgood --- she looked untroubled and serene. An exquisite mole tapered out on one of her cheeks. Further along, and to the side, came Butler James; an underling who continues to massage the left-side of his face with a scrunched up silk handkerchief. Quite noticeably, a trickle of blood passes down his physiognomy like an unclean eye-wash. Could it possibly resemble an impure variant on Optrex? No matter… "Let us skim over our deliberations once again", mused Heathcote Dervish. His scarf appeared to be pulled down under his chin – albeit even in an all-encompassing or thorough-going way. "But how can we trust the insane violence which exists within you?", contradicted Butler James from the cab's far corner. "We already have before us such a blitzkrieg – and it relates to a public house's pandemonium."

LIFT UP THE VERTIGO OF AN ISOSCELES TRIANGLE: (95)

Our hulking rhino, Mastodon Helix, has now broken free from any cages which might have closed in upon him in the past. Whereupon his misshapen claws or mittens – when constructed around their own shafts – reach out towards Heathcote's visage. It comes over all cowled, Hermetic, occultistic and vaudeville in its *de luxe* aspect. Do we see in such a signification (or a post-

87

dated aspect) the Terence Fisher film of Dennis Wheatley's *The Devil Rides Out*? Nonetheless – and despite being startled – Heathcote Dervish continues with his spiel. He is determined to be the king of this particular castle, even though John Cowper Powys' *Maiden Castle* lay a long way off. 'In another dimension, I remained a prisoner of Moustachio Brave Herring, but now I'm back and thirsting for vengeance. Let your life be a bullet passing through screens; only when you hit a level you can't penetrate… that's the end-point. Yet one will enjoy much glory and others' servitude before then. Mark me', growled Mastodon Helix, 'I mean to make of this planet a play-thing of my charms. It doubtless spoke of those games of bar billiards where no-one's allowed to win. Now however – all of existence lies on the edge of this whetted blade ---.' "No, no, you can't --- Fate and those ancient witnesses of the pyre cannot give permission. Do you harken to it, misfit?" This ricocheted around the room as one of Heathcote's dictums – albeit a foray which came reversed out in a mirror. It amounted to scant more than Heathcote Dervish's bleating, irrespective of one error of judgement. Our mage has yet to work out the fact that MASTODON HELIX MEANT TO RULE THIS WORLD!
+
Even if it only occurred on a puppet stage out in Colwyn Bay… with Eric Bramall or suchlike vaudeville *artistes*. It didn't really matter… because any such delirium found its way to a paltry piece of earth. A sod or keepsake which sacrifices its masonry over a puppeteering of strings. *Thunderbirds* aren't always necessarily go, you see!

GIVE OUT SPANISH OMELETTES WITH A KNIFE: (96)
Amidst a High Victorian assemblage our cab rushes on; and it illustrates a whistle-stop tour across so many sun-beams. Again, our three co-conspirators are grist to the mill of their extravagance. This time any such positioning comes to be reversed; primarily by dint of one subdued head that is viewed sideways-on. It belongs to Heathcote Dervish – despite

inhabiting a foreign body and being dressed up in a frock-coat and tails. Again and again, various traffic hurls or whizzes past their window – it could well be careering motor-cycles, autogyros, hover-pads, spendthrift penny-farthings (possibly powered by tame nuclear energy), dirigibles, air-ships and related Phileas Fogg helium balloons; together with gliders, canal barges, motorised foot-pads, pogo sticks and velocipedes. Heathcote Dervish – for his part – lay like a suffragette to the left; while being pinioned next to the cab's décor. His hat had some relevance to the one worn by Mister Hyde in Stevenson's tale; even though his fable's set in Edinburgh not London. True again, his visage looked seedy, disarmed, mummified and bereft of moral candour. A cocoon of bandages left his skull's remit – at once waxing illicit in relation to Bram Stoker's guild. Wherein various editions of his Egyptian novel, *The Jewel of the Seven Stars*, hid the extremity of its end in order to avoid nausea. (*Nota Bene*: the real edition happened to be the William Heinemann one of 1903, whilst later variants by Rider, Jarrolds & Arrow proved to be abridged. Such amendments seemed to be anaemic, weak and foreshortened). Nonetheless, Heathcote's ear is misshapen next to his greatcoat; the luxuriant wove of which completes a Victorian day. Heathcote Dervish mumbles something in reply to Butler James' former assertion – namely, one that had to do with his unreliability; or could it be described as his proclivity for violence? Who knows? "As to any reckless plenitude", asserted Heathcote Dervish, "you can rest assured. My intelligence relies on other things. It luridly examines the matter." "You'd better", pursued Elsa Bounteous Hapgood with a made-up or oval mouth. Her face divided itself truculently as she spoke – and the woman's features denoted a Royal Flush. (Whether it was flaccid, purged, enflamed, bloated or all over with passion). In the far corner sat one's butler – who kept swabbing his wound with a silken rag. A steely if determined look played about his mask... albeit one which seemed to say 'impress me'. Go on...

A BRIDGE TOO FAR OVER ONE PARTICULAR MEADOW: (97)

We left our drama in a situation where Mastodon Helix's massive hands reached out towards the wizard's cowl. Were the aforementioned Mastodon X's mittens rough, chapped and ill-hewn… while stopping short of any perfection? Yes indeed! For Mastodon has moved from the base of the dais; thence grasping Heathcote's cloak in a giant's maw. Intemperate basalt exists beneath them – and it becomes lined with the blue tissue of so much clay. It serves as the cement for a new abstraction. Mayhap it might be what Ezra Pound referred to as *lapis lazuli* – or did Socrates not mention it as cyanus in the *Phaedo*? Needless to say, the behemoth's crippling muscles glow under an autumnal fire: and this originates from some flames of yesteryear. These flicker in an embrasure in the corner – a brazier occurring outside of any witness' sight. Around the base of one's altar or ebon charge, however, one warlock sprinted forward like one demented. He – rather than the master of his coven – seems to realise what eventuates. His name; you ask? Why, it proclaims the title of Splendour Thomas perchance. "Listen to me – to me", came the gasping voice of Heathcote Dervish. It lisped aslant of the moon's own retrieval, if only to brush a cannon with a butterfly's wings. Such obliging gossamer can never bewitch a termagant like this. "Bow down, monstrous one. You must prostrate yourself before me like a votary or a trembling waif. Don't force me to countermand you with radical measures. I summoned you up from the deep pits – by virtue of my own thaumaturgy: and now gratitude is expected in kindred mead. Seek out the help-meet of your witness, I pray you---." "Gratitude isn't an emotion", sneered Mastodon Helix, "but the expectation of it becomes a very lively one. Mark it: my fulfilment of your kiss was to offer you Kronos' backside. Do you fear its impact, belittled one? Let me savour some grace and favour from you… For now that I have returned from a welter of flies, one of my very hands can make away with a city's walls. Do you see me chipping away at its red stone? Nothing else can

90

suffice in my own parlour; within which you have entered as a crepitating fly. Dost thou recall the Vincent Price film from the nineteen fifties called *The Fly*? Under any other semblance though, I, here and now, luxuriate in my power! It emboldens the sport of badger baiting (thereby)... Let me trample you, little man, into the dust beneath my feet. In truth, you are unworthy to cavil before me. Do you reminisce about Franz Neumann's economic survey, *Behemoth*, that was dedicated to national socialist Germany? Why so... Chelmno's rise is the provender of false riches – nor can any offer you relief with the lees of so many corpses. These help to deliberate upon a mummification's interest." With this he started to whirl Heathcote Dervish off his feet. "Can you expect one like me to bow down before those I may squash like ants?", roared Mastodon Helix.
+

"Do something", squeaked an unsplendid Thomas from the basis of our kiln. Quite clearly now – and at the font of his exhaustion – fear mounted upon him like an estranged peekaboo.

DO YOU HEAR ME, SIR CRISPIN, IN THE MORNING[?]: (98)
Our nineteenth century torpedo continues to break the surface of these icy waters. Don't count your blessings, thereby. Put it on hold, my friend, since one of these terror tubes mounts to raw creation as its own after-effect. Let's reckon on this: "You require our aid if thou desires art to be fulfilled", muttered Elsa Bounteous Hapgood. Whilst Heathcote Dervish's *alter ego* bobbed and jigged about like a gibbeted skull. Could it just be the hansom cab's velocity which contributed to this cause? In any event, the old-fashioned film camera came to concentrate on his features in this silent movie. These were a breakaway from customised estrangement. For – when looked at with a closer degree of attention – his burnt bandages or mummification refuses to subscribe to Alan Burns' *After the Rain*. (A modernist novel, this, that had been written in the nineteen sixties and came with a Max Ernst cover). Furthermore, the unlikeliness of

such a source proves its very witness, and it mounts to oblivion thereafter. Surely now the facts may be revealed? *Avaunt thee* – Heathcote Dervish's features were endwarfed, marble-like, rancid and indicated a semiotic of damnation. They are also wizened, mad-eyed, fanatical, monger encompassing and fervid. In all truth, his orbs gazed on with manic glee under a top-hat --- what ho(!), no-one may write this off. Now we can recognise a burnt mustang beneath the hood; especially when spliced *avec* triangular teeth… which refer to a Wyndham Lewis portrait of *The Laughing Woman* (circa. 1910). His molars grip glass-eyes abreast of their own bandages, in other words.

BRAM STOKER'S VISAGE ENCOMPASSES A GIBBOUS MOON: (99)
Back in the relatively late twentieth century, one's drama continues to unfold. Within its compress, Mastodon Helix stands triumphantly on a stone plinth – and a burst of flame cascades around him in order to filter out daylight. Indeed, why so? Because these wizards, whether male or female, scatter in every direction under the impact of Mastodon's entitlement. Various of their number move in a helter-skelter manner, and after a fashion which accords with Charles Manson's crew. (Note: Manson's hippie psychopaths used the name Helter-skelter). One of their number, Heathcote Dervish, was held helplessly aloft; while others prance for cover in drizzle and rain. Moreover – when suspended in mid-air Heathcote's sandals are on show – and they indicate the footwear of one of *Papillon's* extras. Needless to say, one of these reeling images lets out a cry --- surely, he's yet to properly hear about Dion Fortune's Bull God? Never mind it… since a magenta cowl covers his image: and thereby accords to it nothing other than a penumbra above the nose. A factor (let's be clear) that reconciles itself to Warlock Splendour Thomas' grimace. "Flee, flee – all is dead and gone", bellowed this male version of Pope Joan… as was expressively laid out in one of Lawrence Durrell's novels. Irrespective of which, Mastodon Helix shook Heathcote Dervish like a rag-doll. He

held him up to the light, somewhat roughly, in order to purge him of all misgivings. Let everything be frankly dealt with, here and now, when we announce Mastodon's word count. Each and every syllable of this oration then enunciates itself as follows... Might it also be an example of Patrick Magee's voice travelling over Lear's pitch and sound? Again and again, this shadow-land trombone issues forth. It has to do with those key marginals of death.

LIGHTENING-FLASH EPAULETTES: (100)
The Policemen now surrounded Phosphorous Cool in a deliberate circle – a hemicycle (it proved to be) within which our silvery puppet glistened like an optical spectrum. The heavy blue wove of their uniforms closed in under a gas-lamp --- a provender that hinted at one removal too far! Yes again, an arsenic and old lace filibuster intruded here – if only by dint of the Ripper's previous walks... Weren't these indicative of a 'gore bore' tourism which prevails? Nonetheless, one's silvern husk teleported itself above the ruck or *melee*: and with one gesture from the like of Bramall's fingers he's free. A policeman was about to declare: "I think you'd better accompany us to the station, me lad" – but now nought supervened whatsoever. "Lor(')!", expostulated one plane man's copper. "Cor!" expressed another. "He's levitating – out of all witness – up and away from us. Do ya hear?" Certainly, our metropolitan blue noses were flabbergasted by this white ball – as its particular speed traversed a roulette wheel. Surely, it looked for egress in a socket, irrespective of those red-and-black counters? Could they turn out to be plastic – or not?

A SWIVELLING BRACE PULLED ITS FACE OFF: (101)
Meanwhile, in our instrument of fire, Mastodon Helix stood abreast: and he continuously waved Heathcote Dervish around his head. Like a splintering gingerbread-man, he twirled --- thereby resembling something out of *Bagpuss*, a BBC television serial of yesteryear. Whereupon two cowled merchants in the foreground   ran   for   their   lives...

"NNNNNNOOOOOOOOOOOOO!, one of them cried out in livid pain. Nor may such a rhetoric find its form cut off or alone. Mastodon Helix then let Heathcote go – by hurling him into the middle of his votaries. They scattered or found themselves knocked over like nine-pins. As he was cast away – Heathcote's back turned over a mild somersault... whilst moving on from us. In the midst of being thrown among his fellows --- in agony --- Heathcote Dervish let out a masqueraded shout. It had something to do with massacred nerve-endings; albeit after a fashion that ventilated the passions within. All of this involves a scintilla of hurt or victimised pride; especially given the airs and graces --- *a la* MacGregor Mathers --- which Heathcote had wrapped around his own shoulders as a magician.

LET LOOSE THIS CARAVAN OF FOSSILS: (102)

In our nineteenth century vice tablet, Phosphorous Cool --- accompanied by a robotic Tumble-weed --- spirals away from the constabulary. They wheedle off at a spare rate of knots, and each one is given over to a latitude of nerves. Several of these law-and-order officials are thereby dumb-struck --- nor may they recover from the velocity of this escape! Now and again, a gust of very precise wind curls up behind them – it jigs slightly to the side and flows amid pass-port papers. Moreover, a gushing wind-tunnel strives to enliven this process... while seeking to abscond amid a maelstrom. Various middling Victorians – aside from the out-manoeuvred policemen – give chase. All of them grant a 'view Halloo' towards a pursued fox or hare: the like of which have taken off adjacent to a tabernacle of walls. One denizen of *Victoriana* stands out abruptly, and he besports a floppy hat together with a tie-pin, a cravat and extravagant side-whiskers. "Up and at 'em, me lovelies!", he lets loose. "No-one masters this provender or issue better than us... We must defeat this poltroon who ripens with the Ripper's advent. Let it peel away if we're not careful – there can be no mercy for those who dish the plate! Anyone who denies the author James Hinton's nomenclature travels in purdah. He indicates a marauder's transfiguration; namely, one which claims the symptoms of so many gongs and cymbals. Might such a creature rise from waste ground wearing a red-skull? In any event, he embodies the *largesse* of Godzilla in a Japanese monster film, and such a misfit's bound to crash to earth eventually. Like Icarus in Greek legends of yore – he'll fly too close to the sun and singe his wings. We have to encompass its fall or closure (therefore); and the notion of one manifestation shuts down lamp after lamp. It identifies with mischief, albeit if only to lay siege to a Phantom's name."

A MUMMIFIED SIDE-CAR RIDES PILLION: (103)

A close-up of Mastodon's visage occurs now. It wears upon it the mantle of a lizard-like duty, and this is one that afflicts Nature with a forgotten trespass. A saurian complexion abbreviates the eyes; whereupon we come across one battle-hardened entity too large by far. These orbs smack of misfortune or blaze with Fire: whilst the teeth tapered, dragon-like, in a mouth of gold. Can it realise the truth of one of David Icke's shape-shifters? For, in truth, doesn't this writer consider the late Queen Mother to have been a closet brontosaurus? Again, maybe his fastidiousness indicates the wearisome quality of John Gardner's Dragon – when revealed in the latter's novel *Grendel*. A text wherein the entire saga of *Beowulf* is reconfigured, worm's side-up, from the monster's point of view --- never mind its mother!
+

"Avaunt your witness to degeneration!", bellowed Mastodon Helix at the top of his voice. Surely, such a crest or cusp indicated that Spyros has retained his Adamic strength – when ripping off such a cowl or mask?
+

"Your category doesn't fit any relic of inhumanism. Oh no! I will give you the answers to your own counter-blows before they happen. Listen to this: since it was such a gaggle as you who gave me life in the first place – I'll be generous… I shall allow the rest of your coven to live in order to tarry after his mistakes.

95

But never choose to forget my power or puissance – I furnished yonder klavern with existence even in death. Aught is owed to me; especially the circumference of your actual travail! Do you see? It avails no-one to deliberate upon the Bloomsbury Group of yesteryear. May you remember Duncan Grant's art (?) --- tear it to pieces! For morality remains the ability to crush a thousand insects in one palm, or *a la* Palmistry. Let us then deliberate upon the line of talent which traverses a plane of skin from one side t'other. Reinvigorate Great Granny Webster, why don't you?"

TOO MANY SEVEN INCH NAILS CURE THIS BREEZE: (104)

Our two desperadoes are still seen to be running in the direction of so many tomb stones, multi-dimensionally. A colourful advent, this: given that none of them can bring to mind the modernist mausoleum in northern Paris... one which is devoted to Oscar Wilde's after-grief. Still and all, men of iron, Phosphorous and his Robocop scour the entrance to many passages, and they are actually lost in a maze of lanes between Whitechapel-cum-Spitalfields. A gust of blue dust fills the air; it trespasses all around them... so as to discuss one particular imprint or ring. Could it exist in such a Tartarus? Against this favouritism, a number of walls fly indifference's flag. They incarnate --- if only at one remove --- the reality of Iain Sinclair's poesy (or proem) entitled *Suicide Bridge*. Perhaps a deep green advertisement for Cocoa, drinking chocolate or 'ovaltine' can be prepared? Despite the fact that Phosphorous Cool quizzes Hermaphrodite X on the direction they might take. "Theseus shall not entertain his minotaur to a game of cribbage on the way out", Phosphorous evinced. "We may go in circles (round and round again) yet no Ha!Ha! exists to create a fall in a pitch of England's pasture. Do we speak of a Green Man or a Man of Kent? Yet again: will you reminisce about a female novelist who wrote a book called *The Ha!Ha!* (?): meaning a sudden dip or gap in an English garden – often at a labyrinth's heart, and one allowing a guest or a surprised visitor to fall. Didn't Albert

96

Camus compose a novella known as *The Fall*?" "You speak truthfully, master", averred Tumble-weed, "yet examine it this way. Perhaps we should investigate the sewers or an inner parallelism of ducts, in order to elude governance? Or, quite possibly, do you pity the steel of one who leads an entrapment too far... whether naked of each moon-time?"

SAVE THE WHALE; BUTTER ITS SCOTCH: (105)

An arrestation seeks to intervene in our drama presently... For Mastodon Helix bursts through a granite wall which superintends his progress; thereby causing a myriad shoal of boulders and shards to press in. They home in on one especial point – if only to mount unforgiveness and cause a rippling sensation in his licensed back. These muscles soon come to undulate under a parched skin; and they also inundate the wall like so many false phalli in the household of a black witch. Could their crimson cascade indicate a multitude of special colours or tints: such as cerulean, beryl, cornelian, ruby, nacreous impress, adamantine and wax-works? Oh my, truthfully so... this enclosure's mural forms a falling grandeur around him – even if it just contrasts Diego Rivera's leave-taking with it. What did Mastodon have to say about it, though? Why... nought but this: "Enhance the availability of Pickford's model, if you will! Mankind rests on some easy timbers of assault (perchance); and I intend to search for Elderado in the innards of those I have to disembowel... no matter how robotically. Let us examine this filigree: since any desire to wreak vengeance must uncouple itself from unmarinated foreskins. No obscenity – as regards the imagination – can be usefully occasioned here. Even Stephen King's novel *It* (or *Es* in German) definitely assesses the dark red and black tincture of any lamination. Who knows what the future holds? Your carrion must make way and foreshorten the idea of embalming, even if there's no longevity for mankind any more. An atomic clock happens to be ticking already – and a needle in the vein needs to march towards Thermopylae. None of Leonidas' three hundred drummers may be heard distinctly at such a distance. Truly – or by instinct – Mastodon Helix has got much to compensate for. Let rapine feed on my own blundering necessity."

LOOK! LOOK! AN EAGLE PECKS AT A DWARF: (106)
The serrated teeth of Tumble-weed or Hermaphrodite X are set aquiver, now that they're down in the sewers under old Whitechapel. The smell reeks up in an appalling mist, despite the up-turned pavement egg which Herm. X holds aloft. It proves to be grey and textured like pumice in its expanse. Tumble-weed broke the silence first in this dripping emplacement: "These passages of unleaded silt, master, mightn't they provide some false polish to things? Could the elephant – alone in its tower – effectively undergo the torments of a rag-time which outfaces E.L. Doctorow? Nor can the peace of ages – down here in the latrines – be replaced by anything other than an electric chair. Cast in a dark-blue welding towards black – it obviously intrigues on behalf of Andy Warhol's silk-screen print. Cor (!), a little bit of what you fancy goes a long way to alleviating gut-rot, particularly at the public's convenience. Surely a thousand-and-one pipes, inlaid with mirrors, refracts glory on a willed conclusion? And all prisms when metered to these distances, why, they take effect if one balance shoots forth a Newtonian direction. What say you, guv'nor?"

TOMMY-KNOCKERS IN THE NIGHT GO BINGO: (107)
Mastodon's massive physique leapt away in a fit of pique… in a situation where each limb mushroomed to its own cloud or density of steel. Yes again, the sky over which he prances has turned a deep yellow – albeit with a trace of blue cloud across its expanse. It proved to be willowy, abiding, untreasured and otherwise oblique. Mark it down now: each and every outburst manoeuvred various crags behind it: and these were edifices that helped to define the crenellations of a ruined manse. Such runes – most considerably – chose to illustrate a Hammer House of Horror out Peppard way, and this was despite being one which

opened out before weather-beaten elements. Given rural England's windswept and inclement climate, the hollowed out interiors of these dwellings emboldened one over a building like the asylum in *Dracula*. A Victorian mansion, this, it occluded to the indifferent purchase of one whisper too far. Dare you detect a kindred utterance? All of this subsisted in spite of Eric Bramall's puppet-theatre; a domicile or Montague Summers' pit that exercises a cascading branch of skins down the years. In truth, Mastodon Helix scrambled across a windswept scene – itself bolstered by watery painting of an oriental cast. Can it involve Kokei's Japanese *impedimenta*, perchance? In any event, those magicians who were left below issued the following trumpet: "Look at him go, boy! The like of it is rarely seen the other side of H.L. Mencken's noontide. No sir: this time any different result's bound to spark a riot. Observe how – Godzilla-like – his paws or hooves cause him to travel through the air in a manner recalling Armageddon."

A HUNGRY MOUTH CRIES HAVOC IN THE HEAD: (108)
Meanwhile, down in the sewers we find our two cohorts – each one of whom stands astride a gushing vent. These can only help the stagnant waters gathering routinely at a moment beyond. It also transpires that the lichen of so much mould casts a shadow, even a nuclear dust cloud, on a neighbouring wall. Let it rest: since the whole point of this levitation is to indicate the dankness within. Perhaps the following scenario suffices: a playlet in which a well of silvery water rushes from an underground geyser; it pollutes any origin with a mixed displacement... (to speak of). Needless to say, our welcoming arbitrage looks at the tunnels round about and knows wisdom: and these help to manufacture one hungry siphon too far. Might it incarnate the principle of a watery mouth, or even the *Watter's Mou* (in Scots) that Bram Stoker used in order to pen a novel in the eighteen nineties? At once resultant to such an offering – Phosphorous Cool calmly enjoins the following refrain: "I must plumb the resources of my own mentality, Hermaphrodite X. A time always

99

comes in the affairs of men for a silvery sliver. In such a debenture as this, Tumbleweed, I may be able to spy on my alternative's thoughts. Rather like a restless troubadour or mince-meat merchant – somewhat after the facts – I reckon on an element of cage-fighting to maximise performance. If, psychically speaking, I can lock in on their minds… well, many and varied suggestions tumble aprey around my feet. I shall then be the master of their secret codicils. Never mind the Da Vinci code, a rebus' illumination doesn't cause a hero to falter in his task." "Can your prey's locker be left unguarded so easily?", mouthed Hermaphrodite's quatrain. "Oh my yes", insisted Phosphorous Cool, "one license too many will doubtless see me through to an exchange of swords."

SHOOT VALLEY DUST FROM A RAT'S PAWS: (109)

Beholden to a solemn earth our coven releases its former leader – given the conundrum which declares that he lies bereft and listless like a rag-doll. Certainly, his near corse adopts a weakened complexion – namely, one which strives to raise him from a recumbent formula too many. The consideration of these moments wait agape, and they likewise cross a dividing line into Eric von Daniken's territory. Might it just sway the ballast of Robert Bloch? Nonetheless, Heathcote Dervish lay dying with a boulder to his rear – and the latter cut off like a conic section (somewhat unobservably). Betokening the radius of a Praetorian's column, it summoned up the focus or radial of Bulwer Lytton's scope… particularly if it related to his novel, *The Last Days of Pompeii*. His wife, Elsa Bounteous Hapgood, cradled this broken offerant in her hands – even though sundry cowled figures surrounded her in a miserable vein. A few surveyed the scene behind her; and they were spectral, confused or wanton. Yet grief effectively contrived not to find them out. A previous votary in cape and cowl then lit up the sky to its own barn-yard gate. He chose to offer the following solace. "My dear", he attempted to console her, "our erstwhile leader lies comatose as a piledriver's result; the former a throwaway from a

circus strongman who litters one cave too many with its bones."
"I hear you ill, argumentative spirit", interceded Elsa Bounteous
Hapgood on her behalf. "The reckoning that we face is to save
the Master from Pluto's doorway. Tell me – as an aide-de-camp
to any black-ice – can an unknown necropolis filter its ebon? A
way to rescue my saviour from oblivion has to be found. I won't
be able to face sleep's taste else. May the Scientologists then
prove me to be a lackey over their E-meter?"

A BLISTERING ONSLAUGHT ON A FORBIDDEN HILL:
(110)
Under *terra firma*, our Victorian adventurers wait awhile, even
though Lon Chaney's plunge into Parisian tunnels came to be
sepia reduced. Do you remember the remarkable instant in *The
Phantom of the Opera* – the silent film of Gaston Leroux's novel
– where the madman launches himself into the Seine, mask in
hand? Forget not this: because Phosphorous Cool has placed a
thumb and spatulate forefinger next to his temple. What might
our guest from a silvern paradise be thinking...? "A
configuration comes to be apparent in one's divided mind. It
attracts sovran territory – if only to give up the ghost over
primordial tension. Examine this evidence, Hermaphrodite X, a
medley of yellow press publications filter on. These trumpet the
names *John O'London's*, the *Pall Mall Gazette*, *Illustrated
Metropolitan*, the *Gentleman's Magazine* and such like... On its
back cover a frontispiece materialises; and it's been reversed out
in a mirror. Let it alone now... yet, without favouritism, one is
here to see three characters manifest themselves in a forgotten
mist. They are Heathcote Dervish, Elsa Bounteous Hapgood and
Butler James. All of them register some co-ordinates in Camden
Lock, north London, just down from Chalk Farm in the borough
of Camden. Likewise, a covered or established market signals the
likelihood of many products passing by on the other side, *inter
alia*, and despite all such abstracts due to the fog. A pea-souper
doubtlessly covered their tracks in this imagined snow. Does one
even reminisce about the plot of Ian McEwan's *The Cement*

Garden over this particular rise? It registered an untruth… now that vaudeville *artistes* have joined an array of puppets on these trestles. Given all this preparation, though, Phosphorous' meeting with John Dee --- or Skrying --- waxed negative. It definitely blew away the folly of too many tropical fish in a tank. Aren't they restful for one's eyes?

STRAIGHT AS AN ARROW: (111)

Elsa Bounteous Hapgood is speaking forthwith. "Are any able to still the dead beat of a fading heart, even in terms of so much forgotten trauma? Could it really understate a brother's lesion or dilemma (?) – namely, this was one of those pitches which spoke of the body's left side. Let it be: my lord and master lies dying… shall any of you prove fit enough to disprove this junction? Like a graphic novel – such as Peter Kuper's vision of Kafka's *Metamorphosis* – no-one seems alert over emptying out this barrel. Oh, by drear Lilith's nuggets, who will save him from Persephone's broth?" "I may have a go at his liberation of breath", sauntered our silver point. At this intervention, though, Elsa Bounteous scrolled back over her husband's forehead – if only to mount a mausoleum's steps with contempt. They were made from pure marble or *lapis lazuli*, and in such a way as interpreted this reckoning. It shone on towards a light blue impress which is nearly always marbled or veined with pink; the latter reminiscent of what Ezra Pound had said in Imagist diction on many occasions. Her eyes slanted meaningfully to the left during these words, and all of it occurred underneath that white streak in one's hair from early in life. Surely, such a pale path amid the blue-'n'-black is the sign of a witch throughout past aeons? Be still and all amidst wonder – for her warlock's body skidded away to a restful plenty, and appeared devoid of life. Who has been speaking to her trace element, then? Why, it happened to be none other than Phosphorous Cool.

DIGNIFY FRUITCAKE WITH AN APPLE'S TART: (112)
Meanwhile, in an irreducible darkness or sprite, our three desperadoes approach their hidden lair. They tiptoed across a wicker-work of dwarves – i.e.; one which lit itself up occasionally with a passing strobe light. It came affixed to the wall via some tracery or other... even though a finger of lightning lit up the scene. All in all, it seemed to embody the aftertaste of John Cowper Powys' novel *The Brazen Head*. Irrespective of such detours, however, our three characters moved along a darkened alley under golden globes. At first sight they looked like a pawn broker's embrasure, but now strange spheroids or globules intervened. Didn't they incarnate the principle of a lamp rather more? As we said before – our three intimates proved to be Heathcote Dervish, Butler James and Elsa Bounteous Hapgood. Each one of them crept along this duct sideways on – and it articulated a triangular vertice, albeit reverse ways. Can you feel a natural outburst coming on now? Truly, a rich incline pins the bricks to this particular plane; the former a horizontal bar (or access) that doesn't add one jot to the distant church steeple. It towers over a city's artery; a mere underground portmanteau (here) which occasions those curved entrances in Bath, Durham or Chester. A brief raised promontory on stilts led to the door... and it came constructed from fine old wood. A knocker of polished brass studded the willow; and it recalled Durham's cathedral. Butler James – the furthest forward of the trio – made to pluck it first.

IMPRESS A VAMPIRE WITH GARLIC IMPALEMENT: (113)
Let's thrust forwards into the twentieth century with our tale... For now, Phosphorous Cool has risen from a stone dais whose brick kiln was sovran over so many lost offerings as these. Like those theatres of yesteryear, today's actors are oblivious to such vaudeville turns who proliferate all agog. Every such music-hall act indicates puppets holding onto a trestle, or possibly Patrick Magee playing Krapp. This is in Samuel Beckett's drama about an oldster with his tapes in an aged audio machine that magnifies

a metallic strip. It stands next to him on the darkness of an unlit stage – where only a lead actor (like Magee) sits illumined. Everything else remains darksome. Around Phosphorous Cool various cowled denizens move away, and they proliferate around so many beach-combers looking for shells... each one of whom shares an internal echo within. "You deserve no pity save rapine", mused our hero. "But – despite the fact that we are wooden spectres – our Animism gives us an insight into mankind. It understands why a factor of three score and ten isn't over till the fat lady sings. A death before its time cannot suit Ombre's finality, after all. Nor can it liberate the climax of a Patience game played by three hands." Still backing away or seen in profile (m'lud) Elsa Bounteous Hapgood acknowledges: "Yet let us undo the fastness of a lost keep. What can you do? A principle which imprisons nought loosens no molecules. Neither may a hungry man salvage steak from some run-of-the-mill soya beans. I don't understand, my vainglorious marionette... cease to offer false hopes offshore. Again I repeat, whatever shall you accomplish?"

SELF-PORTRAITS IN OCHRE HINT AT A SHADOW WORLD: (114)

Back in the late nineteenth century, our three emigres from east London have made their way northwards: and they circle an arctic doorway. Might it embolden some sort of honey trap? Let's see: now that one's distracted trio have effectively surrounded their wasps' nest! A vague feeling of triumph seems to glow in our three musketeers' loins. Elsa Bounteous, in particular, stands adjacent to a doorway, and the ramp + panel by which it's reached. She wears a fur travelling hood or wrap; the likelihood of this excludes a provocative ball-room dancing dress underneath. Moreover, a silhouette covers half her face and it exists under one tent pole too far. Does one see its configuration of fives? Anyway, a series of interchanges or wooden blinds lay to one side; and they came louvered up to a sinister point... a medley that harkened back to Angel alley in Whitechapel in the east end. (Truthfully speaking, this is where they had just originated from). Certain barred windows also slandered or occluded their path; and these all strove to achieve an effect halfway between Gilbert & Sullivan and Edgar Allan Poe. Most noticeably, however, we have to treat of the masterful impress left by Heathcote Dervish – especially given his genuine reduction to a phantom this time around. An event – the secret consequences of which – prove to enforce a Ripper's surreal quality! No wonder that the journalist Patrick Lavelle's study of the hoaxer, *Wearside Jack*, had to be published by Ghostwriters incorporated... A spectral essence or bogle, now, Heathcote Dervish passed along like a phantasm or its envelope... that is: an entity which left its own etheric spore *a la* Adolphe Constant. Never mind the fact that he crepitated in London against a dawn's light! The knocker – for its part – keened to a heavy or progressive abstract; and this represented a nomenclature which lost Durham cathedral in its red eyes. Wasn't such a crimson seat over-burdened, octopus-like, unfastened or estranged? Our butler James continued to sound his horn – but in a manner altogether distinct from Sarban's pornography. Suddenly – and with only a momentary warning – he heard that bolts were being shot on the door's other side.

PORTCULLIS BEETLE; A SHALLOW ENTRANCE: (115)

In one abstract or neon of sound, an exposed palm can be seen limned against the blue. It denotes an imprecation from a panel drawn by Herb Trimpe; and such a story-board senses the outstretched palm print of Phosphorous Cool. He stands adjacent to this undelivered paw; the fingers of which are uncurled before a Thorakian torso. Doesn't his silvery upper body strength then glisten in a wasting light (?); and it's a deepening of pthalo into turquoise via a golden span. Now and again, his saving grace alters its compass – what with such a hand signal mushrooming out in order to arrest Fate. No vaudeville act other than this can ask for penance by way of a witness: since a doom-laden palmistry enters the frame here. Nor may it be said that one line within a creased palm, crossing over from left to right, shall traverse a minor irritation's absence just as well. Surely, it prefigures a talent which curdles to its own astrological profile, given an impediment over such a game of draughts? "Await the witness of my fingers and thumbs", declared our silver-top milk. "Any power of restitution in me comes from the cosmos – at least in terms of a rectilinear energy-flow. Alternatively, and by means of a hidden ventriloquism – my puppet-master speaks through me in relation to an endless misstatement. *Avaunt thee*, make him whole I tell ye! Deliver up the quarterstaff of a Demon king in English pantomime... let it be. Transfix this audience, I command you, with Stravinsky's *Petrouchka* and its basic spirit...!"

A SLUG – THROW SALT IN ITS PATH: (116)

Bolts in our nineteenth century door shot back internally, and it reluctantly began to open with an abiding creek. Here and now, slowly, oh so slowly, the wooden door slid open in its portal of rectitude. Oaken or teak in its continuing frame – one yet came over a metal jamb + lintel across its sill. But again, our egress opened inwards – if only to unburden the penumbra of an unshaded light. In the doorway stood an ill-formed or hump-backed nurse: one who alternately held a flickering oil-lamp. Without a book or its candle, it played up one flavour in this set aside glass. To be honest: the sister of mercy wore a tight and low-cut dress; one which was an altogether more provocative answer to a question posed by Florence Nightingale. Do you see it? Because such an object doubtless resiled to a new prospect, in that couldn't she embody Elsa Bounteous Hapgood when facing off now or etherically sporting new vistas? Above all, any detective work has to seize a mirror-effect – even after its reversed out imagery. In form, though, she wore a belt and a nurse's cap with a red cross on it, and this Swiss badge proved to be monstrously scarlet in its steadfastness. Doubtlessly again... her brown hair came parted under a white cap... one whose nature is cast aside by a perfect moon face. A plate-like or oval status that belies yesterday's hump! Moreover – if we were to trip over into the semblance of Igor, the good doctor's familiar or assistant, might this not be a female variant on the theme? In any event, the matron's face swivelled like a doll's; at once porcelain, ovalesque, plaster painted, ruby-lipped and even perfect in its innocence. It evinced a dulcet quality which understood the compression due to Russian roulette. For – rather like a spastic librarian in Henley-on-Thames – she existed deep down inside this basement. Given that the ancient or pre-modern library happened to be situated under the town hall. Didn't she allow the author to enjoy adult books from the age of nine? A factor which seemed contrary to all known rules. A notice that itself existed irrespective of those numismatics – namely, the enshrined Roman coins existing in so many cases. Still, in keeping with the early years of silent cinema, our matriarch has yet to vouchsafe a word. No sound passes from between her lips.

A DRAGON'S BREATH MELTS BEOWULF'S GOLD: (117)
Furthermore, bolts of liquid flame passed from Phosphorous Cool's distended palms; and each palm-print contained within it the witness of one blast. (Could the *desideratum* of Wyndham Lewis' cultural magazine from early in the twentieth century not come into the frame now?) In this tableau, the manikin known as Phosphorous C. arches his back, primarily so as to launch blistering bursts of lightning upon his prey. These are co-ordinated downwards in parallel beams: and they have occasion to meet in Heathcote's corse. A body or lamentable object (this is); the likelihood of which almost sports a mummified air… as if it existed in Luxor under a night-shrouded mystery or deeply buried in various sands. Crackling electrical energy inundates Dervish; it provides a coursing vanguard so as to fill the air with swarming fire-flies. An agency that susurrates to a witness, this – if only to divide a realm between Heaven & Hell with pinkish sparks. "Let the power cosmic bask in my plenitude", declared Phosphorous Cool. "If any existence or under-nourished life

exists here, *inter alia*, let it be summoned forth at the flick of this giddy switch."

+

Silence then billows asunder, in order to reign after a few brief instants of action… may it drown.

CYRIL H. LOVEGROVE; A VICTORIAN MORTUARY: (118) The crippled nurse gestures with her index-finger against a yellow background; and this is one which transmutes light blue into gold. Her other hand, however, upholds a flickering oil-lamp; the latter a glass space or chasm that contains within it a spluttering flame. Like a candle in the wind, we find such a taper mushrooming into an unappreciated cloud. Further on from this, our nurse has turned slightly to the side in order to reveal her hump; a promontory which issues forth as a muddy vanguard like Spion Kop. May it not bear comparison with her mauve or otherwise brunette wig: a colouring that gives a flaxen wash to Thomas Hardy's *The Trumpet Major*? Needless to say, her gestures indicate the finality of a new disclosure; and it also bears witness to her starch, lintel + cape. It all occurs in a situation where the silhouette of her dark eyes ramifies with a red cross – the former contained on a bonnet above. "Good evening", averred Butler James in a sombre voice. It reverberated like a distant bell calling the faithful to prayer in a Khitian temple. "Mistress nurse, we have called at your establishment this evening in order to visit your master. Is the mortuary superintendent at home; or mayhap he's concerned with one of his gruesome experiments? For – like James Hinton's philosophy regarding fallen womanhood – no deviation from Peter Cushing's test-tubes can be tolerated. Similarly, Wise's *Introduction to Battle-Gaming* must never deflect from other truths – namely, the fact which states that Doctor Seward walks alone down his asylum's corridors. Are you aware that Charles Bronson, the most dangerous man in Britain's prisons, has written an autobiography? Less widely known, though, remains the information declaring he wore a cage around his head.

Reminiscent of Thomas Harris' characters; and, in particular, where in flickering blue-light Andy Warhol's electric-chair performs... its wicker format spoke to pthalo's enclosure." "Oh my yes, welcome all", replied our ward sister. Her name was Ms. Igor; and clearly she had refused to peruse Sylvia Plath's *The Bell Jar*. "The professor has been waiting for your tinkling sound. He will see you now. Do not fear."

LEAD ON INTO DARKNESS, RED-EYED ONE; DON'T SPECULATE[!]: (119)

Let us fast forwards a century to an on-going drama... wherein Heathcote Dervish's corse has risen off the ground in casual surprise. A reckless puppet to the last degree of its performance – a look of somnolence or calm crosses its features. May the wizard just be dead or sleeping? Who knows? Yet – poltergeist like – he certainly rises from this dais: and his warlock's vestments flow underneath him in the haze. Yes assuredly, he floats with a calm or benign mask o'er his face – a visor or its kindred which is clearly oblivious to the unbearable lightness of being. Examine it in this way: a shower of sparks envelops his advanced corpse and streams it with psychedelia – rather after the fashion of Timothy Leary's brain liquefaction. One model stands out abreast of everything, and this has to do with the puppeteering of so many toy-theatres. For no-one other than their historian, George Speaight, can effectively see the strings marshalling such objects. Off to one side, however, Phosphorous Cool gestures imprescriptibly, and in a way that causes him to stagger back and forth like a marionette. Could it be an example of transference; or a scenario where the sap of one plant masticates another's rheum? Have you yet to register whether a venus fly-trap feeds on insects, or not? After all, one's first instinct when left alone in a room with a *Drosophila* is to kill it. In the words of an American crime fiction writer of yesteryear – Goddamn the blue-tailed fly!

109

HAVOC IS THE HEAD-MEN[!]: (120)

In an alternative vista of Victorian London, my friends, our narrative grows apace. Yes indeed... For, on the left side of our haversack, Butler James stands to. He obviously wishes to introduce one and all to everyone else, and in accordance with the manners of an Edwardian music hall. His features – when hidden within this temperature – came to be regarded as smooth, ovalesque, unprincipled and relatively untroubled. Leastways – one element immediately stands out: and it has to do with the scar tissue down his visage's left side. Seal and paste wise (now) it travels down one aspect of the face... whilst being active on a physiognomy's sinister tracing paper. A feeling of vague uneasiness (this is) that becomes even more pronounced, especially when the mortuary's guardian was introduced. He happens to be such an ossuary's lord and master --- officiously so. A brick kiln exists to one side of him, and a deeper recess continues to exalt its shadows. Nor can we understand so sweetly why blood flows over those unwhetted blades...

+

In front of us, a man's vista becomes apparent. He wears a silken waistcoat taken together with a large cravat; and it sports a tie-pin by way of lustre. If we consider it movie-star wise, the skull is long and thin... and it evinces a prognathous jaw or a coif of hair over the forehead. His non-wig proves to be brown in colour. All in all, his cast of character --- even reminiscent of vaudeville or puppeteering --- seems to be familiar. Butler James deems it necessary to do the honours. "My brethren", he remarks with a flourish. "Mark on your calendars the following treatise, at least in terms of Germany's forgotten art concerning the Ph.d. Yes sir and above: since I would ask you to put your hands together for Baron von Frankenstein... the scientist, mortician and brain-digger of this establishment." (In fact, our particular physician harkens back to Brian Aldiss' thesis in his book, *Frankenstein Unbound*. A tribute, *ceteris paribus*, which preceded the post-modern or electronic folly of William Gibson). Never mind: all of this subsists due to the fact that our

Frankenstein looks back to the example of Moustachio Brave Herring. Surely, the existence of one precedes the other's tirade?

BREAK THE EGG-SHELLS OF A DELUDED YOKE: (121)
Elsa Bounteous Hapgood lets rip – once she becomes animated by concern for her spouse. "Certainly, my beloved husband rises in the air like a subaltern of non-identity – not that a sleeping prince necessarily mirrors its absence. He floats off the ground etherically; or in relation to one of Albert Louden's obese women. These cry havoc in an untroubled mien over their bed-sheets – especially when compared to the pseudo-intellectualism of a Tom Stoppard play. I actually prefer Ron Hutchinson's *Rats in the Skull* about Ulster loyalist paramilitarism. *Avaunt thee…* to my side, gentlemen of the coven, this silvery puppet happens to be killing my husband. To my help --- attack him; devour him: prevent him from doing harm." In saying this, Elsa throws out her hands and her capacious robes then billow behind her. What of other gestures, though? Because a fellow mage, Warlock Splendour Thomas, looms nearby with his cowl having fallen away amid flame. He looks both animated and ill at ease. "We dare not creep upon him out of Nosferatu's bidding, Elsa. No penumbra may shield us from his wrath. Given the strength of such a silvery titan – one false mood or move could destroy us all! In such a labyrinth, an English Ha!Ha! spots a macabre bend. Likewise, a seventeenth century text like Vondel's *Lucifer* hints at a magic camera or a purple wine stain too far."

GREET THE LONGITUDE OF A GRENADE WITH APLOMB: (122)
Heathcote Dervish and Baron von Frankenstein are found to be conversing with each other way back in the nineteenth century. For – irrespective of Audrey Beardsley's artichoke – any black-and-white drawing must hint at Heathcote's spectre. Given that a graphic impress lies upon us here; and it imprisons purport and hints at a hidden trajectory. This is artistic or happens to be a tendency which moves via Beresford Egan towards one that

signifies Ralph Steadman. Doesn't the line stretch back to Rowlandson or Gillray? Didn't it also satisfy the savage or monstrous, thereby?

+

By virtue of such a panel, Heathcote Dervish undergoes a spiritual tide – and this was one which cleaves to a ghost at Banquo's feast. His triangular head waxes pyramidal now – whilst an impress of these stalks continues to surround his limbs. It all denoted a thick bracket or a lock of hair behind a portal, irrespective of a corn dolly that stands no chance of being consumed by fire! Never mind a redundant soliloquy… Later on, these imprints lurk in some sort of spiritist guise – only to lay siege to phrenology's brain-pan at one remove. Altogether now, his lustre waxed apple-like --- at once becoming pith to its own severed core. Or – without being fermented into cider – could it be reduced into crab apples step by step? "These matters resile to nothing save a sovran indifference", elicited Heathcote. "My health forced me to requisition your aid, my dear Baron. I require a new corse, compaction or body." "But, of course", composed Frankenstein, "you were right to consult me through your allies. Since a voodoo doll can always be worked from wax; at least in terms of another's available lair. Or might such an offering impose hair? Because one item which differentiates its revenge hints at a prior nullity. It holds to a comparison with a skull, a token or a cranial midget that provides a rendezvous *avec* the red and the black. A mediaeval mystery play thereby cradles a white doliocephalic bone in dark light."

MADDEN THE RELISH OF ONE VOODOO DOLL: (123)
Elsa Bounteous Hapgood continues her spiel; and (indeed) there's no stopping her pronouns or received pronunciation. It all happens to be delivered in a format that Nancy Mitford called U rather than Non-U. "Address our witness", she hailed with glee. "It doubtless speeds across the grass towards one's croquet hoop. Our love quits the advent of a new future. Given that the silvery puppet's energy flows into Heathcote Dervish, primarily so as to

retrieve him from oblivion's gate. Must you observe its concourse (?); even if the manikin's very sustenance floods into our warlock. Look! Oh rejoice; let it be released or engineered from beyond a grey matrix. No commingling with nothingness has an opportunity to intervene now; nor can we discount the electricity which surges around his eyes. These orbs --- momentarily disfigured in their frequency --- flicker into an awakening or some such semblance, or absolute. Rejoice! Rejoice! One's king never dies in a salutation owing to Ombre; and never mind the stanzas of Alexander Pope. In these circumstances, a red inundation of lace looks out beyond its trellis and it incarnates a hop-scotch; even an abstract expressionist design *a la* de Kooning. A painter or dauber who definitely does not record such scarlet embroidery. Recall this to our minds, my friends: this lattice or crystalline structure has an echo: and it proves to be diaphanous, shape-shifting, unbalanced, even propositional over Lorca's blood wedding."

RENDER GRIEF TO A STAINED-GLASS WINDOW – IT'S IN HEREFORD: (124)

Irrespective of any other developments: Baron von Frankenstein leads the way down a brick incline which surrounds the possibility of such a descent. A wall bracket exists high up and to one side... and it occasions a niche that reconciles itself to flaring torches. These are not out of place; since our *troupe* are making their way towards a fully stocked charnel house. Also, Frankenstein's baron has taken to explaining about the rejection of living tissue. "Heathcote, we've been working on a livery of soft flesh; and now you'll discover which jelly mould can't contain all those brains. It emboldens so many gadgets. Like those galvanised or twitching limbs in hoary Frankenstein films by James Whale – one dictaphone stands out aplenty. Similarly, it understands that a votary may kneel amidst a roseate mist which shimmers over such captures amid leaded planes... prismically speaking. These events cause the religious and body snatchers to bend down – at least once we have filleted such lintel as wraps our corse. An envelope it testifies to being; the like of it cascading down to an opening witness. Let us pray that one anatomy lesson causes us to celebrate a pride drawn from Gray. All of it repositions itself next to an enabling wall like Humpty-Dumpty."

PING, PING; BLING, BLING: (125)

Husband and wife have been successfully reunited by this time, albeit after Heathcote Dervish's near-death experience. It likewise let rip the mantra of so many preying mantis' silent cries. Listen to me: our chosen couple then choose to grapple with each other... and this's despite any premature defeats. Various cowls or votaries surround them – seemingly oblivious to Phosphorous Cool's existence. His silvery beacon has been weakened by such a definite chase. A certain expanse of energy also creases his palm; and it proves to be a nimbus that cannot call upon a hurdy-gurdy man's witness. We must reckon to such a smoky embrasure --- at a moment where our puppet's hands deliver the steam of a necessary awakening. Does he eventually stare down from on high to see – what? Well, it may be nothing other than a reddish pilgrimage... one whose kindred basks before a Fauvist screen. Loops of colour then promenade down in a cascade or spectrum. Eventually a scimitar – drawn from Robert Musil's notion of the man without qualities – enters into one eye-socket over time... by virtue of a serpentine exit.

MIRROR, MIRROR ON THE WALL – WHO'S THE WORST OF US ALL? (126)

Proportionately speaking, Heathcote Dervish's spectre passes down a line of freshly minted cadavers: all of which were found to be laid out on trestle tables. These parted with any percussive daylight, as soon as the eye could see. Whereat – by dint of this particular collusion – corpses were laid out on either side: and faced off against one another in accordance with damnation's fatalism. Observed from this angle, then, Heathcote moves down each aisle by acknowledging silver, or examining those specimens indicative of Hell's Kitchen. These variants entomb a massive presence in all their livery; and they lie atop one another sarcophagi to sarcophagi. One token admits its fellows at a moment like this, even though Butler James exults at Death's panorama. "Incredible, my man", he enthuses with a favourite spleen. "Let's look upon an unfolding nightmare that cradles malevolence at Heaven's Gate. It basically intones a recess from Wyndham Lewis' *The Childermass*: where two public school boys, killed in the Great War, await the Bailiff's permission to enter the celestial city. A rufous brown or ochre covers our domain; and it maims a colour scheme which draws a finger across an adult face. Could it be a visor; or an iron man who understands the gesture of one deluded eye? Such a socket then became unstuck in one of de Chirico's depressions. Unhallowed of all main light sources (forevermore) – it dimpled before the Hell-Fire club's stewardship: and nor can you easily forgo such a coin. This leapt out at yon; and it joined hands while brushing a concrete wall. Surely, this was one of le Corbusier's efforts deep underground?"

PADLOCK THE DUNGEONS OF A MIND: (127)
Reject Jurgen Habermas! Indeed, a conversation now ensues or breaks out roundabout a coven's overall significance. Elsa Bannister Hapgood decides to begin the task. "Your plan virtually led to its creator's demise, my husband. Surely it's better to live a full life than strain for a purity which exists over the gate's other side? Certain wags say that with nought above you there's nothing to aspire to. But – my spouse and warlock – I beg you to reconsider. Our plan has merely been ground into millet, in order to suffer the weak to die." "Their death rises exactly as the progeny for our raging talents", urges Heathcote Dervish by way of a ready assistance. Moreover, his asservation might take the bark off a tree in order to solder its roundness. Are we aware of what Max Stirner meant by such creative nothingness? Any road up, Heathcote proves determined to justify his actions… at least in a like manner or kindred. "*Avaunt*

thee, spouse – master of magicks and other tokens of Mordred – we must belabour a puppet's face in order to achieve our destiny. No campaign of one's own vintage can ever really treat what Emily Dickinson called a 'zero in the bone'. No way and et cetera... All that really matters is our manipulation of transcendence. To teach the masses or *lumpen* to dance to our tune plays an infernal organ – this was itself well ahead of Bach's peace-time offering. Necessarily so... For, my brethren, the way to activate one's struggle has to be to ennoble *Jihad*. (Don't we remember, in truth, a dissident football fanzine of yesteryear... one which went under this title?) No consideration and a mass of bunkum... since the holograph of a warrior's imprint adjusts to a tracery of spent leaves. It understands what the philosopher Julius Evola meant by *The Metaphysics of War*. Let none other than the late John Aspinall subscribe to each kindling's trust over his gorillas. After all, the natural habitat of Man becomes a jungle of his own making. A notion that happens to be true – even if it's covered with asphalt or tarmac at the time... This much waxes evidential by virtue of a voodoo doll. It delimits the prospect of the authoress Donna Tart's forbearance, in a situation where each wax figurine holds a sensibility in trust. Needless to say, any skull-head oft comes delivered in clay or as a maquette; the latter a semiotic for the mongrel who's born well outside its customary time. Yes indeed, such an experiential locomotion harvests a field near the edge of death's row: a conundrum in which various skulls are seen nestling on stalks of wheat. Does your understanding differ – and if so – may not a grim reaper offer to scythe down so many heads? In all honesty, it emboldens the spirit of a thirteenth card in a Tarot park. Let us seize its offering: when we find such a skeleton placed next to a bridge of sighs or moans."

A YELLOW BRICK ROAD MANIFESTS ITS CAUTION: (128)
In a nineteenth century turn of phrase, perchance, Heathcote Dervish's spirit passes along between sundry corpse-lines. These

recollect the words of Butler James concerning such an ossuary. "Masterful one, thou art free to choose a lissom grove from amongst the most handsome features, largest muscles, mightiest thews and most attractive lineaments --- all of these are yours, albeit when given a placement by Caspar David Friedrich. Alternatively, you may feel that one factor writ large comes abreast of its pace. You are now free, Excellency, to choose a perfect form from this Hall of our Dead." "Assuredly, my servant from a distinct age of yore", repeated Heathcote, "nothing suits me better. A factor of oblivion will never fascinate my vows over Sir Peter Maxwell-Davies' Fourth Symphony – in that the reanimation of spent matter has eluded science's refuge for many a year. Let the Age of Reason not collapse before Buffon's existential headgear!"

ONE NEGATIVE IRON MASKS ITS ANSWER: (129)

Elsa Bounteous Hapgood continues to speak within a burst of aplomb or necessary angst. "A failure, husband, to enact Beowulf's vengeance upon Grendel need not detain our majesty. Nor can we trouble ourselves within a bedizened stupor." "Regard me, wife, our combined visages might prove sufficient to wrest victory from defeat. An admixture of pain can doubt its own dotage; and none have to properly witness it otherwise. Do you see? Whatever we decide upon now – the fate of so much dye is sealed in terms of a preadventure. No welcome tune finds our accommodation to be licit at this time – given that a memory persuades an ocean to peel back from our chair." "Unlike Canute…" "That's correct." "Yet, if we consider it in terms of ripe corn, Phosphorous Cool saved your life." "It scant matters save the offering of spent gravy. No such repast crosses my lips. It must engineer the destruction of one cook who exists in clover – despite spitting in a broth which comes destined for a giant's bowl."

ZIG-ZAG FROM BISHOP TO ROOK, WHY DON'T YOU? (130)

One head in particular has taken Heathcote Dervish's fancy; and it embodies those qualities of power and malignancy that our mage had come to respect. Each one intoned the spectacle of a local landmark, after all, and this happened to be the Combe gibbet in west Berkshire. Wherein – and contrasted against a spectrum of burnt grass – a high pole measures its length aslant a pale blue sky. The faintest scintilla of cumulus passes overhead, if only to contrast with the ethical high-jump underneath. Its livery stood forward most definitely in a longitudinal aspect; and this wasn't any sort of a helix (to be sure). This trestle or counterpart faces off across the beam: and one can imagine two cadavers hanging from either side, and many of them would have worn leg-irons or been caged. A facility which reminds us of the Black Acts during the eighteenth century – together with an after-echo of the same existing well into the nineteenth century. All of these moments of bourgeois ferocity found themselves ably chronicled by a very English, if marxist, historian called E.P. Thompson. Also, didn't we mete out such punishments to those who had brooked our will in India, especially if gibbeted thuggee happened to be the devotees of Kali – the goddess of destruction?

+

In any event, thoughts pertaining to the manufacture of dead bodies flitted through Heathcote Dervish's mind. He had long ago mastered the fact that any new visor must evince puissance and menace rather than good looks. To this end, he stopped next to a jagged edge remarkably like Boris Karloff's Frankenstein's monster from the early 'thirties. Do you wish to enlist its aid without a camp or louche boulevard?

DANCE A HOSE & HAIL ABOVE THE EMERALD[!]: (131)

"See", cried one of those warlocks… a man who went under the moniker of Splendour Thomas. Could not a tincture of Welsh blood be traceable here, even though no connexion with the

118

doleful stanzas of R. S. Thomas becomes apparent? "His strength seems to be unsupervised due to this latest draught. Our legend – or silvery puppet – keens to a moment of weakness, thereby. Can this vessel be half full or half empty, perchance?" Given such an observance, Phosphorous Cool leans on a stone balustrade to one side. His back is curled away from the viewer; and blue-to-white vapour circles up from his exposed hands. These lie flat out or palm uppermost before the Fates! Never mind... since Heathcote Dervish and Elsa Bounteous Hapgood were still conversing. "Dearest one – and yet graven in our absence – we must endeavour to finish our task. Phosphorous Cool and Mastodon Helix shall be allowed to fit their commotion to each other. They will be encouraged to fight, even to die, should it prove to be necessary." "Requisite for what, Heathcote, or whomsoever else?", enquired his wife. Her voice betrayed a plangent quaver. "Why", he responded, "so that mankind comes to tremble over our control of unseen realms. The general commerce or ruck only begins to quail when they reckon to our command over daemons like Spyros – otherwise known as Mastodon Helix. Our ability to summon up one to quell the other merely contrives to send our voices right round the world. 'twill envelop a seedy globe with flame! We alone deserve to take the credit hereafter. The science fiction writer L. Ron Hubbard distributed an incorrect view, you see. A new religion can indeed be created in the modern cosmogony, contrary to science's wiles. We are striving to bring it about."

LOCK UP THE POLE STAR; FORGETFULNESS AWAITS: (132)
Carry on from here, my friends and acquaintances... Given the fact that Heathcote Dervish has flitted down a row of cadavers – all of them lain out on various trestles or plinths. Whereupon these events happen to be occurring in an alternative Victorian England, and in a dimension as yet unknown to our kin. Moreover, a hemispherical East End looms up before us, and this was long before a Kray shot an informer in an evening's pea-

souper. It took place in 'The Blind Beggar' on Cambridge Heath Road... where Hackney's fag-end meets Bethnal Green. Heathcote moved with aplomb above all those corses which met his gaze – or travelled under his finger-nails. He proved to be both present and alone. One cranial embrace sent Heathcote Dervish into raptures! Whereas such a waxen skull looks like Boris Karloff from a 'thirties flick by James Whale or Tod Browning – to use a term of American slang. A phrenology like this distilled its own essence --- whether it came to be tapered, patient, heavy or blanched. A lugubrious fracturing then mulcted its purpose towards grey; while some untransparent eyes existed 'neath blue lids. Face the facts now: because Heathcote's jagged talons caressed the side of this death's-head; and it seemed to be pregnant with awe... albeit primarily in spirit. A rough wooden work-bench existed underneath this Frankenstein's monster. He looked altogether alien aslant some frightful intent, and appeared to be dressed top-to-toe in a mauve jump-suit. (Could it be one of David Icke's notorious shell-suits?) Surely, every recognised catholic school-boy knows that purple amounts to death's colour or tint?

+

"This one, thinkest me thou", pronounced Heathcote Dervish in a stentorian voice.

AN ENGLISH HOBBY-HORSE APPROVES ITS KLAVERN: (133)

"We are only concerned with a planned observation", affirmed Elsa's husband on a rival plane. His wife now hangs back to the side... and her features gather up a latent uncertainty. Let it all rise above you as a spent carrion of Self... Her husband – by this adventure's mist – finds his aspect to be convulsed: and it then comes across as galvanised, unknown to quicksand or beckoning over any prospect. It also offers little by way of a sandy relief. Listen to this announcement from a forgotten Leyden jar... "An eventuality – such as the one you are determined to dispose of – could occasion yonder puppet's death. The massive thews of

Mastodon Helix could well 'do' for him – particularly if they came to blows or even fist-to-fist." These were the words of Elsa Bounteous Hapgood. "No matter, my dear – death is life… as the sages of an unknown Nemedian chronicle beg leave to say. Occasionally now, we are wont to witness a world wide wrestling or cage-fighting bout. Do you bother to repossess one memory; namely, the one of Dickie Davis introducing Saturday afternoon wrestling on independent television?"

BAKE A CAKE BEFORE THOSE RED QUILL GIRLS STEAL IT: (134)

Heathcote Dervish rears up before or above Baron von Frankenstein (MD); the latter being observed from the side after a primitive German wood-cut. (A very worthy art-form this happens to be: the after-effects of it can be seen in many a graphic novel by Steve Ditko or Frank Miller). His silhouette limbers up towards a solidly Teutonic profile; and it's one that recalls the administrator facing off against Rowolt in Fritz Lang's *Metropolis*. Heathcote D. has to be clearly aware over whether Professor F. truly amounts to a reincarnation of Moustachio Brave Herring, or not! In locomotion, though, Heathcote Dervish crepitates on a grid-iron – while a susurration twinkles around his apertures. It all betokens the heaving otherness of H.P. Lovecraft's Old Ones, to be precise. In a similar vein, then, the dehiscence of Dervish's form causes a fractured lens: and it demists, oscillates, bifurcates or twists. A hole gathers under the surface of an elongated mouth, and it subsists unto those flashing orbs… especially when taken together with his pustules, burps, fake bubbles, weird splices and tentacles. All of which doesn't even mention the triangular head-piece that adorns his hood. Do you remember the villain in Gerry Anderson's *Thunderbirds*?

A CLAXON OFFERS POWER ITS HALBERD; LET'S BREAK EGGS[!]: (135)

Heathcote Dervish continues to apportion blame to a silvery doily... one whom he proceeds to lecture amidships. This is irrespective of those manikin wires: all of which continue to trail tendrils from the ceiling of our imaginary puppet stage. A template (thus) that endorses Eric Bramall's hair-and-wire act up in the fastness of North Wales. No-one can foreclose on its offering of yesteryear. "Like a latterday Olric, silvery one, you must anoint your libations with the blood of many an alien. Get this: a quest against dangerous monsters --- such as Grendel or his mother --- lengthens glory's aspect. You shall have to pursue Mastodon Helix. Do you wish to be part of his destructive reek?" "I will hazard nought of a like kind, temper or kindred", issues forth Phosphorous Cool by way of a reply. "I remember all too clearly the rectitude of your treachery. No-one plays me either for a Fool or King Lear's Tom o' Bedlam; a figure who's quite transparently Edgar in disguise. Let us choose to rendezvous with a puppet-playing barge underneath the bridge at Henley-on-Thames, Oxfordshire. It exists on one side of the Thames when marooned by the Leander club – replete with its pink tie. I choose to fight only in those quarrels which interest me. You waste your breath on what words you have to offer, mischievous one! I shall no longer interfere in the maddening affairs of mortals. Have regard for the fact that Phosphorous Cool battles solely on his own behalf. My bishop moves diagonally across the board in order to take refuge in iron, Heathcote." (Note: it's the first instance in this long adventure where Phosphorous Cool has acknowledged Heathcote Dervish's identity, albeit in passing. Nor can he throw a defaced coin against a wall so as to drift into silence. Wouldn't it be regarded as a downright game of craps?)

A CORN DOLLY FIRES ITSELF ON DISTANT PLINTHS: (136)

Baron von Frankenstein moves to make a gesture with his hand; and it relates to the way in which Ralph Richardson carried himself when playing Julius Caesar. In this particular tournament any gestures estrange themselves: and they limber away into silence with the nervousness of so much grief. Moreover, Doctor Frankenstein's face looked avid, gleaming, refulgent, expectant and lit-up with the forgotten glow of so many test-tubes. For – in the words of a near namesake like Dr. Moreau – Frankenstein has fallen prey to the colourlessness of pure research. (A doctoral thesis *manqué*, this, that searches back towards the testimony of Sir Fred Hoyle, the Huxley brothers, Carletoon Coon the anthropologist, Phillipe Ruston, Jack Kevorkian and many another scientist of similar ilk). Listen to his flavoursome rhetoric now… "The operation will proceed smoothly – if we descale your cadaver of all other skins, my friend", declared the Baron reflectively. "Can or should our approach level out any other distinctions? But you must recognise one elixir or remedy, Heathcote, and this has to do with your corpse's sundered nature. Once you have entered into its portals no escape is possible… I feel it incumbent on me to inform you of this transubstantiation, my mage of another age. It flickers like the wing's candle; and comes at once to be blown hither and thither unto dust. All in all, Frankenstein's second monster rejects travelling barefoot in the head. He shall strive --- rather more --- to avoid those ice-flows: wherein a nineteenth century authoress had her creature finish up."

TRAVEL ONWARDS TOWARDS A BEAR'S SPINE: (137)
Phosphorous Cool still continues to reply to Heathcote Dervish, primarily over his refusal to confront Mastodon Helix. "Your rage won't transfix my heart, O misery", he transposed. "No articulation can cause me to wage war against my wishes. I only have to yank myself up over the tram-line and away from those who wish me harm. Bless me! Nor do I need to stoop to erect soldiers as my new carrion or provender --- one only has to think of the B-movie with Jacque van Damme and Dolph Lundgren, for instance. They are not the necessary scarecrows of any forthright identity. It is not an example of fire one and see; at

least as regards one of your bubbling poisons or water lilies." To face off against this, though, Heathcote Dervish had swooned to a deadly quiet. He stands directly behind our magnesium oxide puppet; especially as this manikin's making every gesture to depart. All of a sudden, Heathcote Dervish looks uncertain or slightly forlorn in his conduct; it's the first time this has happened. One also can't help notice the rocks lying roundabout; they embrace a character of sandy brown and illumine one too many craters. Surely those beached wrecks and solitary houses, existing out on the margins of Salisbury Plain, won't prove to be inextinguishable? Perhaps one or two exercises in Dennis Wheatley's ritualism isn't always good for the spirit?

CASTLE FRANKENSTEIN: BUT WHERE IS IGOR[?]: (138)
Back in Baron von Frankenstein's laboratory an arcane experiment is taking place; and it's one which proves indicative of a hundred Hammer Horror films of yesteryear. Look at this spectacle in front of us: it is a tabernacle to alternative science that seems to splice David Icke together with Guy Debord. Now then, several large condenser batteries lie off to the left, and these are cylindrical in their electromagnetic measure. A system of levers or pulleys then limbers up behind-hand --- all of them connected to various hooks, stanchions, grappling irons and interwoven cross-beams. These delineated some heavy joists made of wood or darkish timber, and they took place in a medley where 'twenties electro-vascular gear gives up *Victoriana's* ghost. It shadow-boxed with those rather camp Hollywood films depicting Frankenstein in the early 'thirties... particularly at a time when the talkies were mushrooming and Boris Karloff adopted the title role. Likewise, a bank of large galvanic generators supported one wall or mural, and each one had obvious connexion switches like burdensome dials. All sorts of trip-wires, meters and registering devices chose to o'erlook this plot. Above Baron von Frankenstein's scenario – and like in a 'fifties Bacon painting – a naked existential bulb illuminated the scene. Whereas our aristocratic scientist – for his part – worked

124

away steadily on his monster's body; a massive forearm of which straddled a podium and let itself off to the side. Can't you detect the criss-cross marks of so much stitching on this cadaver's skin (?); it has literally come to indicate the charnel-house offerings of a man-thing. Certainly, our mortician had dwelt long enough in a death-house or an ossuary to collect these distracted bits. Nor can Shaun Hutson's literature take us away from this lab's iconic status. Also, a drip led up from the dais wherein Professor Frankenstein's operation took place, and this eight foot corse found itself covered over with a diaphanous sheet. It was brilliant in its necessary whiteness... even though a limp and massive arm lay off strangely to the right. It successfully concealed the corse of Frankenstein's monster. Whereupon Baron von Frankenstein's crippled or hump-backed nurse made her approach... and she carried a small basket or trug of medical implements. Could these work out to be an array of retorts, ampoules, needles, pipettes, draining boards and egg-timers, perchance? Our female Igor cradled them lovingly in her hands. Has she yet outlived the fact that our ward sister was an emanation of Elsa Bounteous Hapgood... at least ectoplasmically speaking? Furthermore – and as a final closure – Heathcote Dervish's spirit or *anima* floated over this operation. It appeared to be a jumble of jellified blobs – the remnants of which oscillated in a coagulated way. Above it all, something reminiscent of a Padstow hobby-horse (or hose) loomed in a fractured display. Who isn't to say whether the Ku Klux Klan originated from these western parts? All in all, Heathcote circled atop a fidgety Frankenstein his wonders to perform. Don't you know it all bears upon it an X-certificate film classification?

A TERRIBLE ANTIQUARY PLAYS CHESS WITH HORSES: (139)
Meanwhile, Phosphorous Cool jigs up abreast of his twitching wires; namely, these are those tokens of puppeteering that he intends to make use of in order to disappear. He has certainly planned his escape from this particular pit. Is he not prepared to

liberate his skills by hopping, skipping and jumping away? Yes indeed, our roles seem to be reversed – and now it's Heathcote Dervish who looks troubled. He travels along in Phosphorous' trailing wake – while one of his shadowy minions makes up the numbers. On closer inspection, such a hooded votary can only be Warlock Splendour Thomas. Doesn't the cowl pulled down over his face indicate a forbidden pleasure... even a guilty secret? Anyway, we have to observe whether this stick or hood obscures his features; in a dramaturgy where these items wax lyrical over a prepared mixture of purple and yellow. To be sure... Heathcote Dervish enunciated his clarion thus: "None may know of our witness before the truth... Understand this, my stranger and enemy, if you desert us the consequences will be grave and unforeseen. Do you occasionally watch me when masked or in a vermillion oblivion? In this lexicon, my body lies strapped to ancient or galvanic machinery; the like of which saw me shaping up to a blue haze amid dandelions. These also found themselves to be connected by a thousand wires, in a conundrum where each azure spiral reckons on its own spit. Dare one cross this favourite line – primarily so as to understand my swooning beyond a remit? Am I cast in cerulean dye amidst the flesh of my ligatures; a seasoning otherwise bound to liberate me from the banks of machinery above? I plead with you to avoid deserting us, Phosphorous. Examine a puppet's kindred or kind, I beg you – let it all fall down amongst a drizzling downpour. Surely, it's electrostatic in its allure; a sparkling raiment (this) liable to refract a body in its walk-on part... when doused with fire? Do you remember Ezra Pound's beard waving its surrender over a brilliantly squared blue? The whole assemblage then rose and cast aside its offering – a debenture that (in turn) rendered mute a modernist rapture by Chagall, Lowry or Roualt... all of them arranged in no special order. To be certain now, a shimmering excalibur or a tincture of sapphire'd horses lit up a corse. It came encumbered with so many links to the Frankenstein machinery within which I was trapped – have pity, if only by dint of another's dimension." "Sympathy multiplies misery for those who suffer in their weakness", intones Phosphorous Cool. "We basically acknowledge a knife of destiny that cleaves a bondsman to his yoke." Cool breaks off momentarily, and then comes up against some liberal treacle... albeit from a most exhausted source. An exercise in *salon* theatre which can only be Heathcote Dervish acting against type. But – in the war of each against all – yesterday's bravery becomes the carrion for tomorrow's crows. Let us see...

AN EGG-CUP VISITS HADES WITH BLOOD ON ITS RIM: (140)
All of a sudden, the spirit of Heathcote Dervish looks down on Frankenstein's body from above: and the latter's cadaver comes stretched out on a dais or slab. With every move and gesture, now, the movie history of the 'thirties returns to haunt us – it definitely busts a gut over its trespass. Whereupon we notice that Frankenstein's monster lies in a prone position which merely draws the eye towards his coarse trousers, belt and flaxen jacket. A kind of transponder or electrical head-gear cups his skull; and it doubtlessly serves as the feeder for the electricity that Baron von Frankenstein wishes to impart. "All is ready for your metamorphosis... from one changeling into Thomas Middleton's escape", interpreted the good doctor from below. "To begin", our Man of Science averred, "prepare yourself to enter into the matter of this limitless corse. Do you want it to be restricted to merely those freak shows of yesteryear?"

DEAL IN THE GREATNESS OF SPARTA'S HAND AT CARDS: (141)
Why, let us fast forward to events which pretend that they are occurring in the twentieth century. For Phosphorous Cool was about to cast off and fly into the night-sky above Salisbury Plain... even though such a starry backdrop might be a painted board on a puppet's stage. Haven't you interpreted this as an offering to George Speaight's history of the toy theatre? In any event, Phosphorous cascaded away into the firmament – and it's

almost as if he can fly without the aid of Icarus' wings! In his mind's eye, philosophically speaking, he recalls Heathcote Dervish's fondest forgetting: what with the reality of a blue electrocution victim who fades away to nought. Similarly, Dervish's body manifests itself anew and it rears up with an elongated eye... or possibly misshapen teeth. All of our vortex swivels around the smoke of a translucent fire. Discounted and yet counter-penetrated... is this how such loftiness should be? My children, listen to me... an account of one of our ranges measures the distaff side (somewhat falsely). "If – as you attest – Mastodon Helix lays waste to a world of paste-board and putre, why, be it so. I shall shed no tears, withal. Surely, such a mastodon must relish the task of exfoliation – rather like one of those Assyrian bull-gods in the British Museum? Further to our analysis, strength begets its own morality which is bereft of guilt. It luxuriates in a plenitude due to puissance alone, thereby. I will intervene in no quarrels that don't directly involve me, but Helix's vengeance strikes me like the roaring of a circus lion. Has Clown Joey proved facile enough to free him from his cage? Regardless of these pageants, though, one's tempted to declare whether Mastodon Helix embodies this type of deity. One who exists mounted in red nacreous stuff or cornelian; especially when possessed of eight arms and filling a niche in a temple. It subsists in a pale emerald light which was illumined by smoky braziers. Look at such a forlorn temperature again – given that the masses swarm around its massive pedestal like so many ants. They are countless in their irretrievable nothingness. To some witnesses – like Joseph Goebbels in his expressionist novel *Michael* – such an idol represents Christ. It's a type of re-christianising in other words... but, in fact, it turns out to be a travesty of the case. Idol-worship, shamanism or fetishism of this kind has to be decidedly unchristian, to be sure. It must have more to do with the religion of the Assyrians than anything else. Didn't the old testament Hebrews or Israelites call them the 'accursed of god'? Yet, in these days of days, the culture of

philo-semitism will have to be rejected if the West is to revive. No occidental renaissance can be contemplated without it.
+
Could the quest for such a grail be regarded as a fanatical pursuit of purity?

LIBERATE THE SNARES OF SO MANY BORES: (142)
Meanwhile, our Frankenstein's monster lies alone on a plinth – whilst an electrical generator hummed to itself near his massive head. A cranium which was better illuminated by a spot light that refused to spear its contours! These were heavy, somnolent, unfolded, graceless and yet powerful – whereupon his visage definitely possessed a menacing aura. A pair of head-phones existed on either side of the creature's skull or stitches, and they looked – for all the world – like an alternative iPod. One large buckle might also be observed at the nethermost extremity of this Frankenstein's monster!
+
Girding his loins, then, Heathcote Dervish's spirit passed into the inanimate corse; and it did so through an ectoplasmic transfer… skin to skin. Yes, Heathcote slipped in like a divine vapour or gas: one which may osmotically filter through any partition. What is Heathcote's astral body thinking during this triumphal moment? "Nothing but the following assists me over wrath's plenitude", he mused. "In the offering of my new kingdom, I shall visit any new understandings with a sword… these must remain unfocused forevermore in such avenues. It depicts a grief deep down in one's well of suffering – but by no means at all congruent with Radclyffe Hall's *The Well of Loneliness*. Since the truth is that this magnificent new body shall bequeath to me conquests unheard of! Hitherto, all I lacked was a stalker to my prey. Forgive me, great Odin, a cup of bitterness runneth over into a murder of crows."

A DEEP SIX HEIGHTENS RAGNORAK: (143)

A century farther on, Phosphorous Cool jigged away from Salisbury Plain's scaffolding. In the background his wires trailed over the trestle of such a puppeteer's hand; and these were tendons (in turn) which levelled off down the back of the stage. It took the residual form of Eric Bramall's ornate stage-set in Colwyn Bay… wherein the twentieth century's dark and baroque prince adopted his motif. Phosphorous flew up a screen at once cadenced with azo and cadmium; and it shook at this gesture of a prior engineering. Look at you, O my brothers… Phosphorous' identikit picture co-existed with an orange sun. These factors certainly couldn't help but listen to its process of awakening. May one hear a trident being scraped across a floor (?); itself carpeted with the retrieval of so many lost souls. Phosphorous is still liable to turn when startled by such a sound, even if he happens to be in mid-air at the time. Why don't you follow such a motion with your opera-glasses, honest to goodness…?

CORPSE REANIMATION IN FRANKENSTEIN'S BOUDOIR: (144)

We now proceed to the energisation of this particular corpse in the nineteenth century. A moment where Frankenstein's corse lies prone on its slab; the former being an industrial stanchion with brass-work fixtures and fittings. These articulated a sort of fairground or workplace apparel – above which the eight-foot cadaver lay dressed from top-to-toe in serge. Furthermore, an enormous cavalcade of electronic sparks fizzed aslant, and they gathered around several globules… each one of them alive to the chance of a molecular fulfilment. Given the fact that we are speaking of mesmeric turbines – every one of 'whom' charged itself over a galvanic shield. Globular they happened to be: and basically lit off against circumstance; as a trace-element limbered up so as to free Frankenstein's monster. A tourney which then involved rescuing him from coldness. Behind this lightening-cube transformation (sic) a medley of gears superintended; and, like some sarcophagi or coffers of yesteryear, such structures shipped up to a darkened ceiling. --- Even though we can easily see these dials and grids being lost in an electrical haze. On a feminine front, however, both Elsa Bounteous Hapgood and the hunch-backed nurse look away. They are intently surmising Baron von Frankenstein's features... irrespective of his early origins in Moustachio Brave Herring. Likewise, Butler James also has his head skewed in the Baron's direction; and he's wearing a duffle-coat at the time. Our narrative's mortuary professor – for his part – encodes an obsessive mien that's redolent of a mid-fifties science fiction film. Around his temples a spectrometer or a hidden mirror does the business: and it appears to be taped to his upper reaches by some lint or other bandage. But such mummification otherwise leaves him cold – particularly when these hands stroke or caress the dials in front of him. They understate their own purpose in the finality of causation... especially when one understands that a spectrum inundates these rods: one which negates our circumstances with a binary level of switches. "How goes it, good Professor?", asks Butler James *apropos* of nothing in particular. "Are you any nearer to your goal in terms of animating a corpse? Will Frankenstein's monster ever live again outside of celluloid's lustre? Nor may any discount the progress of science – wasn't Mary Shelley herself keen on galvanic agency? A progeny which led all the others around Lake Geneva to adopt a similar genuflexion, thereby. Didn't she compose a novel years later called *The Last Man*? Yes indeed, natural science shall animate dead flesh by freezing out the marrow from its fist. No other exchange can then guard against unregarded bone. Electricity is obviously the means adopted by a modern Prometheus. Harken again to my cry, almighty Professor; does your experiment bear fruit?"

SAVOUR A TAMBOURINE FOR A MILLION DOLLS: (145)
Phosphorous Cool has now surmounted a mausoleum of expectancy; the former a structure that's left way beneath him in a dip on Salisbury Plain. This had come to be characterised by a

constellation of out-buildings – all of them wrecked, semi-abandoned, all at sea, left over or circumscribed. For – truly and above board – these pylons looked adrift or otherwise lost. At a time when the edifice's hulk seemed to be bereft, stilted, dispirited, and with triangular or conical roofs levelling at nought save silence. Whereas sloping planes of light green --- never mind cantilevered installations --- gave off a pessimistic reek. A folly which led off from the open spaces within; especially given that these extended dwellings were open to the elements. Behind our distracted hand (so to speak) we can spy various whiffs or trails of vapour. Might they be clouds, mist or ascending steam? It matters not: since Phosphorous deliberates on this dice call... while he scrambles up a puppet's backdrop. "I refuse to strive for those who wish me harm. The wise man husbands his own strength, in order to strike with the keenest brand. None shall accuse me of procrastination or letting the Devil take the hindmost. I have always striven forward with intent... so as to impress one's face upon the mud. Could it be (alternately) one of those death-masks by Marc Quinn? They are kept extant by freezing – seeing as how they're made from blood."

A LIGHTNING FLASH WITHIN A CIRCLE INDICATES MOSLEY: (146)
Meanwhile – back in our impromptu nineteenth century – the eyes of Baron von Frankenstein's monster slowly open. Each lid rests on an eternity (albeit of lead) before it chooses to slide apart. Let's break free from post-structuralism, now... At first, the flesh appears to be pallid, unbestrewn and patched up with a quilt of stitching. Do you effectively take stock of this awakening? Moreover, Heathcote Dervish finds his new body difficult to deliberate upon; and it seems to be vaguely strapped down or maladjusted to such deviance. "My eyes (which were once bloodshot) gaze aslant. They stare across a tongue of flame or light situated on a sun-dial... a device that characterises a late Victorian garden. Many a Sherlock Holmes story was discovered to possess one. Rest easy, now", murmured Heathcote in

132

Frankenstein's corse, "but congratulate me, Herr Professor. I breathe in and out of these new trap-doors of provender. All systems are go; they swell the glands and pass blood through these veins. Surely – in terms of a multiple cadaver – we come face to face with one metamorphosis too far? Wherein the black blood of a thousand gibbets cries out from the ground. Answer me this, good Herr Professor", intoned Heathcote Dervish, "can't you interpret my release as a new life?" "Yes indeed", conceded the Baron, "his orbs have refilled --- but not with cherubs. The lilypads are bloated and twice their natural size on stagnant waters. Frankenstein's creature lives!"

A NIGHTMARE CRINGES BEFORE ITS GREED: (147)

Phosphorous Cool has come to pass a willowy hand across his eyes. A silvern gesture (this) which sought to hide those wires that stretch down from the puppet-board lying ahead. Furthermore, the manikin known as Cool had to take stock of one cognisance too far, in that he felt a weakness within him due to his exertions. Also, this voodoo doll in reverse recognised a hint of prior exhaustion, primarily after expending so much energy in returning Heathcote to life. On our anti-hero travelled across this crown's illumination of brilliant azure – it all seemed to be painted rather spaciously with a golden tint. "What do I reckon will be the outcome of this adventure?", fated Phosphorous all by himself. "By virtue of the fact that a dream impinges itself upon me – it is at once plentiful and lucid. Might I yet star within its labyrinth; in a manner rather like Ken Russell's film version of *The Lair of the White Worm*? Necessarily so… given how a blue face has become translucent now. It releases a shoal of electrical sparks; while each socket came unbroken in a shimmering haze. It intoned sapphire's break with Heisenberg's uncertainty principle, thereafter."

TARGET A TERRIBLE BEAUTY TO ITS CRADLE *A LA* W.B. YEATS: (148)

A century back in time, Frankenstein's monster's face creases into a grimace; and this giant homunculus is now fully alive. Likewise, there was no need to essay the art of Val Mayerick: since sundry electrical pulsations are seen to engulf our man-thing. Mary Shelley's most famous creation was fully awake (forevermore), and this involves a bold glimmer in a cadaver's eye. Large head-phones inundate his skull from either side, and these provide cups for each ear which locate a binary system in the brain. One's attention is also drawn to those ligatures around his scalp – together with two eyes, both from separate corpses, that lit up the night-sky. They existed on either side of a head's fulfilment – if only to liberate one of Peter Cushing's witticisms from memory. Whereupon the mouth --- in such a drama as this --- signifies a misplaced fracture, one which grimaces before its own wakefulness. Some sort of rough cloth lies neatly underneath this bag o' bones. But – all of a sudden – Frankenstein's demi-urge lets out a confused shout: "My arms and legs are trapped in a vice of impermanence... a fact that renders me helpless over biological momentum. Yes, locomotion remains the key to Lon Chaney's silent cinema, even in relation to a film dealing with a circus' saturnalia. It had to be called *The One Who Gets Slapped* in 1924." Given such evidence as this, the requisite degree of power has not been provided to enable bodily motion. His arms and legs waxed stuck or immobile, thereby. "Yessss", replied Baron von Frankenstein --- in his guise of Moustachio Brave Herring revisited --- more juice is electrically needed for your appendages to be granted a due velocity. Let not the millipede strike out beyond itself... now that Farmer Jones' spade exists to cut an earthworm in half. Have you licensed your own crow-bar yet? You're certainly unable to move – lest we permit it."

+

Does an electrostatic dream filter out its own observance, if it's contained in cerulean? Especially when we understand that what

134

subsists in the mind of one character can very easily move across into other brains. Aren't we dealing with puppets herein, irrespective of Carl Jung's ideas about the collective unconscious? Never mind any more detours... because a bearded apparatchik swoons under wires. These are of the brightest blue, pthalo, sapphire, beryl, French, nacreous with a glaucous tinge, as well as cadmium sulphur. He comes latticed to a statement of phantasm, merely being circumscribed now and filtered via Varese's tight-rope... albeit in terms of sound. Here and now, though, any self-portraits wither before their casket; and they festoon an azure silhouette with a spiralling blue danube or Monday. Could D.H. Lawrence come to be crucified on a pine like Attis of yore?

RESIST THE CANNONBALL WHICH BISECTS A PLASTINATE: (149)
Meanwhile, Phosphorous Cool catches one glimpse of a city on fire down by the corner of his retina... it depicts an avalanche of flame reminiscent of Greek fire. Wasn't this a liquid or phosphorescent agent used hitherto in mediaeval sieges? Let's look at it more closely... can it resemble a toy-theatre which blows up or is otherwise ablaze? We are dealing with Eric Bramall's wagon-load of marionettes (anyway). Another feature also flashes into the memory, and this has to do with a situationist art-work – possibly even one that harks back to child art. Why don't you take time to consider Peter Callesen's *Big Paper Castle*, but now ringed with a fiery halo? Phosphorous – intrigued as to the cause of this devastation – moves closer to it, primarily so as to examine any holocaust at first hand. No revisionism shall be enrolled in these early stages! But still, one cadmium filter articulates its mayhem; and it travels onwards with the digital simulacrum of so much light. Wasn't an ultra-modernist opera by Karl Heinz Stockhausen called the same name? It impresses one immeasurably – given the facsimile to Zeus that fades into what Paul Raymond once dubbed 'electric blue'. Whereupon a bearded ascetic swoons like one attached,

135

prior and forevermore, to Andy Warhol's electrocution chair... one making use of bluish dye or woad in a silk-screen print. Listen: a form showers sparks amid toadstools, each one an electron and awaiting Farraday's nonchalance.

TORPEDOES STREAK AMIDST ONE'S WAKING PURPLE: (150)

Back in an identikit nineteenth century, we find a nullification of our desires... For Frankenstein's monster lay awake on an adamantine dais, but his limbs were caught in an infraction. They cannot move. "What ribald implementation of dreams is this?", averred Heathcote Dervish. (Remember now: Heathcote D. spiritually animates the corse of our junior Frankenstein – yet neither of them may shift a muscle.) "Like a Stan Barstow novel about impoverished emotions, my form cannot rise to an axiom of forgiveness. Look at this: these callow youths have come to inundate their own shores. Why not effectively shoot a hand off an arm that holds an orb (?) – for it's only then really free to go and plunge into the heart of a nuclear reactor." "Don't confuse us with any false heroics or otherwise", resourced the voice of Baron von Frankenstein. In offering this dictum (though) Moustachio Brave Herring's *alter ego* looked down in a condescending way. Moreover, we find that those fire-lighters which covered the professer's eyes have been displaced, and these were those spectacles that protected one's orbs. It all came in most handy when electrical fire-storms were being discharged roundabout. All in all, this scientist's livery seemed to be supercilious, congealed, touch and go – and even latent with potentiality in terms of phrenology's impress. Do you realise that – in many respects – phrenology proved to be a Victorian precursor to most forms of modern psychology? "Granted, Frankenstein's creature", muttered the surgeon, "your limbs are paralysed due to a want of resource. Because power – in other words – has yet to kindle its litmus test over some spilt crab-apple juice. Why don't you just refuse to see it?"
+

136

A gap of a few moments began to intrude, hereupon. Could it then be preternaturally quiet – like after a barrage during the Great War? It was only resultantly that Heathcote Dervish recognised his entrapment. Like yesterday's iron maiden, he proved to be bound up within the body of Frankenstein's monster.

ZEALOTRY RETURNS US TO THE TRUTH: (151)
Phosphorous Cool makes his way now through a medley of carnage, or misplaced desires. All around his skimming and silvery tone... the world has gone up in flames. Great gusts of fire are consequently blown hither and thither... despite the fact that many a wall is down or had been knocked through. Also, at the periphery of his vision, a crowd of humans gave chase to lies – abundantly so. Their faces are convulsed with fear or perturbation, and they run, jump, procrastinate and then lurch forwards without plan. All around them mistress pandemonium girts her skirts... particularly at a time when Robespierre's brother was led to the scaffold after his more infamous cohort. Maximilien's jaw had already been shattered into many pieces and held in a silk handkerchief, irrespective of the Thermidorean reaction setting a seal on revolutionary leftism. It arrested or cut him off by dint of the guillotine, and this is even though the chairman of the Committee of Public Safety had begun his career by inveighing against it. He later chose to become its very personification. All around Phosphorous Cool, though, a Comus Rout circled its cause at the heart of oblivion – especially when no loyalty can be bought without a bullet in the gut! Such masses are illustrative of Gustav le Bon's conservative metaphysic, as attested to in works like *The Psychology of Crowds*. Truly, this assemblage ranted and raved like Ensor's masks – or possibly, those pencil-works of his whereby a skull looks at itself in a fording river. "What's ours comes entombed in a golden casket within a white rhino's tower. It may be translucent, limpid or up in the air. Xenephon no longer needs to avail himself of his electorate... and any forays up-country could be limitlessly

exposed. Aren't such creatures nearing the end of all sorts of tethers? Might one detect an Ollendorffian beggarhood – one which dances on the tip of a diamond-headed needle? They were like pin-balls in a slot machine. But what must be the cause of so much riot, distress and folly?", asked our silvery captive. A moment later Phosphorous Cool spied the genesis; and it was a rampaging Mastodon Helix!

A FACE REFLECTED IN A WELL'S STRANGENESS: (152)
"What treachery is this?", expostulated Heathcote Dervish from well within the body of a Frankenstein's monster. Are we not really given over to considering James Whale's film of 1931, *Frankenstein*, at such a moment as this? It starred Boris Karloff as the monster – but now a subtle difference cloaks such an affair. For Frankenstein's monster lies prone on his dais and is incapable of any movement; when taken together with a pair of electrical ear-plugs that give witness to his prison. Like a man who has been lauded as Scaramouch – but who's been tied to some rags of straw and a mask – one factotum waits for the blaze that'll set it alight! A strangulated sense of arson --- after all --- acts as the basis for Guy Fawkes' drama. Above this exultation, though, we can see an exhilaration in all the other characters: whether Baron von Frankenstein, Butler James and the female nurse/Igor. She exists to one side of this special tournament. James holds Elsa aloft now (and interestingly) she can be described as wearing Victorian underwear, such as bloomers, serviceable or robust shoes, a bodice and one make-shift bra. Most noticeably, an old-fashioned military revolver lies aslant her left hip; and it finds itself within a sabretache or suchlike contrivance. The nurse – an ectoplasmic relief of Elsa Bounteous Hapgood – just smiles on. Her lips certainly betray an oft-slanted leer, and it's a sort of biped smirk. Whereupon Baron von Frankenstein, a eugenicist or dysgenicist who is certainly part of his time, speaks first. "'Tis no betrayal at all, my monstrous bevy. We have merely captured and made use of you here… in such a way as suits your necessary ambition. Don't you

recognise the circumstance where a wheel-chair enters a tombed gulf, and it closes down the path of a concrete corridor? Namely – one which has been revived by an ancient patterning of pipes that exists above it. Such a tableau seems to trespass on a dank or dismal tomb, a rival which contrives to forever betray the prospect of le Corbusier's unfinished dream. Brutalism or whatever else now, eh (?); given that these ducts will draw down such a chair to a new oblivion under glass. All of it goes to show the sepulchral darkness of a pit: when light plays its relief on raw concrete, itself untreated and painted white in accord with Albigensian brightness."

WRESTLE, WRESTLE ON THE GROUND AMID ABSTRACT EXPRESSIONIST PAINT: (153)
Down below – and amidst a maelstrom of frenzy or smashed cars – Mastodon Helix hurls his imprecations against the world. What can really be going on here? Might this amount to a puppet-theatre played in the mind for laughs – wherein a Strongman endeavours to rip up a telephone directory on one of Aleister Crowley's tarot cards? Don't reach for those stars again 'n' all… since Mastodon Helix luxuriates in pure power, malevolence and the rites of destruction. A prognosis which contains one implicit outpost; and this has to be a saurian monster shambling forth under candle-light. At first, it casts a necessary shadow on a declining screen – one that recalls the final curtain on a miniature stage-set *a la* Montague Summers' Restoration drama. Examine this entreaty, my friends: such a mastodon moves against a criss-crossed pattern of blue-glass, and in a sylph-like manner. May it altogether signify – here and now – a mesmerism or illumination due to the unconscious mind? Could it truly be bred in the bone as before?

PRISE OPEN A DEATH'S-HEAD, PREPARE ITS ONSLAUGHT[!]: (154)
Meanwhile, our plotters have moved in so as to counter-act their coup. Have they been making something of Curzio Malaparte's

book about how to carry out a successful conspiracy, perchance? Anyway, Baron von Frankenstein leans o'er his charge with a menacing aspect – and he seems to have forgotten all care and consideration over the doctor-patient relationship. Do we have another example of Doctor Shipman on our hands? Nonetheless, Frankenstein's monster looks convulsed with ague or grief, primarily under the influence of Butler James' and Elsa Bounteous' arrogant stares. They wax both imperial and inscrutable under this sombre jade. Truly, the after-effects of Heathcote Dervish's incarceration are borne in on him... one after another. Most particularly – now that a repeated image flits into their creative minds... oh so suggestively. It has to do --- as before --- with a cripple's movements in gothic stained-glass. Especially when this occurs at a time where smoky beams come up... via a grill on a far wall. These hint at a new token within identity – when taken together with a rubber-plant underneath. The creature in question definitely wanted to transgress the actual; or to leap beyond one forcing ground-cum-prison. Let it be understood... because, in terms of appearance, our guest limbered up to a palsied freight. (That is to say, *mon ami*, it's one which spoke of crumpled newspaper... while riding aslant of a wheeled chair.) In deportment, such a miasma blinked before its own stain – particularly given the momentum of a thalidomide's release. Again now, such an offering betokened a liquefied spectrum; one that appears lonesome, rag-tag-and-bobtail, spindly, leprous, skeletal and mildly electrocuted as to hair. It all continues to go on now, you see. Further, his chair slides like a metallic contraption across the floor, and it's one which blossoms, negatively, in accord with fate's reverse dye.

RAISE THE GATE FOR WARM-BLOODED DINOSAURS: (155)
Phosphorous Cool finally decides to give courage to Mastodon Helix who lies beneath him on the ground. For just moving in a puppet-theatre's fake sky – when manipulated by Montague Summers – is enough to give one a case of the shakes. A muscle-

bound Helix also ripples with various tendons of subdued folly -- all of them liable to let off depth-charges deep down in his anatomy. *Avaunt thee*! Mastodon glides up to meet him afterwards; and the two plummet down into the sovereign ground.

+

Against all this, a mortal 'gator or reptilian entity bulks large in an enabling gloom. Let's behave now towards those you wish to defeat with a sense of unction (!); and it alone can penetrate the uncouthness of a leathery hide. Will one be able to get a fix on such a transcendence, thereby? Especially given that a Cyclopean red-eye transfigures a slit, if only to create the possibility for a nuclear quake later on. Let it all slide out from under a branch or a cloud of unknowing (now) – particularly if an amphibian's gesture be mulcted in a Charles Atlas advertisement. "Don't spray sand in my face, squirt!", mused a message from one's sponsor. Do you remember them? It even occurred at a time when a black lagoon creature missed one heart beat too many – only then to explode in a gathering of withered scorn. Still, he came on across the threshold again – all of which had to do with a carrot before the stick… in terms of a reptile's enclosure. No more disclosure was allowed, inevitably so. Still & all – and against a gate's witness – a 'raptor moved onwards in this quiet ossuary. It doubtless stood as an emanation from Mastodon Helix; at once spiritually speaking and amid all such Masonic tardiness. But Mastodon's third-brain or reptilian entity travelled its course, and it loomed as a hulk within dreams which offered no quarter over Eros… either in terms of aggression or territoriality. Do you see? Count Richard von Krafft-Ebing then contextualises no greater grief than this.

A BULLET RACES TO ITS TARGET BEHIND A THOUSAND SAND-BAGS: (156)

In a nineteenth century fastness or set of dreams, Elsa Bounteous Hapgood's features came up trumps. They position themselves over the foregrounded domain of a Frankenstein's monster –

141

only to thereby liberate a phrenologist's regard. Because – momentarily and all apace – she releases the fact that noughts can effectively be crosses for those who play this game. Moreover, her iron mask – when delivered in a spectrum of Dumas' London Dungeon – glowers down on her trapped prey. A Fury she besports herself to be, primarily in order to enforce one's will over and above the ear-rings with which she is decked out. A rather glacial Butler James stands behind her all this while... in a tableau where sensitive observers can discern the scar down his left side. It was delivered by Phosphorous Cool during their duel in Whitechapel several moons afore. Does one recall that, criminologically speaking, the left side or eye gives a clue to the inner persona... at least from the perspective of folk wisdom? Let us continue to feed on a parallel bar such as this... for, as a metaphor to the above, a cripple raises a hand in order to draw sand-castles in the air. His extended mitten traverses an open doorway – the aperture of which leavens off to a golden blackness. It follows one's coat-tails all the way back to a yawning grave!

+

Now then, a grubby T-shirt festoons an absence of electrocuted hair; and a medley stands up from the scalp like a mohican's shock. It's delusional, don't you know? Yet our movie director moves onwards continuously towards answers in dun-coloured rooms – possibly then intoning other jails within the mind. Again, in terms of a bell-weather, a thin hand delivers its consciousness aslant one more vista of sand. The sound is also deafening while the wheel-chair slides, and it definitely has to do with an echo occasioned by rubber on concrete. Yes, such an offering causes our mummy to reach out in the direction of silence, even within the perspective of 'her' own grave. Listen to me awhile...

TERROR ANTHRAX STALKS ITS GOLDEN FRAMES: (157) Mastodon Helix and Phosphorous Cool are now engaged in mortal combat... in a situation where these two puppets' wires become intertwined. Each one engages in ferocious wrestling, neck to neck, only to discover that the other one has beaten them to it. Must you disseminate its witness? In a conundrum where one large reptile holds with trespassing against a glow: a factor which causes him to slope down corridors of yesteryear. Seemingly though, one question mounts another in terms of a scaly hide – since this checkerboard suits the grievances of so many doves, let alone those squares existing on your average chess board. It eclipses all other shames, you see… despite the fact that a reptilian eye opens to an enclosed windrush. It's a speck on the old pin-hole camera of yesteryear: and it certainly registers one complaint above Pepper's Ghost. Most particularly – given that a saurian orb fancies its chances, if not necessarily when tied to a post during the day-time. A scenario in which a retina flecks in the direction of a scarlet livery; whereas its pupil happens to be a dark strip, longitudinally speaking. A matter of scales --- thereafter --- surrounds the blinding susurration of this Eye. It knows no other pineal orb – save one that hangs over a transparent tomb… primarily during an instant where Phosphorous' challenge has yet to materialise. Certainly, one ormolu glow must transfigure itself abreast of a cosmic emptiness. Belatedly then, the reptilian part of the brain has to come to the rescue of a cerebration which knows no tics.

BLAISE CENDRAR'S *LICE* WEARS A GAS-MASK: (158)
Frankenstein's monster is responding assertively to such blandishments (or wiles) at this time. These give out before one a fake certainty. Whereupon – looking down – we can see whether Frankenstein's homunculus wears a furrowed brow; together with a snarling mouth amidships. All of which has to be topped off by those Singer sowing machine marks that cross atop a rather square-shaped head. Rectangular it be – or somewhat given over to a combination of those corses from which a man-thing was made. Such a mastodon exists outside of many a helix; and it can only promise never to grant the request that conspirators desire. Do these individuals recognise one particular

cat-call; wherein Heathcote Dervish, disguised as already mentioned, refuses to administer one last request? It concerns the truth of transcendence as the gateway to endless inequality. It is always an elixir in relation to the above. But what really builds up in the mind of a new Prometheus had to be the following...

+

For a cripple's wheel-chair draws nigh to its necessary conclusion tonight. This helps to assuage the 'Rocky Horror Show' awaiting us... somewhere or other. In a set-back like the present one, remember, a spectral chair carries itself forward on wheels of gloom. To one side of his carriage's egress lay an oblong fissure --- it betokened a new watchfulness in ochre that lit up a smoky halo over its den. In comparison to which these shadows snake away, and they are like ebon marble or sepulchres made from similar sandstone. This greater darkness released the template of a thousand wrongs – itself a slide-show which delineated the reality of two dolls or manikins further on. Each one trespassed on a brief subway: namely, one that continuously saw the sleek planes of two perfect heads. Both of them existed – furthermore – aslant of various longitudinal gaps. Doesn't Newtonian physics come to the rescue of Dior's or Tamara de Lempicka's world? Most assuredly – in a development where the purple planes of a tonsured beauty offends even pink. Likewise, as in the purely visual era of silent cinema, our liver-birds limit this peculiar impasse and each one stares into the distance like a store-dummy. A distraction then plays upon its necessary witness; and this was one which leads to those smooth arabesques of Paul Bowles' fortune. The phrenology of a retrieved witness also intrudes here, and it's an image that tests those oval moments of poise. Can a shaven-headed supermodel, with perfect bones, successfully play Satan in Mel Gibson's *The Passion of the Christ*?

LOOK OUT, LOOK OUT(!); THESE STORE DUMMIES PASS IN REVIEW: (159)

Our two protagonists, Mastodon Helix and Phosphorous Cool, continue their brawl betimes. It threatens – most definitely – to open up the Gates of Heaven with its travail… now that these two puppets, wrapped together in mortal combat, grapple for the future prospects of the earth itself. Listen to this ready temperature (most assertively): since their forms are interlinked and even our marionette's wires threaten to cut the other off. Let's look at this conflict once more: as Mastodon smashes our Phosphorous tinted one into the ground. A solitary brigand [Mastodon] has successfully outmanoeuvred t'other, so that the silvery sliver lies underneath Mastodon Helix. The latter specimen then lances our anti-hero into the earth; a manoeuvre seemingly reminiscent of a spear tackle in rugby league, for instance. Nonetheless, Mastodon cups his hands together and wallops Phosphorous Cool in the stomach – thereby causing him to stagger backwards and subside upon the loam. Various boulders, bits of rotten sod, turf and a violently green sky all radiate this pasture. Mastodon Helix shakes his fist in power and pride throughout!
+

Remember now that our objective correlative, in T.S. Eliot's terms, leads Phosphorous Cool to surmount a latticed structure which has been suffused by a tincture of the deepest red. For – no doubt about it – a stroboscopic indent infuses this pillar like an old factory chimney rising up from the ground. It also finds itself pulsating to one's lunar gaze, primarily by virtue of an arc-light shimmering over such crimson with a netted effect. It's a process that wakes up a momentary oblivion, you see, if only to subsume Buffet's observance amid an abandonment of squares. A perpendicular assemblage, this, which somehow pin-points the evidence of so many oblongs, given such ludic density and torment. But none of the above can do anything in relation to the immense saurian existing below. Can it re-interpret one's dreams… in a manner reminiscent of the creature from the black lagoon?

WE DISTANCE OURSELVES FROM HOP-SCOTCH AT OUR DISPLEASURE: (160)
In Professor Frankenstein's mortuary-cum-laboratory, however, we find a wheel-chair which is next to a bank of electrical equipment. Whereupon Frankenstein's assistant/nurse brings forward a cape and its triangular hood – a barrier that will soon cover a monster's visage. All this time, he (Fervent) lies on a dais in suspended animation; while Elsa Bounteous Hapgood stands further out and massages a syringe. It happens to be one of those pipettes or museum pieces which adorn the shelves of old labs, or alternately the Royal Museum of Surgeons in South Kensington. Moustachio Brave Herring/Baron von Frankenstein – for his part – looks down upon his charge with a microscopic air; namely, it's one that finds him exultant over the prologue to a modernist opera. Seemingly then, his features at once wax sneering, over-confident, condescending and easily defined. One of those surgical mirrors also comes attached to his scalp by a band --- it primarily asks surgery to relieve pain by inflicting it. Wasn't this the inner surface of Robert Selzer's book, *The Story of a Knife*? "Our witness statement coughs at the interlude of such centuries", purred the doctor who'd achieved this feat. "You will recognise the truth of our demands when we put them to you. It certainly won't help if you forbid our manikins their customary pleasure. First, let's control the outcome of one of Moreau's experiments… so otherwise facilitated by Peter Singer's advocacy of animal rights. No – you remain completely within our power: and it doubtless indicates a foray into grave-time which pensions ease. Do you detect its worth? Anyway, a brief injection of a mind-control serum shall soon place you entirely under our sway. Nurse Igor (he addressed her directly) get Heathcote Dervish dressed as speedily as possible… then place him in his wheel-chair for onwards travel."
+

146

Look you: our metaphor holds as good as before. Leastwise – we now find a situation where the wheel-chair squeaked its way forward. All and everything happened to be closed off in somnolence and gloom. Also, ever since his entrance into this Hilton, one scarecrow illumined a way towards an unlit pavement. He admittedly crossed the threshold in order to remain in the game... *squeak*; *squeak*. Yet the mobile chair carried on across one gifted mansion too many; and it basically charged out in an ochre bestrewn haze. A playlet wherein a movement occurred over dank concrete --- the former echoing to a sensory deprivation chamber's distaff.

A BLACK ENVELOPE CARRIES A SINISTER MESSAGE WITHIN: (161)

Truly and again, these monsters clashed when they're juxtaposed against the paste-board of a toy-theatre. A minor boardgame (this) upon which the festivities of London town find themselves washed up. One factor necessarily elides into another here, particularly given that the painted fun of a "peekaboo" knows its place within folk culture. Yes and yes some more... because Mastodon's massive thews now stand in victory over a crumpled Phosphorous Cool. He lies smartly to the left and definitely under the thumb; by virtue of the fact that his silver-toed body lay prone amongst some rocks. It appears to be mildly smouldering, confused and beaten down. Similarly, Mastodon raises two slab-sided fists in triumph --- both of them encompassing the size of hams which hang up in a butcher's shop. Mastodon Helix continues to celebrate anew... for he wallows in the character of his strength! Nought else but this can prove decisive in life's struggle (necessarily so)...
+
Let's look at a spectacle that is drawn from the reptilian part of the brain... especially when we have occasion to understand a crystalline shattering overhead. It tears apart the transformation of its own viaduct – in a dramaturgy which smashes a domain of black opal. The glass tinkles on and sets itself the task of

147

rebuilding a stained-glass window; i.e., one that's been burst asunder like an effort by Stanley Spencer in Cookham. Most assertively – when a spear reaches across these tendrils of destiny; and they were found to be floating amid so many stages! Shards of crystal began to deliver their promise, and they lumbered forth in a mastodon's direction. (Namely: one that sits precisely with those accusations over whether the dinosaurs were warm-bloodied, or not). No scientist can really act in the affirmative yet... nor need we fall on a red-eyed reptile who looks on undisturbed. His essential deportment recalls Godzilla – albeit in those Japanese science-fiction films of yore. Never mind the fact which declares that a champion, such as Phosphorous Cool, falls upon our brontosaurus from above, even if he grasped the Spear of Destiny around his midriff. A sigil which has escaped from Trevor Ravenscroft – whether or not James Herbert chose to get involved in it. For his declaration – and at the foot of a tunnel marked 'arousal' – the man-reptile stood on his hind legs. From one perspective, the EU matters very much – but you have to recognise that nothing will change, irrespective of another's lustre. Here and now, an overall menu delivers efficacy. It helps you to drop your mechanism and cleave to a professional gentleman! *Ceteris paribus*, these homeland security measures were overseen by players in a culture where they can be tacked on a blackboard. Spiritually speaking, the truth saw our amphibian looming up bulky, amoral, razor-jaw like and caged at London Zoo. His squat or flat-faced features beckoned to one's attention... if only to protect many of these crippled stoicisms. They certainly stalked the backline of insouciance!

OUR SOVRAN CORNEA SOUGHT *KRATOS*: (162)

Back in Frankenstein's laboratory, swirling circles of flesh surround their prey. Each one of them then asks the same question in a different way. Perspiration broke out on Boris Karloff's features (now), and these were over the facts or *impedimenta* at issue. A blue streak transfixed this available skin – making it padded up to the cloth, studded and quilted, as well as sown up. In the manner of *White Jacket*, a gory medical novel by Herman Melville, a Singer sowing-machine lay at its base. Sweat then clouded a brow without cognisance... assertively so. For what have we here? Heathcote Dervish was crippled within the body of a Frankenstein's monster in a 'thirties horror film. Whatever did he think of this – in all inevitability? You see, Heathcote required a permanent cadaver for the future, primarily *quod* his spirit might be lost forever... it could never be at peace as a flibbertigibbet. Perhaps our New Prometheus thought out the following? "Can our treacly one's chair jerk about alright – either plagued over its stillness or gloom? A form lay to the right in this sepulchral dark --- it caught all of our witnesses unawares over mistreatment. In these circumstances, even a smoky calm ministered to turquoise's glare – whereupon a single wheel-chair travelled about. A symbolism which hesitated in this glowering cubicle... at least when a spastic had refused to douse himself in flames in order to deliver aught. Could such a visitation be Hermaphrodite X reincarnated? The wheels (meanwhile) seemed spindly; the legs like a stick-insect, and the hair electrocuted! "Where are you, Heathcote?", whined our visitor. "I need your assistance, if I'm to achieve traction... leastwise, if my conveyance's to move. All around me, though, the sepulchral engine of an NCP car-park glimmers. It chooses to speak --- necessarily --- of le Corbusier!"

FOLLOW THIS ENGINE WITH A THOUSAND FACE-PAINTINGS: (163)
Our hero or anti-hero, Phosphorous Cool, lies adjacent to one craving... although his body's doubled up throughout. Might all its joints be specially painful? Mastodon Helix – in a customary way – gaped in triumph at Wrath's gateway, and he definitely hadn't forgotten his origins in mediaeval corbels. (Those in and around Castleford had transfixed the young Henry Moore). We know such answers now, most truly. Because any news agenda caused him to beckon on in quietness, and his muscles rippled under a bright orange hue... one that guided the Hyperborean

within. A factor which also extended to chthonian precepts, and these milked the scene of their own disgrace. He bunched up his fists into two great mallets; whereas his features limned up altogether diabolically. They were at once seen to be heavily browed, fossilised, rasping and aught like a great tortoise! Eventually, he forced his hulking frame in the direction of a classic colonnade. A red number 38 bus – all the way down from Hackney Wick – led one of its number to a Flaxman portrait of Donatello. "I must smash the living daylights out of Punch, my lord. It likewise causes my gigantic feet to rise over Tartarus' stillness – albeit with various spatulas in tow." Whereupon – during this discourse – our Mastodon strode across balustrades of wood that have been blown hither and thither; and these were symmetrical as to purpose & size… nor may we forget the streets of 'sixties London town closing around them. Then again, a Renault car lay bounced off to one side, with a curved or steaming bonnet. In the background, many building fronts and their appurtenances were bubbling up amidships in neo-classical splendour.

TORMENT THE MAN WHO PULLS OFF HIS METAL FACE: (164)
In disregarding one warning ahead of time, Heathcote pressed on apace… Didn't he recall that moment of splendour… wherein he approached his fifth wife, namely Elsa Bounteous Hapgood? All of this took place in another or possible dimension (perforce). A scenario inside which Heathcote Dervish's limpid spectre neared her form… as was indicated by the triangular head-piece and its tapering externals. Such a self-questioning led to these expansions (so to say); wherein globular redoubts hurtled around the circumference of this frame. It mulcted towards a decidedly purple glow – within which medical attention, over Butterworths book about tumours, caused him to filter out any osmosis. While, directly behind her, a series of interconnected stained-glass windows were to be found. These saw themselves laid bare by so many entrapments; the like or whose kindred remembered

Salisbury cathedral, for instance. Likewise, Elsa Bounteous Hapgood sat on a clawed seat; the temperature of its solace finally being measured with a sword. A few negative tarot cards (or possibly disabused playing cards) fell to the ground at such a moment. Each one then chose to mention its stylistics or variance. A table of excellence (thus) whereby she looked back on the phantom with a withering condominium... even fear.
+

Now then, in this incarnation, Elsa had about her the look of a troubled blonde beauty... much after the fashion of a young Brigitte Bardot. Fish-net stockings were seen to hinder a short or chav like dress, while her blonde mass of hair streamed down her back like a great body of fire. It chose to forget a folly of cascading water... thereafter. Given all of this, her face, breasts and hands seemed otherwise perfect. They continued to taper to the finish of one of Eric Gill's resolutions (in other words). Oh my yes... it especially has something to do with those metal objects in her hair, and these were like tendrils of steel within driven snow. Or, somewhat alternately, they fitted onto the Catherine Wheel of Kate Bush's own nature... and this was never mind the fact that they resembled the minor spokes of a wheel twisting to gold, on rind stone, amid a vehicle of burnished pumice. Each and every ormolu abstract, then, sign-posted a certainty which said that – within a peroxide mop – she wore bullets in her hair. Let's sign off for a Mary Rose, in terms of a spectator's apparel...(!)

ENDURE THE END OF CASTOR AND POLLUX: BETRAYED TO A PONIARD[!]: (165)
In any event, Phosphorous Cool staggered from pillar-to-post in a reluctant fit of strength, and at a time where St. Paul's loomed in the background. Surely, one can see Wren's dome limned against a bright yellow sky – namely, one that illuminated one of those grand city buildings set up roundabout. True enough, the mausoleums of these city banks struck us as real; while Phosphorous clutched at a wall *avec* trembling white fingers.

Such silvery ducts as these stroked some chalk, even though the masonry had more to do with classical bias than anything else. Its brickwork became chipped by kindred mortals *et al* – save alone for the grief of one alleyway too far.

+

Related passions come to radiate sulphur, though, in a playlet where a boot levels off against a cripple's back. It gives a rejoinder by means of some faint praise... i.e.: one which condescends to spin its own tail, insufferably so. For – rather like one of Edward Muybridge's moving photographs – this sequence depresses a spinning diatribe o' wheels. Do you reckon on it? Most definitely, such a doleful ardour moved its sparkling tracks forward – and each link in this daisy-chain chose to dun its mixture. Against a dulcet grey drop, then, some transparent concrete planed itself off against granite. It spun the embrasure of distant watercolours – if only to sweep across this particular wash. Nor can such a cripple stop himself screaming when the blow comes. The boot of either Phosphorous Cool or Heathcote Dervish follows through on its own aftermath (now); at least as regards a livery of electrocuted hair!

BOVINE, BOVINE: WE MEASURE THE UDDERS AFORE SLAUGHTER[!]: (166)

Meanwhile, another scenario sought to die before an edifice of wish-bones; and these were liable to creep back into so many funk-holes. Granted: the spirit of Elsa Bounteous' husband approached her like a flat-nosed lynx betwixt so many liars. Above all else, her husband's triangular head hoved into view, and it hovered as a magisterial tripod next to some flickering candles. Elsa Bounteous Hapgood – for her part – looked rather despondent and downcast... with a suppressed mien afflicting her lips. These were cast floorwards in an attendant slope – namely, one which curled up around the dolefulness of its pout. In these tram-lines, therefore, her face headed south towards its nethermost pole: what with upturned nostrils and eyes that came half-closed above. Likewise now, the tattoo between her eye-brows seemed locked in its own gammadion or swastika. Also, her blonde mop of hair was all shot to pieces – it essentially cascaded to left and right, with metallic impediments adorning its tresses. These items of subliminal jewellery proved to be like spokes, spikes and tendrils of spume! Heathcote Dervish's spectre broke the quietness by speaking first. "Ho! Wife, why so silent a look before Portia's uplift? Isn't she – when I come to think of it – the wife of Brutus in Shakespeare's *Julius Caesar*? Wasn't she also proud and doughty Cato's daughter?" Silence ensued on this waste of warfare, thereafter. So – in lieu of nothing in particular – Heathcote Dervish tries again. "I beseech you, why has a frosty stillness crept into your habits of late? I sense a cool nimbus radiating from you, in a manner which recalls Anna Kavan's novel *Ice*." Still no reply found itself recorded before these griefs.

PANDEMONIUM AT THE ORGAN INDICATES A CAPRICE: (167)

Meanwhile, up on our puppet stage in north Wales the following tableaux has played itself out. It occurs on a template where Phosphorous Cool jigs about amid piles of smoking masonry; and these exist levied on either side of various redoubts; namely, one, two, three, four and five. Moreover, smoke also swirled up from broken mens' bones --- it knew no limits of percussion... necessarily so. A lone Rolls Royce or silver cloud – possibly of a light green colour – stood to one side of this imaginary aisle without a border. Yet Phosphorous closed on his absence and he thereby moved to indicate a new frequency – but he dimly perceived that a revenge against Mastodon Helix loomed closer.
+
Simultaneously, we find a cripple thrust forward in his disabling chair; i.e., one which leaves a token of respect behind it even as it careers. A cry is heard on a white satin o' sulphur; namely, one that negotiates a Herculean rejoinder to a plummeting stone. Furthermore, under any impelled blow the toy-swing slips and loses sideways momentum, only to slide and shift. Its emptiness

153

then becomes a travesty to forgiveness or unforgiveness... and any backing swims before the aft, even if one para-olympics cannot vouchsafe its response.

MASTODONS FROM THE DEEP ACCENTUATE HELIXES: (168)

Now and again, a sacred claw moves closer to a blonde tress, and it indicates nothing save a partial witness... not just with lustre, but also over the prospect of rolled gold. A spectral hook (to speak of) almost alights on his wife's hair, but then it turns around in order to scratch a gaping nostril. Were not these the openings for a new enclosure – one which forsakes all answers, whether steely or determined? It deliberately sets itself afire – if only to start complacency running with a few candles between them. These are small, cylindrical, tapering and white – each one flaring so as to accommodate its own answer. For her performance, Elsa Bounteous turned to look at her husband in profile, her hair (jewellery aside) proving to be turned down... and it smoked to no tricks. Listen to this now...: "I fear that I cannot adumbrate the nature of my disregard", cautioned Elsa Bounteous Hapgood. "Possibly I may share the fate of your other lamentable wives, if I go public on this. Like one of the heroines in a von Stroheim movie, I might be too young for decadence before my prime." "I told you", snorted her spouse, "I had nothing to do with their very tragic and unfortunate depths. Their violent deaths grieved me – I have to tell you. A situation which harkened back (for us all) to the desperation of so many renewed states. It didn't even reveal the mayhem of Bartok's *Bluebeard's Castle*... irrespective of those secret chambers containing his wives' heads." "I remember Charles Perrault's fairy tale as if it was yesterday", she answered.

HARPOON A JESTER'S FOLLY[!]: (169)

So Phosphorous Cool looks up with a despairing glee; and his calm --- if placid --- features are transfixed by a passionate concern. Cannot a passing brave or missionary characterise it as a fanatic's pursuit of purity… almost after an exercise in religious iconography *a la* a host of Renaissance artists? These were Botticelli, Mantegna, Fra Angelico, Titian, Tintoretto, Cimabue, Giotto and many another one. Yes sir: Phosphorous Cool's brow indicated an unction that was rarely seen – save in the idealistic representations of Leni Riefenstahl's transports, for instance. It basically instills in one what the religious mystic would call an instrument of yearning; a Nietzschean phrase used by Arab police services in the Middle East. Needless to say, his eyes hold in their sockets (without pupils) the prospect of every future development – save only one which portends to a captured nerve, let alone dishonour. Our division of joy stretches out towards a new galaxy – never mind anything else, even a blue Monday. To be sure: any new order of Aryandom has to be based on a progressive instrument or iterisation… it will have to face off against nothing other than the nobility of loss. Do you see it? Surely one recognises now – in terms of Time's apparel – that the limitations of skywards movement can only occur on steps of yellow flame?"

FORGIVE THEM, LORD, FOR THEY KNOW NOT WHAT THEY DO[!]: (170)
Listen carefully now, my children… since Elsa Bounteous Hapgood felt moved enough to come up with her grievances. It took the form of a limitation upon speech – despite the fact which sees an amber wife tilted away from one reclining hand. It essentially went near to stroking her mitten, but missed and had to settle for the guardian's zone instead. Does one comprehend it? Also, her look waxed to a terror in the eyes one was reluctant to see… Yes truly, these adventures into oneself can always comfort such misgivings. These – irrefragably – were Fate's repercussions. All that her husband, Heathcote Dervish, might ejaculate proved to be the following: "My dearest one, is aught amiss? A problem with one of our three off-spring perhaps… or something to do with one's great uncle, Hermaphrodite X or Tumble-weed?"

+

To whit: the wheels of a disabled chariot tip up in a sibilation of Blue – neither of which can then escape from the Newtonian device of perpetual motion. It freezes over any promontory that faces us amidships… necessarily so. Likewise, the punishment for such transgressions has to be a fall from the stars (*viz* Icarus). Yet again, each offering knows its sense of placement, when one causes this chair to hurtle through darkness towards a transparent floor. None may occlude its ebon tint or exclusion now!

A METAL SPINNING-TOP JETTISONS IMMOBILITY: (171)
When we come to consider it, our future pathway is delicately mapped. It must have to do with Mastodon Helix's desire to smash a wall to pieces, brick by brick, and this was primarily by hurling a great fist in its direction. It struck like a pile-driver, throwing masonry from side-to-side… and spraying cement shards after a swarm of locusts. This much happens to be clear… yet, amidst an evident majesty of commotion, Phosphorous Cool draws near. Especially when we consider that the wires which hang over the stage were the gossamer of forgotten dreams; they linked to one haphazard account over time… the texture of this making a bee-line for so many extremities. All of it occurred in a smart puppet house in Colwyn Bay. Again and all, Mastodon glances upwards now in order to spy his veriest jigging fiend. It certainly has nought to do with a puppeteer's sound – let alone a salvo of unquiet graves. These relate to the fact that Mastodon stands, hands on hips, looking up at a silvery one on a northern compass. "So, miscreant of our finest hours, you've come crawling out of a fox-hole, eh? How can you bare to stand up with those trestles lying above you – each one connected to a thousand wires and attendant pulleys. Listen up, fish-face: my witness to you is a circle of destruction! Might it shadow its kindling to a tainted source; wherein a range of half-heads and mandibles, blown apart, are held in a cyborg's hand? Oh my yes… come on down to my level, silvery one, even if it cuts up a somnolent disrespect. I shall await your evisceration (now) and

thrust you into the flames of a new Kolyma --- to be sure. Come in and die, little one! Lucifer makes work for idle hands, boy, and my novelist's career has to begin with my first capital letter. Look you to it... I have spied on yonder victim, primarily so as to pulverise thou without grief! Heed me!"

DEATH'S-HEAD MEETS MEAT HEAD: (172)
Finally, we can see that Elsa Bounteous Hapgood had squeezed her hands together... and screwed up her features, withal. All of which was done in order to provide a scintilla of dutch courage... so as to face her husband's ire. During this process, the woman's blonde coif hesitated at its own rainbow, and it also led her to blurt out: "I want a divorce!" Tears were actually rolling down both cheeks as she said it... as well. Now then, Heathcote Dervish reacted with scorn, alarm and as if he'd been stung. Furthermore – in the teeth of this display – we gain a close-up on Heathcote's features. They are slightly helpless, diseased yet undiseased, fissiparous, uncongealing and fraying at the edges. All of it occurring in a conundrum where a brillo pad turns up at the corners... and becomes spotted with brown dots. Each of these crepitations teases out the ropes of a new enclosure – primarily so as to enliven such blood-shot eye-balls within a decrepit frame. Again and again, though, we come face to face with a visage that's characterised by the following words: fey, stray, hey(!), pay, may, can't relieve that day and Quasimodo's red-letter display. Don't you recall Lon Chaney's depiction of him in a silent film during nineteen twenty-four?
+
In a parallel dimension to parallelism's locution, (sic), the following has to have its sway. Do we need to cultivate a rhapsody towards Paul de Mann's indeterminacy – the latter contained in a text like *Blindness and Insight*? To which one is tempted to say – in post-structuralist vein – whose blindness and whomsoever's insight? Nonetheless, an endwarfment had taken place; whereby a figure lies at the basement of a hooked cross. It embodies less a Christian sigil... and more an Indo-Aryan

symbol. These beams criss-cross the corse when viewed from above: and its light-space is limited to the bare concrete lying beneath 'it'. Every item of this *Pieta* seems determined to play its part in such a threnody; i.e., a dramaturgy that was devoted to various reliefs from le Corbusier. Hadn't it all been occasioned by kicking a cripple down-stairs in his wheel-chair?

TWO CYBORGS MEASURE UP BEFORE A WOMAN IN GREEN LYCRA: (173)

Suddenly a piece of wall comes hurtling at Phosphorous Cool's head; and it reflects the efforts of unspecified mountebanks. These messages of hate must pass on from an understanding of murals, even in terms of Diego Rivera's wall-painting tradition. (A necessary counter-point, this, to Gabriel Garcia Marquez's logorrhoea in *The Autumn of the Patriarch*). Yes... since the masonry speeds upon him out of all premiums: and it virtually shatters the glimmering of a silvern puppet. It dances and spins, of course, after the fashion of any marionette enjoying a garrotte. Thanks very much... Yet by jigging to the side in an adroit manoeuvre, aided and abetted by strings, Phosphorous Cool avoids these hurtling bricks. They – and their attendant brick-dust – shift by at a fast rate of knots. Momentarily, it appears to be a house on the move – after an effect created by William Hope Hodgson in his *House on the Borderland*. Again, when witnessing a violent calm, Phosphorous comes to realise the closeness of such javelins. Each one essentially passes by virtue of a millimetre in either chest; nor can the hurt occasioned by Carl Andre's bricks intrigue any change here. It definitely looped the loop and turned back, if only to hurl David's sling-shot in Goliath's way. Look you: Phosphorous – at the behest of his invisible puppet-master – zooms down towards such boards. A structure of balsa parchments (these were) the likelihood of which backed away from a midget's theatre. Anyway, no Euripides of the minor stair proved available, so Phosphorous Cool dives down to the final act. A curtain, then, goes up on Restorationist drama in order to indicate Montague Summers' staging. The playwrights in question happened to be Rochester, Shadwell, Congreve, Wycherley, Aphra Behn & so forth. "Let the final drama begin", mutters Phos(.) Cool, "in an aeon like this fighting waxes immortal. It overshadows the grief of Achilles over Patrochlus in his tent. No sir – what avails us now has to be the strongest vision possible of one man's going too far. It occasions a knock-about with one's fists before the greatest care, and it likewise strikes down those craving the knife. Dysgenics rules (in other words); it carries no other valency. In the whole of the world let's prepare for some *English Martial Arts* by Terry Brown. May the fire-fight commence…"

TRUTH IS A KNIFE PASSING THROUGH MEAT: (174)
Heathcote Dervish lay alone in one of Peter Cushing's sepulchral chambers; the former having much to do with the English atmosphere of a Hammer House of Horror. Yes indeed… for within its confines Frankenstein's monster (or the new Prometheus) lies abed – together with a clutch of also-rans who gathered around like vultures. During this moment, the impish nurse – replete with a hunch-back – brings up a holding chair. Does it signify --- even in memory --- the fate of the wheel-chair user with whom we've been dealing? Herein, our character or freak-show *artiste* had plunged to the bottom of an abyss… and inside this a lone hand reached up into an upright posture. It (the MS sufferer) felt beholden to the reality of a splotched and blood-flecked sponge. These events, in turn, sprawled adrift of le Corbusier's concrete panels. Our mystery play also had something to do with an exercise in misprisionment, whereby a swirl of imagined paint susurrates from below. It travels via the conspectus of Michaux's art – without really suggesting anything substantial. A violent impasto of such paint likewise hints at de Kooning's work, if little else. Above this fetish swirl two spiritual essences in blue mist. Could they incarnate the principle of a good and bad guardian angel? Yet – most evidently – one shape on the right suggested a half-naked Edwardian gentleman. Whereas – on the left of our plate – a daemon appeared in its

vortex; at once horned, beast-like, unsacrificial and reminiscent of one of Aickman's wraiths. Didn't the London poet Iain Sinclair once call it *Suicide Bridge*?

A NOBLE AFFIDAVIT OUTWITS A PURPLE HEART: (175)

Battle has well and truly been joined (now) between Phosphorous Cool and Mastodon Helix on a puppet's stage. Surely, this happens to be a scenario where any puppet-board theatre, such as Eric Bramall's, must face demolition under these weighty blows? To surrender to them remains the thing... Whereas Phosphorous drops directly like a gymnast or wrestler into Mastodon Helix's mind. Or – more pertinently – does he fly like a speeding dart or arrow right into the heart of its trajectory, thereby? Our phosphorescent one merely slows down now in order to navigate one plot too many (*per se*), and once there he glows like a sword quivering at a dart-board's centre. He squirms beyond recourse to available duty; and all of this subsists in a way which causes Mastodon to reach up by flexing his enormous muscles. A manoeuvre that's calculated (quite evidently) to hurl his assailant from him with all speed. In all of this violent shambles, Mastodon Helix and Phosphorous Cool represent those wrestlers from the nineteen seventies like Big-daddy and Giant Hay-stacks. Does anyone remember Dickie Davis with affection? To be sure: our protagonists are now given over to pawing, mewing, shifting, gouging, slanting-in and otherwise man-handling. Each and everyone has their favourite holds or grappling-irons of grief. These were occasioned by an advent where Mastodon Helix gave notice of a throw; a feature which leads one to wonder what else might be going on. Yesterday now, such an adventure might have announced a new triggering, but (withal) it seems to confer dangerous possibilities which involve being thrown overhead or crushed like an egg-shell! Why don't you desist from this, do you hear? For the suppleness of Phosphorous Cool's body indicates that he stands ready to react to any such spearing. Moreover, the knowing observer recognises a sporting contest once considered to be Ambrosia –

or the food of the Gods. It definitely fed off the reality which says that naked, oiled, sun-swept or tanned – and inevitably adrift of the Aegean's golden & settling light – we understand the enthusiasm of such 'gods'… wrestling… for what it was.

DOCTOR FRANKENSTEIN LEADS NONE TO VICTORY SAVE SEWARD'S DWARVES[!]: (176)
Do the Shah of Iran's Invincibles or the Waffen SS hold the keys to this kingdom (?); itself a moot point given the spectre of a nemesis who's dressed all in black. But to differentiate ourselves from a long-standing debate over L.S. Lowry's cripples – let's consider the environment in Professor von Frankenstein's laboratory. It occurs in a playlet where Frankenstein's monster lies adrift of all consciousness – what with electronic ear-plugs over both ears and wires superintending above. His face limbers up to a flatness irrespective of its regard… the chin of which jutted out abruptly and under various temples. To the side of his animated corse lurked Baron von Frankenstein – or possibly it's Moustachio Brave Herring in another incarnation. Look you! For he crept on our reanimated cadaver armed with a malignant syringe. Doesn't he play games with a conspectus of Doctor Jack Kevorkian at this moment? Furthermore, various items of an electrical agency travel around this lodge. What do we have here (?); why, it's merely nothing more than cables, binary switches and certain items that go back to Babbage care of Burroughs' computing… not to mention a fluted or electronic conch. To one side of this foreplay, and right on the button, we notice Butler James in full military livery. He's positioned with flashy Victorian epaulettes, a sabretache and a handle-bar moustache. Indeed, each end of this walrus peeks out from beyond his cranium. It masters itself thereby; and it chooses to recognise an example set by Lords Cardigan and Lucan. Further back from such a medical pallet – and on the other side of our energised man-thing – stands Elsa Bounteous Hapgood. Or – at the very least – this figurine has to count the cost of being her simulacrum or *alter ego*. By way of dress, perchance, she had on a nineteenth

century bodice --- naked to the waist --- as well as stirrups, jodhpurs, sparkling ear-rings and the accoutrements of Fanny Hill's underwear. Surely, she melodramatically indicates the turn-over of a music hall *artiste* or vamp? No such estrangement from 'Self' can otherwise be permitted…

WE RETURN TO THE HIMALAYAS OF A NEW WITNESS: (177)

Look at this, my crowds, and roll up to feast your eyes on a puppet fair most brutal! *Avaunt thee*, two strongmen – one more lithe and subtle than the other – wrestle together on a parchment now. It definitely goes to show that nothing hinders glory save its own execution. Formally though, our two titans clash in a ready tournament of battle. For – surrounded by boulders, rocks and the hulks of abandoned buildings – what do we find? Why, an amazing or astounding complex results… whereby Phosphorous Cool somersaults gymnastically over Mastodon Helix. He then locks his silvern or shinty legs around his assailant's head, in a double head-lock, from which he will have great trouble in extricating himself. Momentarily speaking, Mastodon is then caught off-guard in a bout or rumour monger; wherein Phosphorous turns the tables on him and causes his foe to plummet into the ground. Spear-tackled in this way – Mastodon Helix was momentarily stunned… and the strength in his limbs became flaccid or watery. Do you assess correctly what our manikin has achieved? Because by twisting like an eel over Mastodon's bulk – he frees himself from a terrific grip, only to pulverise the other's head upon forcing it into the ground. A semblance of ready dust particles rise up at this juncture. It also goes to show that no-one's necessarily afraid of Virginia Woolf. On the impact of Mastodon Helix's big-top with the earth, an onomatopoeic 'THOOM!' was heard. Does the latter have the stomach to come back or renew the fray?

ARMAGEDDON'S VILLAGE WEARS RED HAIR: (178)

Elsa Bounteous Hapgood became the first to break a laboratory's silence. "Once reanimated and in a new physiology", she seemed to be saying, "we knew that you would attempt to double-cross our potentiality of sorts." (During this disquisition, the bogle of Heathcote Dervish in Frankenstein monster's body, could only think the following…: "I began cavorting with multiple corses, charnel house derived, so that my spirit might have a resting place in this bay of leaves. Let's regard it by virtue of a sacred flame… since my hidden journey, via the example of Samuel Beckett's *Molloy* or *Malone Dies*, has led me to this pretty pass. Yet maybe not everything is as it seems from the outside of such a pericarp or rind?") Whereupon – in his mind's eye – Heathcote dwelt instantaneously on the following vista. A diseased theatre must know its own advent, and there happens to be a strange feature of limitation here. It also has occasion to do a walk on the wild side under an electric eel. "I'm dressed in black, together with a white collar and cuffs, and I traverse the concrete corridors of a forgotten enclosure. It denotes an NCP car-park crossed with le Corbusier – even when it's suggested in jest." Likewise, his features masquerade under the shadow of one tremulous gesture. "Physician heal thyself; do I not hear its quatrain? Above me, though, the canopy of a blue spirit-level rises in mist, and it harks back to old silhouetted days of yore. May – after the fashion of Jung – these moral trampolines exhaust themselves on a bed-of-nails? Let it depart quietly, my friend, now we find a tocsin sounding out the quarters – albeit with the bells' campanology muffled by felt." Still and all, Heathcote Dervish – in his distant recollection – wandered around an ouroborous' circuit… the latter entwined on those circumstances which lifted everything above it like an electric eel. When all he wanted to do was dwell on a necessary contagion called madness…

MASTODON HELIX VERSUS PHOSPHOROUS COOL: W.W.F.; HEAD-TO-HEAD: (179)

Phosphorous Cool has now succeeded in leaping on Mastodon Helix's head – all of it occurring in a tournament or wrestling bout... where one masters the other over ten or twelve rounds. A few sorry rocks lie in parallel around their feet, even if Helix's misshapen toes do not have it about them to gain a claim on porous sandstone. Viewed from another angle, though, Mastodon Helix's features are hit savagely and repeatedly from in front... they begin to wilt (then) under the onslaught of these thunderous slaps. Mastodon's visage, *ceteris paribus*, knows its own gateway and detracts from it... seemingly forever. Yet further, the molecular embrasure around each eye-slit becomes noticeable: and it resultantly puffs up in a scaly, amphibian, porous or handicapped way. Might it go very far down the track in illustrating a species of white leprosy, or quite possibly, those bags around the casements that interr some strange dermatology? Likewise, in and around this demand for lift off, we come across the lightning-marks of such a fusion. These streak away towards the halo of a new sunrise or forgetting...

+

Nonchalantly – by all accounts – another conflict is occasioned by the inner mind of our combatants. Whereupon one prairie fire looms upon a distrait retina. Yessss... For here I find a trail of brandy-wine under my feet --- its splendours turn out to be red and are not looked down upon as regards haemoglobin. You take leave of your senses if you attempt to fashion a future from flood-gates; and these often open up a forest to new beginnings. Still and all, one's organs petrify before a sand-storm; i.e., an event which was whipped up and spills aslant of any attendant fogs. Listen to such a dance, why don't you? In a carry-on where Phosphorous Cool comes face-to-face with Mastodon Helix... But now the latter has been transformed into a gigantic reptile; thereby lapsing into the brain's third quadrant. (If one chooses to quantify such researches into a saurian stem – namely, one that lies at the base of consciousness. To be sure: Eysenck or Koestler

164

may be right or wrong over such difficulties). Furthermore, a Darwinian like this breathes in its own enclosure, and it disacknowledges those scales which seep from its crust. These take the form of a rubbery hide. Cellular these were; or definitely liable to build up into a cold-blooded edifice. --- A Scandinavian offerant that was linked to no time at all...*viz*.: it effectively came fixed to a dark spectrum around its mouth. (A reptilian version of the surrealist magazine *Minotaur*, this, it fed on serrated teeth). Will we ever know more regarding insouciance's medley(?); given its red, avid and staring eyes. They possess a darting quality all their own; at once blind, staring, strangely refulgent and yet condensed. Who can operate on such reptile-house disclosures?

METAMORPHOSIS; DOCTOR FRANKENSTEIN'S MONSTER LETS RIP: (180)
"I congratulate you on a beginner's nuisance value", assented Heathcote Dervish from his position on a medicinal slab. After all, Heathcote D. has decided to opt for a new physiology; and it is drawn from multiple cadavers... Why so? It was basically because his family and blonde wife, Elsa Bounteous Hapgood, worried about his corporeal future. Could he really survive as a spirit? Yet again, my friends, fate had a way of acting on men's affairs like the movement of chess pieces on an Icelandic board. It's not bad for tyros and upstarts, eh? But Baron von Frankenstein, his hunch-backed nurse Ms. Igor, Butler James and another Elsa Bounteous... they'd all forgotten this surgery's object. Over-confidence, in such circumstances, can prove inefficacious over purgatory's results... most especially. It happened to be that our caged waif sought manumission. Surely, his detractors must focus in on a mage without compare?

SHOOT A CYBORG IN THE FOOT WITH A CROSS-BOW: (181)
Phosphorous Cool then brought his palms up in order to slap Mastodon's face; and a terrific clap or wallop is thereby

administered. In this instance, Mastodon Helix's head hurtles backwards with a snarl – if only to border on near insanity. Paradoxically, Helix seems to stultify and weaken under this onslaught – whereupon our silvern one goes from strength to strength. Or alternately, he incarnates a forgotten spirit of yesteryear… one that's embodied by those pearly Kings and Queens from the east end. Further – and amidst a blaze of blue – Phosphorous Cool grasps this hulk in a vice-like grip. --- A three minute bout or cage fight (*per se*) in which his adversary goes down under magnesium oxide... He wilts over cosmic radiation drawn up to this particular. Whereas his frame – even when demarcated from a puppeteer's strings – slumps down to a music hall's boards. For Mastodon Helix's irretrievably broken now!
+

Likewise, in a tunnel of cerulean or agate, Phosphorous Cool tilted against a lurking reptile. It all caused one stanchion to break down, limit its toxicity and fold-over (thereby). Such a development also occurs in front of an abstract paw – namely, one that's outstretched after a Pre-Raphaelite painting of St. George and the Dragon. This recoiled suddenly o'er a sound temperature: in a situation where a limb pulsated with its execution… even on granite. Pebbles were then always shovelled up to the side, and they often made up the numbers over nacreous discharges --- at least as pertained to a thrown-out or put upon limb. To re-adapt Karl Marx: saurians of the world unite; you have nothing to lose save a pterodactyl's mirror! Why don't you climb over a picket fence, in order to see Gabriel Rossetti's portrait of St. George and his dragon? Because its head has been definitely severed at the tooth (that's why).

FEAST ON A SCARLET ARM TRAVERSING SAPPHIRE'S SPACE: (182)
Behold! Just like a Masonic prayer-board, our Frankenstein's monster bursts from his bonded garlands. All in a trice (therefore) he raises himself from the dais – irrespective of any compass signals to the south, west, north and east. These

surround a wooden casket of the most violent red… on which has been burnt a skull and its attendant cross-bones. The lettering on these meditation squares has faded, basically due to the influence of ultra-violet light. Nonetheless, our Boris Karloff in another medium jerks up from the deck – thence causing his bonds to shrink away from him with so much aplomb. They shrivel and die like electrocuted bounds of leather… no matter what. Especially since this particular Big Daddy is home free of all electrons; nor does he take any chances in relation to convulsed iron. Immediately – and upon receipt of such power – his head becomes encircled within a cyclopean glow, and it filters everything out of an orgone lustre. (In this regard, then, his entire corse comes to be enraptured by an etheric pulsar or quiver). During the course of which, his fists knot and his eyes & mouth become flushed with anger – despite any other perversity. Electrons whizz about and cash in on a sundry brouhaha! Whereupon both Baron von Frankenstein and Butler James are knocked for six. Like a selection of west country skittles left in a row – they are mowed down by one ball travelling at speed. Don't you reckon on it? Because Heathcote Dervish's fists – like in a Sarban short story – smash into his nearest tormentors. Moreover – in a manner somewhat reminiscent of puppets or manikins – Doctor Frankenstein and his erstwhile servant are thrown away. It inevitably recalls a moment in Gerry Anderson's real life drama, *The Protectors*. To which the spirit trapped within the new Prometheus' body adds: "I AM THE MASTER HERE!"

RING-A-RING-A-ROSES, ALL FALL DOWN: (183)
Phosphorous Cool and Mastodon Helix are still wrestling with each other… even though Mastodon is clearly wilting in a beetle-like mania. (Remember: Franz Kafka's short story *The Metamorphosis* was written in German as early as 1915). Irrespective of it, lines of cosmic force radiate out from Mastodon's head – in alignment with the grip that Phosphorous has on his features. These necessarily congeal under the issue of

such a rise – nor can one illustration really offer its tommy-gun throughout. All of a sudden one cuts to another image; a scenario where two hands of polished pewter grasp a mainspring. Each silvery palm stretches upwards around a tonsured cranium (now) – one that's enlivened with either fury or hate. Alive; alive-o, during the consequences of this, various sparks of metal flew off a deluded scalp --- and slowly --- oh so slowly --- Mastodon Helix's eyes begin to close. They are heavy and somnolent with the dew of unforgiveness. Now then... the jaw-line cracks and falls aslant, if only to witness a croupier raking in the chips... prior to a new insanity. Avaunt thee!
+

In a new world of unbelief, though, a silver bullet detracts from its target. Can it be living on in accordance with such a surcease? Whereupon a gauntleted hand grasps a spear – in pursuit of lightning's quandary or one jagged edge. It breaks out into barbed patterns of spray behind-hand (thereafter). Yet again, a saurian out-rider travels down this circumference, and it's one which glances a blow from a speculative glove. It --- the forked lightning --- also passes along against a dulcet trembling of fives... namely, a barbarism that continuously favours the criss-crossed lattice of a blue screen. Like a ludo board or some form of cribbage, it inundates the half... even though we find ourselves in a vortex or gust: where a mastodon clings to its dinosaur's course. Does it really mount this passageway safe in the knowledge that warm-bloodedness is the last needful thing? Such an assemblage won't pursue Godzilla to its grave. No way: when a shape with exposed limbs wanders or shambles about – only to reconnoitre the dreams of dwarves. Look you... shall a red eye reflect like a Belisha beacon in the dusk?

NO DIATRIBE AGAINST APPROXIMATE ZEROES SUFFICES: (184)

"I will show you the future in a handful of dust". --- T.S. Eliot, *The Wasteland*

Does one care. Given that our imp of the reverse screams like a good'un. Have we not made use of a title by Edgar Allan Poe in the nineteenth century, here? Especially when we consider that the nurse about whom we are speaking wears a starched apron and cap. These happen to be the accoutrements of Igor's feminine regard --- much after the example set by Terence Fisher in a Hammer House of Horror. Examine this... her face remains open to a sleeping grave, and this occurs at a time when a series of liquid dials brooks no reprieve. They adumbrate an old-fashioned radio study... or possibly a modern car's internal design. Don't we forget how she incarnates the principle of Elsa Bounteous Hapgood(?) ... a woman whose spirituality exists on several different planes at once. "We face an enormous power-source; yielding to nonesuch above us. Observe these Babbage pre-computers --- my masters: and must they communicate anything other than a dancing demon who's minus its electronic nimbus?" These were exact words which soared above the available *terra firma*. (Irrespective of any enabling light, you wouldn't even know of the girl's disfigurement. A factor found to be reminiscent of the nurse on the Odessa steps in *Battleship Potemkin*, that is. On many occasions Francis Bacon, the painter, tried to capture this as exemplifying the modern cry).

FASTER THAN A SPEEDING BULLET: (185)
Meanwhile, Mastodon Helix lay sprawled upon the ground, and was otherwise over-ridden by a mantle of fire. This proves to one and all the burden of such an affidavit. Certainly, the hulking orange mutant's fallen into a state of sleep; i.e., one which enables him to dream of unhatched dragons hitherto unknown. It is no longer berserk. No mediaeval bestiary, in short, could be said to have catalogued their name. Against this, Phosphorous Cool staggers back slightly and passes a silver-foil hand across his forehead. Clearly, this cage fight without walls --- levelled against Mastodon Helix --- had exhausted him. While, in the background, behind his trailing wires a mural rises up, and it happens to be slab-sided. A series of arranged bricks serve as

cornice blocks on either end or throughout. The sky remains a dark ultramarine during this tableau, however. Let's listen to what our gleaming puppet has to say about it all: "He shall sleep the long night under opium's agency or rest. Like a babe or stripling it will be his/its semblance of slumber. Granted these divine hours: many grains of sand are chosen to pass through the funnel of a timer, there to fete a Sahara's loss. Do you reckon on it?"

+

Our reptilian nether entity cascades aplenty; and he continues on amid such corridors as these (regardless). Above all else, this erect saurian approaches in the dust... in order to set free a rectangle of blue. He or 'it' moves along in somnolent darkness, abreast of a stillness that is occasioned by red eyes. Look at this now: the lower part of its anatomy lies in shadow; or it speculates about the patchwork quilt of such a leathery hide. This --- again --- manoeuvres so as to crystallise a draining of the deep end, and it signifies one intrusion too far into the reptile house. Has anyone ever read Angus Wilson's novel, *The Old Men at the Zoo*? Similarly, an orange to brown hue temporises its scales --- whilst it's busy receiving the livery of crocodiles as yet unborn. It likewise transfigures an early Renaissance map of the world – a panorama which dyes its own skin in order to limit its rawhide. Only one thing can obviously save it – and this must involve the opening of an eye. It spectres to crimson against a loss of identity – what with those oval shields that have an amphibian's impress laid across them. Given such a future, this eye blinks amidst leather --- at once scarlet to its core --- and comes over all mulcted, unblinking, shiny or laminated, et cetera. It possesses, again and again, a pupil or inner iris of a stretched black pointillism. Who belabours the serpent folk's cruelty now then, eh?

A DIRIGIBLE RELEASES ITS ELECTROSTATIC CARGO OF LEAVES: (186)
"Those who dwell in Hell are not dead!" – the Tallis scholars

170

Above Baron von Frankenstein's mortuary – and witnessing the heavy artillery of so much lightning – an advertising balloon hovers in the celestial aftermath. It glows with the spectacular core of its messages (abundantly so). Could it be piloted up above by a distinct variant on Warlock Splendour Thomas? Never mind… for like a First World War airship, it traverses the green air beyond our template. But the point here is that a massive surge of power flashes down to an aerial on the building's roof. This fluted stack delimits a grief pole, if only to soar astride the sort of appurtenance which features in an old episode of *Doctor Who*. Can any present recapture the BBC serial – albeit mesmerically? Nevertheless, Frankenstein's slate roof encoded many turrets and flowering rifles, and these then apportioned blame between planes… at least in relation to gabled windows. Such sheets of glass are brilliantly illumined and they trespass on yellow against the dark. No-one fears this resolution again, you see, because our impish dwarf correctly calls this particular shout. It electronically shimmers down from the heavens, and thereby animates the rictus of Frankenstein's dead hero. Surely everyone can configure, contrary to Mary Shelley's statement in *The Last Man*, that galvanic action animates a corse? It runs contrary to Vesalius and Galen, after all --- but aren't these supposed to be 'enlightened' times? (A *soi-disant* enlightenment, one might say…) But it's also licit to point out whether Phosphorous was used on the ground, in parks and elsewhere, to confuse Zeppelins in the air during WWI.

ARIES RETURNS TO HIS FLOCK CARRYING A RAM: (187)
Look at this measure of fortune and listen to this… for such a compost manages to combine hope and despair all in one go. First of all, Phosphorous Cool has succeeded in hauling Mastodon Helix over his shoulder – and, rather like an ancient Greek sculpture, one man carries a sacrificial bull across his back-line. Behind both of them lies a wilderness of strings, and all of it adds up to a trestle which is held in a puppet-master's

hand. Could it really be the Welsh wizard known as Eric Bramall – especially when one considers the backdrop to one of his vistas? It comes rather painted with the transparency of a million forethoughts… in a situation where the tinsel of London town, as evinced by its paste-board, twinkles below. Some fires are also seen to be burning over various city blocks… and to westwards points of this. Yes again, the kaleidoscope of a Gotham in darkness lights up below, and it conjoins the mixture of certain elements that refuse to die… such as the blinking of unknown eyes, towers, armatures and signals. Can these be habitations for those damned by Fate? A magenta-to-blue sky supervenes over everything else.

+

Now then, one rise in this rictus has to be a lizard which blossoms into a stone, or who continues to face down such qualities with a startled eye. A creature that inevitably looks to open up the nature of an obelisk or its tower, even though such a structure corrodes its witness. It can only really be described as immense; given its penchant to rise majestically like an old-fashioned chimney. It proved to be darksome against the lineament of a red sun; itself a glowing favourite which suffuses the sky with the peace of haemoglobin. As a proposition, it moves out from its retinal filter – only to encompass a watery web: when illumined by such rubiate clusters. These arrow in upon magnificence; and at once become a tracery for small fractures of chess-board. Or might it refer to squares, in relation to whose temperature one loner appears? You see – on a sulphurous template, riven by rectangles, he holds aloft a spear or the lance of St. George!

WHET THE BLADE OF THOSE WHO SCREAM AT BAY: (188)

Harken to what I utter! For a growing Frankenstein's monster has been energised by such a release; and he now springs from the dais with his arms pumping, and even his head held up high. An electrostatic cackle continues to discharge its static around his cranium; while his bloated blue-skin finds its husk extended by a thousand lines. Yes…, our deliberate framing of this embargo denotes silent cinema – particularly over James Whale's *Frankenstein* talkie in 1931. Likewise, the inner animation of Heathcote Dervish waxes as free as a day; whereupon the energisation of Frankenstein's monster comes to resemble a Clive Barker foray. All of this occurs in a tragedy where he grabs hold of Baron von Frankenstein, and nimbly throttles him to death… (---) During a period characterised by his life draining away without a gurgle – even though salient retorts, on the other hand, burst under its leftwards drift. Above all else, though, a convulsive hoard of black electrons gathers around his skull, and it mantles to a radioactive oscilloscope… especially when bereft of stroboscopic lights. Whereas Boris Karloff's physique came across as darkened, replete, untroubled, phlegmatic, self-distanced and unsparing. It doubtless deliberated on a solitude capable of mastering its nature.

CRY HAVOC; A BLESSED BONE SEEKS MARROW: (189)
Suddenly, Phosphorous Cool and Mastodon Helix are seen from afar… as they approach Stonehenge's outer limits, or one of those shell-like dwellings where covens' meet. The exterior battlements stray forth like dinosaur's teeth – albeit in a way which lets in the light from a distance under a baleful moon. An orb (this is) that cloaks its character in the mantle of some cloud – themselves amounting to a darkened orange on purple. It swirls like a kaleidoscope; or a vortex in one of Wyndham Lewis' paintings. It's a matter of lines and longitudinal breast-plates (now)… all of them stripped and in black ink. Similarly, this movement fades to an ochre – by virtue of its dimensional relief. Below – and amid these crenellations – Heathcote Dervish gazes on askance. His head (when seen in profile) indicates a paroxysm of self-doubt; i.e., an indication which speeds up its accomplished gesture over one noon-time. It has spent its last adieu now. Whereupon the two hooded cowls of other warlocks are discerned, and they look upwards after the fashion of

denizens in a Robert Aickman story. "NNNNNNNNOOOOOOOOOOOO(!), it cannot be", expostulated Heathcote Dervish. "Phosphorous Cool has worsted our champion and knocked him cold. Now – like a felon in *Spartacus* – he drags him through the dust and halt of a manger. Will Peter Ustinov lean forward, in Lewis Grassic Gibbon's remake, in order to scalp our termagant at a hint of day? Lo(!); all comes to be lost or given up for one spinning British guinea. It revolves under the moon and proves to be bereft of warmth. Nemesis has occurred in the format of Oswald Spengler's *The Decline of the West*... Our courtly jouster is slain and abbreviated tokens are squandered. We have lost our shirts ---."
+

Given these developments, a red replica seeks some solace in its squares. Wherein a scarlet pillar looms up within an oblong's satisfaction, and it seems to pass muster over a prospective dive. A promenade that finishes up over a beckoning tower of black glass; even though such an effulgence releases shards of oblivion... all of which fall foursquare of a dragon. Every shattered pane leavens towards some smoke --- no matter what the discharge. It all tells a tale, in an instant, of the West's revenging spear. Also, this Parthian shot casts everything asunder... primarily in order to mount a grey gargoyle. Could it prove to be the dragon who waits below amid some mist(?); the latter an accompaniment given over to one plentiful gasp. Our massive saurian then stares up at a crashing Phosphorous Cool; and its scales or torso is promptly delivered from zoology to anthropology. Let it whimper as it rides... for such a Spear of Destiny (or Longinius) seeks out a reptilian heart. Irrespective of these eventualities, short limbs like the ones described taper away from the body... don't they recall William Roberts' constructions? Weren't they altogether barrel-shaped? No-one crosses its destiny – if we are to believe a saurian's snout. Nonetheless, our 'raptor's teeth have become razor sharp, ungauntleted, trespassing on the lower lip and alone. Likewise, each eye glowed redly in cruelty's aesthetic --- with or without Antonin Artaud.

BORIS KARLOFF'S TALES WITH A GOLDEN KEY: (190)
In this ultimate scene, our Frankenstein's monster stands above his former clients or collaborators in war. His massive frame fills the very vaults of such a store; and one gains an assessment of his gigantic thews. For Frankenstein's creature – in the guise of Heathcote Dervish's spirit – fulfills the role of Mastodon Helix at the eleventh hour. Yes again, his heavy and lugubrious prospect towers over Elsa Bounteous Hapgood, the dwarfish nurse and Butler James... all of whom are turning and running as we speak. An arch, gateway or tunnel lies further away from them – what with a series of sequential steps slanting upwards and outwards from the mortuary. Only a haughty Elsa Bounteous --- of these Edwardian fugitives --- refuses to buckle and wishes to stay her ground. A risen Prometheus faces her amidships. Whilst as to dress – and contrary to a prevailing prudery – this post-Victorian vamp posits boots, supported mid-riff, bar (if not bra), bodice and a porcelain undercarriage. A keen observer notices how she has started to fidget with a revolver in its holster next to her hip. Perhaps this Browning or Luger is already drawn halfway from its place of concealment? (Don't you remember whether Herman Goering remarked, 'when I hear the word culture I reach for my Browning – meaning the author of *Men and Women*, *The Ring & the Book*, etc...?) Still though, and served up as Nelson's column above them, a dark penumbra or livery of ebon suffused his backline throughout. Whereas above his cubed head – when adjacent to those massive hands criss-crossed by stitches – Heathcote Dervish's *alter ego* holds up two conductor wires. These were massive electrical cables which had been severed at source, and carried aloft beyond a giant's musculature. Surely, such galvanic agents have been retrieved from the laboratory's surrounds; especially after Frankenstein's corse faced reanimation at a stretch? It proves to luxuriate in an architrave of skin – at once bluish to the touch. Baron von Frankenstein's

mattoid stood over them, though, and threatened Elsa Bounteous, Butler James and Ms. Igor with juice-splitting threads.

A COVEN OF WARLOCKS BLOWS OUT TEN BIRTHDAY CAKES: (191)

Our license to sin has relapsed from its own tomb-stone, in that Phosphorous Cool had landed in front of Heathcote Dervish, Warlock Splendour Thomas and the other ones. All of them exist in their cowls somewhere at the rear... and as extras in a Dennis Wheatley script. A tendril of smoke rises up from the left-side of a hemisphere; and it wafts across the back of our klavern... let alone those shattered towers within which they enjoy their feasts. Oh yes – it's Heathcote Dervish, above all, who seems to have had the stuffing knocked out of him by this experience. One imaginary face-mask may've been unhinged in order to reveal an array of maggots. They turn out to be breeding fast and loose behind such a cover-all. Yet the threat to Heathcote's armour is proprietorial, perchance, and it limits his seigniorial pride. Nothing more... was he not the Lord of the Manor roundabout? Yet the efficacy of his conspiracy or plan – to showcase aristocratic magic – lies smouldering and broken at his feet. Acting as if within a haze, (sic), his lordship recognises that Mastodon Helix's body has been placed on the dais. Remember: it betrays a lively mosaic; or an exotic saraband in red and green bricks. Dimly, he understands the fact which says that Phosphorous Cool was addressing them in an oratorical way. It takes the form of a peroration or proem.
+

In the shadows of phantasm a time has come to die, now, abreast of a tabernacle otherwise devoted to sleep. In it, we discover the inner meaning of some of John Strachey's books before he joined the New Party... because a distinctive pathway through the jungle had opened up for this demi-god. For example: the reptile's skull seems to concentrate on an aberrant shadow; namely, one that passes over the image of a warrior who's come for it with a spear! A troubling thought intrudes, though, and it all relates to a bean-feast where the saurian attempts to eat its prey. One scarlet orb always happens to intrude in such circumstances; and it measures grief by how quickly we can turn into a chameleon. But now Phosphorous Cool, the one lodging the spear, swivels atop our spawn's head and throws himself nethermost-wise. Against and behind him, there intrudes nothing other than a sea of blue rectangles. It's a cornucopia (you see) to an unconscious version of the Crystal Palace – an edifice way out in south London; and limbering up to the prospect of a gyrating lance. It cuts through the air like a clock's aggressive balustrade. Could it really be the hint of a tolling bell? A notification which was raised aloft or in silence; as Phosphorous levelled his javelin. It then passed through the ether akin to a supreme testing or darting; albeit in a conundrum where the spear shears into this rhomboid's stomach. Once lodged there it will definitely test the providence of a new saviour --- whether it's kitted out in green or not! Can a redeemer thence stand before him (?), and penetrate a scaly hide with wounds? An arrow-head resultantly impinges on these tendons or unripeness, if only to visit a new Golgotha with such twinning. Do you notice it? Most particularly – given the absence of vinegar on a sponge that is held on a spear's prong and proffered by Longinius. Might those who buy into the luxury of this western weapon articulate a reptilian lobe – i.e., the lowest feature of an evolved gland? To whit: it happens to be the one which filters into consciousness what the animal biologist Konrad Lorenz called *On Aggression*.

ELECTROCUTE FRANKENSTEIN'S BIGAMIST BRIDE: (192)
"You were playing with us all along", expostulated Elsa Bounteous Hapgood... a Victorian woman who happened to be half-naked in her underwear. A pistol attempted to smooth down or lacquer her thigh (residually speaking). It sped on beyond the stars in the sky; and yet continued to sacrifice its own halo. "Like orchestrating a child at battleships, cribbage, noughts and crosses, snap, snakes and ladders, etc... you have flattered to

177

deceive a dying butterfly. It was afire." "Your voice limits its correction", murmured Heathcote in tones reminiscent of a spirit inside the body of Frankenstein's monster. "A strapping idealism always leaves us flapping if we play at dice. It rather amused me to see you making your bids and counter-blasts... yet it only served as a fleeting pleasure. Games in the temple of leisure must list sideways over, especially when it comes to blood usage. Necessarily so, a dosage of angel dust causes one to plunge downwards even at roulette. Listen to such an expectoration... a game of brag played with tarot cards has to bring up the number 13 --- thirteen --- namely; the value of death, transformation and transfiguration." With which sound-bite Frankenstein's monster brought the cables together *avec* a thunderous clash. They spat fire and coursed onwards towards some renewed doldrums. These also fabricated the facts of either pitch or Greek Flame. It tongued forth angrily; at once spitting, salvaging grief, mushrooming onwards and filling the air with electrostatic shots. At the centre of this remained Frankenstein's M. or monster. His arms were coiled like tendons of steel; the face flickered massively in the resultant mayhem and each silver bullet tasted like phosphorous (here). While – at random – the bodies of Butler James, Elsa Bounteous Hapgood and the impish nurse were routinely thrown about. Each and every one listened to an extraordinary witness – albeit a metaphor that recalled a pumpkin which was tested with dum-dum bullets in *The Day of the Jackal*. All of these characters died, therefore, in a surfeit of electronic spume... one that caused them to be electrocuted many times over in such a wind-tunnel. One responds now to the death of little miss imp or our female Igor – she's been effectively cremated. A hand came to be thrust out, her cap left her head, the nurse's uniform became vaguely starched, and her body moved in an opposite direction to a counter-vailing force. Soon all three of them were smouldering corpses – but can gross puppets really perish? Likewise, a blue electrical mist enervates our performers (thus so); within which the source of so much pride hastens to its petri-dish. These fly off like notes of star bait; each item becoming acclimatised to its given spore. It cascades from a raiment of sapphire; there to understandably chill to the bone a filament of white-on-blue. This whole scenario savours a xeroxed skull or a cranium that lights up a fluoroscope with stroboscopy – and it cushions a shot from Gray's *Anatomy*, if only to emblazon a Jolly Roger (*a la* Warhol). It radioactively shimmers and then dies... like a puppet muffled to its very jaw-line.

THE FANATICAL PURSUIT OF PURITY: (193+)

Truly, Michael Farraday's galvanic agency has proved to be resourceful... never mind such past breakthroughs. Especially given a template where Phosphorous Cool's wires have raised him above his fellows. Such charges as these gaze up from below. In Beowulf's final hemicycle – doesn't our epic hero approach a dragon who's asleep on his gold?
+

A yellow beam or luminance falls upon our stage with a certain pellucidity, and it limns the curvature of all available spines, as well as counselling against shadows. Beneath our hero's raised finger these magicians look on with an upraised nod; while each of them, to be certain of our ground, seems to be dimly askance. They appear to be fazed, uncertain, hesitant and otherwise hedged in with doubt. Next to them – and slightly further afield – one detects several Doric columns, pillars, rounded cubicles or ventilation shafts. Whereas, in accordance with Solon's judgement, the body of Mastodon Helix lies prone on an outcrop. It happens to be a natural or prehensile capturing o' rock... a philosophical posturing (this) which sets aside due indifference to fate or fortitude. Yes, dear sirs and brethren, our hulking brute lay astride a dais of calcified stone – the latter veined by the course granite of so many sulphurous discharges. These collaborated in order to raise each stratum of rock to the level of an art-form, geologically speaking. For his part, Phosphorous dangled one particular finger – and made moves so as to cast down anathemas from on high. A wisp of ashy smoke curled

179

around him as he did so. The mages --- for their indulgence --- gathered below: and formed a phalanx that they might listen to his judgement. "You practioners of the occult proved to be mistaken", entertained our mercurial one, "when you sought to conjure up a Trog. He was down to fight me, eh? Let me spare you the blushes of your present and future lies... It all betokens the fury which one should feel when an Icelandic geyser shoots up from the earth. Please exempt me from your speeches – let alone your mendacity and deceit. Suffice it to say that your plan to use Mastodon Helix against me has failed --- take it all back now and transport him out of our dimension on double quick time. Patience grows short for all those who might add to your jeremiad – do something about it, I beg you without surcease. Your period --- in terms of a magical fulfilment --- to remove him from the earth shall prove to be strictly limited. Act on it immediately or forever learn to reprieve the anger of his awakening. I would ask you not to jeopardise this orb's future by procrastination or delay. Utilise such wisdom without a remit of pity. By the look of yonder denizens, you wear the dress or vestments of an ancient cult... one which the novelist John Cowper Powys, in his book *Porius* about the dark ages, linked to chthonian excess. Perhaps you feel yourselves to be gifted in this regard? Yet – for my own sake – I find your ransacking of Dowson's *Yellow Book* to be immature. It also rises up to a gate of splendour – an understanding of a stargate that refuses Terry Pratchett's witness. Listen to me: you mouth the proems or versicular of an ancient cult, even in Enochian --- you may go so far as to call it witchcraft. But to what object? To my mind, men are still children who repeat profound platitudes bereft of internal depth. Consider yourselves to be mediocre wretches themselves set down at a Giant's table. This happens to take the celestial form of a bridge which you can never fully understand. Yet (still) your cardinal mistake was to forget the error of forgiveness. Because – in order to travel onwards towards the sun – you have to reach out into fathomless depths and unchartered territories. *Ecoutez moi* (once again): the fanatical pursuit of purity begins

180

with a radical 'forgetting'. It transcends the prospect of yesteryear... in other words. Such a semblance even goes higher and higher up – in accordance with Nature's plenitude. Can it be driven justifiably mad before the sun's concealment? For no-one may properly understand whether morality lacks dualism and it must then find a balance in contraries... a conundrum that has to offset creativity and destruction within an ascending curve. By a deliberation on Abraham Maslow's hierarchy of needs (however) we finally come near the truth – that is: to avoid either madness or boredom Man requires a purpose. In consequence, teleology proves to be a matter of mental asserveration... by virtue of the fact which says that without a kindred spirit one shall fall back towards the pit. Certainly and again, an ideal or archetype cannot but remain before one in concert... albeit with a definite grip on reality. Whereupon the seeds of the Superman – whether or not he had about him a skin of delicate silver – have to grasp the tenements of a compacted sun. Unlike Icarus one must never be worried by the approximate impact of flying too close to the solar orb... there to singe one's wings. Do you hear? The real fault of Mastodon Helix lay in basing victory around violence alone. Mere puissance partakes of the physical matter which has to be transcended; yet everything else proves to be based on an outstripping of such levels. Leave jealousy, material ambition and resentment behind --- I urge you to this without any assurance whatsoever. Ascend towards the star-gate, my mages, and do so in alignment with a small figure in purple armour rising upwards into the firmament. He moves tier on tier or in terms of the justification of an epitaph... again before any semblance of the same. A new compact with Aryandom has to be discovered now – a transcendence towards an iconic status that liberates energy from above to even beyond the most advanced state. As Savitri Devi once remarked about her own formulation... what I admire most is the prolonged impress of perfection. It's the notion which posits that Man can maintain or establish an ideal... this remains the heart or kernel of the matter. A refusal to compromise might sustain such an elixir and it speaks of a perfectibility for each species or race. Every *ethnos* must then seek its quintessential *aporia* or upper abstract – possibly to limitlessly extend it farther afield. Remember: even within an august grouping the difference between the superior and the inferior man will be the distinction between a near-god and a worm. Yet, despite being on the cusp of perfection, the golden key necessitates a further evolution beyond categorisation and towards the 'divine'. It involves the rejection of decay and the emancipation of ultimate forms of strength, you comprehend? Irrespective of the fact that it remains an ascendancy conceived in mortal terms... Man shall emerge out of one unholy egg into higher and more rarefied forms of vitalism. It encodes Bergson's *Creative Evolution*, do you take my drift? Caucasian eugenics will ultimately reckon on the rise of those who represent the suns of their own solar systems... do you partake of this *elixir vitae*? Within our dramaturgy, then, a meteor towers over a parabola of rocky asteroids. Reach out in order to release the power within you, therefore. Although one always has to bear in mind the fact that to progress to eight-limbed status from a termite heap one must have plenty of fuel! Recall also --- my former enemies --- that movements like european revolution virtually flirt with madness by opening up to the solar glare. Never mind: let us examine contrary valences which come to mind. Given the pabulum wherein an unknown Nemedian chronicle can describe the superman as a rope cast between mountain peaks and over an abyss. Yet such oiled or woven twine can also be said to be on fire... not to destroy it but to release energy, thereby. Hoorah!"

AN EPILOGUE OR *FIN DE PARTIE*: (194)
Beethoven's 'Ghost' piano trio as a portent to his unrealised opera *Macbeth*...

Do we recognise any motivations that besport or bear up a sour face? Do not despair... for such a guardian of the tomb always flies in the face of a distracted rapture. The West's Spear of Destiny doubtless penetrates the torso of a gigantic lizard – one which evinces some grey solitude (or leather) aslant of some blue-ribbed gaps. These press or question those who might go forward towards oblivion, in a manner whereby a lance penetrates various amphibian cover-alls. It all occurs in a drama where a weapon levels distress upon a darksome bulk – thereby to crystallise nothing other than a fragmented Golgotha. Moreover, this javelin transposes its residue of passion, primarily by taking off into another generation of suffering. At this pitch, however, the magnitude of such broken lips calls up to those who wish to take breakfast with cannibals. Surely, a blessed relief shall come from this carnival of spirits – thence indicating a grave folly that speaks of a grinding of teeth? Might we surmise over whether a breakthrough against all forms of orchid can take place(?); an impromptu dive into the depths, this, which comes up trumps over Longinius' shaft. It remains transfixed in a saurian's stomach; at a time when Mastodon Helix's arms spill open in supplication or appeal. Ultimately, they must cast off in the direction of some extra time; the like of it resembling an armature or mediaeval joust... a shafting or break with the past that seeks to deny the cedar of a rare tree. All of our Greek tragedy of the north, though, came to be occasioned by the deepest sapphire tint – an arrangement almost designed to spread the word as to its viciousness. Let this go why don't you... (?), now that one particular stick casts itself freely from its broken-backed magnificence. Could it illustrate Odin's or the Wanderer's staff? Needless to say, this tip of the eye-sore burst its bounds over perfection; the latter illustrative of a segment where an unparalleled jump occurs against an indication of deepest blue. Didn't the author Malcolm Lowry write a novel called *Ultramarine*? To be sure: a spear of Longinius', with or without a vinegar-laced sponge, snaps into two distinct chunks... and without the benefit of a residual crack. Whereas – in terms of a microscopic hindsight – a reptilian half-man drops away and this is quite possibly out of all sorts of dishonour. Look here: such a spearing frees itself from a green torso – one which belabours its form down below and that causes any direct claim

183

to cross its currency in blood. Several specks of the above, in a scarlet or abstract lustre, gather around a pregnant female dinosaur at her brood-time. A conundrum which draws its conscience towards an end of all bullying; possibly by backing away towards a template of azure. This emboldens --- yet again and once spoken of --- a spectre of cerulean or pthalo squares. Necessarily so, this saurian athlete recalls a study by Praxiteles – at least in terms of a perfect body or gait. Yet it definitely emboldens one far-flung capturing of reality too far, in that any Charles Atlas poster or figurine has to get away when speculating over a livery in green. Emerald or russet --- in pursuit of blisters --- happens to be the colour here as a frame falls backwards, amid tinkling glass, into a sea of smashed eddies. It all smoulders to a kaleidoscope of broken crystal.

+

Almost forgotten – now and then – in the lie of the land afore such circumstances we can observe a speeding tram. It contains Phosphorous Cool and a robotic version of Hermaphrodite X, the wraith, on its upper deck. Both of them were heavily disguised and the Victorian streets flashed by on either side of them. All of it became an evident or surrealist blur. Nevertheless, at this conveyance's front there stood a perambulating robot. He illustrated a space which was stolid, ultra-British, top heavy, foursquare, top-hatted, Toy town-like and heartily wearing a union jack waistcoat. This figurine also sported gloves and a conical morning-hat above a central piston… or stick. Where are our heroes steaming off to? Quite possibly, it has to be the mortuary superintended by Baron von Frankenstein… a puzzle that Edgar Allan Poe would have left to languish in the Rue Morgue, even in London.

+

But, in such a domicile, we find Heathcote Dervish about to depart the venue. Spiritually speaking – you will remember – he had come to animate the corse of Frankenstein's monster, irrespective of his desire to outwit such facts. In a celebration of this (then) Heathcote lowers an armoured mask or tin-head over his appearance. Momentarily, it obscures the character of his vision and blocks off one star-gate from any new ennoblement. Furthermore, our anti-hero moves aslant the exit – by dint of a mezzanine or a disacknowledged stair. It ceases to reek of corpses in its imagined ducts of air… therefore. Behind Heathcote Dervish – and at the back of his swishing robes – we notice that the skeletons of his victims continue to burn with both error and pitch. Like the master of all he surveys (plus a torch flickering in a distant niche) our tin-head departs. Recalling one of Herge's 'Tintin' villains… these multiple blazes glint off his iron head. A rood or runic symbol (this is) which resembles Sidney Nolan's capturing of the Australian outlaw, Ned Kelly, in paint.

+

To complete a resiling notice from one accomplished reason… let us examine the following facts. It definitely eventuates in a swirl whereby Phosphorous Cool, the silvery one, limbers up the stage: and his progression chokes off one distance or abstract too far. Why don't you deliberate on such an episode more clearly? It obviously leads to the silvern one scrabbling up the sky, and he's destined to be heaved off Eric Bramall's set in North Wales. A backdrop to these wires or trampolines can now be negotiated; nor may Bramall's swift puppeteering prevent a painted globe or earth from soaring away under Phosphorous' leap. Such a mercurial jump will always touch the suit of diamonds in heaven… decisively so. A tinted backing – vaguely reminiscent of a fairground peekaboo – lights up this toy-theatre behind our showman's residual rise and fall. Phosphorous then manoeuvres abreast of certain stars, spheroids, gulfs, small planets, asteroids and orbs. A trail of vapour also follows his cradling. Will a Bottler go out and around the front – so as to collect pennies from those children who are lined up at the crest of their playhouse? Who knows? Root-toot-toot! Yet, in any event, one silvern manikin or his handler knows that his triumph has been laced by transcendence. It reconnoitres the earth anew, but unlike Gaia not as termites upon it.

+

Finally now, he was reeled in towards an overhead lighting batten which existed above everything else on stage. It is situated over the proscenium arch in order to inhibit the manipulators least of all. Doesn't this medley just advertise Vance Packard's hidden persuaders in another way? But Phosphorous Cool had basically vanished – he's disappeared (henceforth) or merges into the strobe lights once and for all. *LUX...* Phosphorous Cool's become nothing more than a bright footlight on a marionette stage. "Goodbye, my children, goodbye!"

THE END